LORD JAMES HARRINGTON AND THE WINTER MYSTERY

1957. Lord James Harrington and his wife, Beth, run a country hotel in the village of Cavendish, deep in the heart of West Sussex. James and Beth are discussing the latest Cavendish Players production, *The Devil Incarnate,* when their cleaner informs them that farmer, Alec Grimes is missing. When James finds Grimes dead, he is certain of foul play. But the doctor says he died of natural causes and even good friend Detective Chief Inspector George Lane dismisses his suspicions. So James decides to put his own sleuthing skills to the test...

LORD JAMES HARRINGTON AND THE WINTER MYSTERY

Lord James Harrington And The Winter Mystery

by

Lynn Florkiewicz

Magna Large Print Books
Long Preston, North Yorkshire,
BD23 4ND, England.

British Library Cataloguing in Publication Data.

A catalogue record of this book is
available from the British Library

ISBN   978-0-7505-4529-7

First published in Great Britain by Lynn Florkiewicz in 2011

Published in Large Print 2018 by arrangement with
Lynn Florkiewicz

Magna Large Print is an imprint of Library Magna Books Ltd.

Printed and bound in Great Britain by
T.J. (International) Ltd., Cornwall, PL28 8RW

CHAPTER ONE

Nestled at the foot of the South Downs in the heart of West Sussex, the village of Cavendish awoke under a blanket of frost which, even by mid morning, had refused to give up its hold.

Lord James Harrington, dressed in chocolate brown corduroys and a chunky Aran sweater, cradled a mug of hot chocolate. The steamy cocoa sent a warm glow through him. 'Begin the Beguine' began playing on the wireless and without thinking he tapped his foot in time with the music.

From the comfort of the lemon and cream lounge, he stood by the French windows and scanned the landscaped garden and distant fields that backed onto his country home, a sprawling red-brick house built in the 1930s.

Terracotta pots were bare, awaiting the green shoots of spring, and striped maple and purple viburnum shrubs sheltered along the low stone wall that ran the length of the terrace.

Trees at the far end of the lawn were stripped bare of their summer leaves and now wore magical coats of silver as they reached out to the winter sky.

The October sun lacked confidence, reminding him that 1957 was drawing to a close and would soon be relegated to the history books; another eventful year in a world that both James and his

Boston-born wife, Beth, had discussed the previous evening.

Britain had elected Harold Macmillan as its new Prime Minister; the Russian Sputnik 1 globe, with its trailing metal legs, now hovered many miles above them in the darkness of space; Lew Hoad had claimed the Wimbledon title, and an outrageous, hip-gyrating singer called Elvis Presley continued to win over legions of fans.

Closer to home, James had been runner-up in the annual village tennis tournament, while the Cavendish cricket team had finished in sixth place – their best position for ten years. The vicar, who, James believed, had preached there since God was a boy, had retired and moved away. The send-off, just last weekend, had proved to be a merry one, thanks in no small part to the appearance of some 12-year-old malt whisky, a gift from his cousin in Scotland.

The fire in the hearth crackled and hints of apple and oak from the burning logs, lingered in the air.

He glanced at Beth. She lounged gracefully on the sofa, reading a copy of *Woman and Home*.

She looked as stunning now as the day they'd met. That had been back in 1930 at a pre-Derby meeting at Epsom racecourse. She had attended with friends. They'd got chatting and found they loved each other's company. Now, twenty-seven years later, they were still good friends and, to James, she was as beautiful as ever. She was wearing a pair of crêpe navy 'sailor-style' trousers with a pink cashmere sweater. A recent boyish haircut complemented her impish face. A big fan of Audrey Hepburn, she more or less copied any trend set by the Hollywood star and, after seeing Sabrina, she'd insisted on having her shoulder-length bob trimmed to this modern, chic style.

He turned the volume down on the wireless. 'I say, Beth, what's happening at the drama club? Are the Cavendish thespians coming out to play?'

Her eyes lit up. 'Oh yes!' She'd lived in Boston for the first fifteen years of her life and, although she'd called England home for the last thirty summers, a faint accent remained.

She closed her magazine. 'While you've been organising Hallowe'en and Guy Fawkes Night, we've set a first rehearsal date for *The Devil Incarnate*.'

'I have to say that it doesn't sound particularly seasonal.'

'No, it doesn't, does it?' She reached for her tea. 'Trouble is, they're all a little bored with doing pantomime, which I guess is a shame. I mean, that is more in keeping with Christmas.'

James had to admit that pantomime was a great deal of fun and, of course, a wonderfully British affair. Where else would people dress as the opposite sex and encourage so much audience participation?

'Shame,' he mused, 'I quite like seeing everyone make a fool of themselves.'

'Well, we're leaving pantomime to the children this year. They want their own show so the grown-ups are going supernatural. And it's been written by a local.'

'Who's our budding playwright?'

'Mrs Jepson's husband.'

11

'What? Our cleaner Mrs Jepson?'

'That's the one.'

He sat down opposite her in a roomy armchair and placed his hot chocolate on the table. 'Won't the vicar mind that we're performing devilish acts in the village hall?'

Beth grimaced. 'I'm not sure he knows. They only moved in yesterday. He and his wife are calling in later for afternoon tea.' She opened a stylish cigarette box. 'Cigarette?'

As he reached over and selected one, the door bell rang, once at first, then urgently.

James expressed surprise. 'Are we expecting anyone?'

Beth looked equally perplexed. She went through to the hallway while James stoked the fire. A few seconds later, Beth ushered an anxious Mrs Jepson into the lounge. She held a cotton hanky in one hand and clutched a small brown handbag in the other. Her face was flushed and her greying, auburn hair was tangled as she wrenched her hat off.

'Oh, Lord Harrington,' she said in a gentle Sussex lilt, 'I'm sorry to bother you, sir, and your Ladyship, too. But I'm so worried, see.'

Behind her, James saw Beth roll her eyes. Their cleaner had a tendency to worry over nothing but he thought he'd better give her the benefit of the doubt and motioned for her to sit down.

'He's not there, you see. He's always there, always 'as been.' Her fingers clenched her bag tight.

'Mrs J, who're we talking about?'

'Well, Mr Grimes.'

'Alec Grimes? Grimes' farm?'

'That's 'im.' She pushed her hanky into her bag, pulled out a fresh one from her coat pocket and blew her nose.

Beth joined her on the sofa. 'Oh, Mrs Jepson, why are you getting so upset? He's probably in one of the fields. It's a busy time for farmers.'

'I've been 'elping Mr Grimes for years. Just a spot of cleaning, you know. Every Monday morning I go there, ten o'clock, rain or shine. I'm always there and 'e's always in. Now, 'e was in at eight, 'cause my John saw 'im, although they did 'ave words. Not sure what about, but anyway, he was in.'

James studied the tip of his cigarette. 'But he wasn't in when you arrived?'

'That's right. Dead on ten o'clock it was. No sign of 'im. And the door was open.'

'And did you go in?'

Mrs Jepson fiddled with her bag. 'Well, I didn't like to at first. I mean, it's not right, is it, walking around someone's house uninvited? But I was worried, see.'

Beth gave her a reassuring smile. 'And what happened?'

'Well, nothing. That's why I'm worried. There's 'alf a mug of cold tea on the kitchen table, and 'is breakfast is 'alf eaten. There's no note to say where 'e's gone.'

James made a beeline for the cocktail cabinet and prepared a small whisky.

'Nothing like a 12-year old malt to settle the nerves.' He poured a small measure into a crystal tumbler. 'Fact is, Mrs J, he could be anywhere. Perhaps something happened to an animal and he's gone to call the vet? He's clearly had to dash off somewhere. He may be back now, finishing off the eggs and bacon.'

He handed her the tumbler and, to his astonishment, she swallowed the drink in one. He and Beth exchanged a grin as she let out a grateful sigh.

'I s'pose. But fancy leaving the door open.'

James checked his watch. Mrs Jepson wouldn't be calmed until she knew what had happened. He stubbed his cigarette out.

'Darling, be a dear and grab my sheepskin jacket, would you?'

Beth went through to the hall and James secured a mesh guard in front of the fire.

'Mrs J, how about you and I pop down to Alec's farm? We'll take a proper look around. If we're unhappy about anything, we'll go over to the police.'

Her shoulders relaxed as Beth returned and helped James slip into his jacket.

'James, don't forget you need to be back here by three. The new vicar and his wife are coming for tea.'

'Ah yes, Mr and Mrs Merryweather. What are their first names again?'

'Stephen and Anne.'

'Right-ho. Look, Grimes' farm is only a couple of miles the other side of the village. I'll be an hour at the most.'

He gave her a quick kiss as he put on his herringbone flat cap. 'Come along, Mrs J.'

Outside, he rubbed his hands together and delved into his pocket for his gloves and keys. He swung open the garage doors and heard his

14

cleaner gasp.

In front of them was a newly purchased two-tone iced blue and old English white Austin Healey convertible with polished chrome bumpers and aerodynamic curves that swooped elegantly down to the grill. Attached to the chrome beam, just above the front bumper, was a blue Royal Automobile Club badge and, either side of that, two fog lights.

James gazed at it proudly: a gem of a sports car and one of the first off the production line this year. He clipped the roof into place and kicked the wire-wheel tyres.

'Beauty, isn't she, Mrs J? I'll get the heating running so you won't get cold.'

'My word, your Lordship. I can't go in that!'

He swung open the tiny passenger door. 'Of course you can. Here you are, let me give you a hand.' They chuckled as Mrs Jepson's buxom frame struggled to fit in the tiny passenger seat.

'Oh my,' she laughed, 'it's a bit low. I'll never get out again.'

James jumped into the driver's seat, turned the key and pushed the starter button. The engine fired up and he revved the accelerator.

'Don't worry, I'll give you a shove out when we get there. She only arrived last week and this is a fine day to take her for a spin.'

He set off down the winding gravel drive and onto the narrow country road that led to the village. As he nudged the speed up, Mrs Jepson cowered at every bend and gripped her seat-edge as they crested every hill. James went up and down through the gears like they were going out of fashion, reliving his brief spell as a racing driver at Donington Park and Monte Carlo during the 1930s.

Back then, he'd fancied his chances as a potential Malcolm Campbell and he'd done pretty well in some of the races. But, after a particularly nasty accident, Beth insisted he gave up. With newly-born twin boys, he'd reluctantly heeded the message and turned, instead, to tennis and cricket. They were enjoyable substitutes, but no match for the adrenalin rush of motor racing. Now the twins had decamped to Oxford University, he'd ordered the Austin as a fun car alongside the more sedate Jaguar saloon.

He pulled onto the verge at Alec Grimes' farm and a few minutes later, James managed to haul his puffing, red-faced cleaner laughing from her seat. She smoothed her clothes down quickly and repositioned her hat.

James studied the farmhouse. 'Right, Mrs J, where d'you normally go?'

She went ahead and led him toward a side door. James looked for signs of life in the surrounding fields but only found them in the form of Friesian cows and Hampshire Down sheep. Fresh bales of hay were stacked ready to take out. Behind them was a pigsty where a dozen piglets flopped on top of one another. Half a mile beyond that was Charn Wood, a small copse, thick with oak, birch and beech.

At the house, the side door was still ajar. He knocked on the door frame. 'Mr Grimes?'

He pushed the door open and stepped onto a rubber doormat and into a sparse kitchen. The now cold egg and bacon remained unfinished on the table. One of three wooden chairs stood in the middle of the floor and a plate from the dresser lay smashed on the scuffed lino. A crude sculpture of a robin lay on the work surface under the windowsill. In the corner, a pile of newspapers was perched on a long oblong board. A dirty mug stood in the sink and, beneath this, a tatty frayed curtain was half-drawn, concealing cleaning materials and dusters. At the far end a door led to a utility room at the back of the house.

James frowned as he made his way through the kitchen and across the narrow hallway. He peered into the lounge and decided Mr Grimes was down on his luck. The dull, run-down interior lacked a woman's touch. A fine traditional house, but not a cosy home and, oddly, no photographs of loved ones, past or present, on show.

'Mr Grimes? Hello?' He felt Mrs J close on his heels. 'Did you look upstairs?'

She shook her head tight-mouthed as James opened the door that led to the stairs.

'I'll take a gander up there.'

'I'll come up with you, if you don't mind. I don't know why, but something's giving me the heebie-jeebies.'

He had to admit that, apart from the odd bleat from a sheep outside, the atmosphere was ominously silent. They made their way up the narrow wooden staircase. Every step creaked and the uneven floorboards dipped as they looked in on both bedrooms.

'No bathroom?' enquired James.

'He's got a tin bath in the kitchen. Underneath

where the newspapers are. The privy's outside.'

James winced. He could never imagine having an outside lavatory. Mrs Jepson stole a glance through the small window that overlooked the back of the house.

'Oh gawd, there 'e is. He's doing 'is oil painting. Must've forgotten what time it was. Oh, I feel stupid dragging you 'ere now.'

Standing behind her, he studied the scene below, then jogged downstairs and made his way out through the back entrance.

'Mr Grimes?' he called as he walked briskly toward him.

Grimes remained still, facing the copse with what looked like a finished canvas in front of him. James felt uneasy and ordered Mrs Jepson to stay back.

As he faced Grimes he felt nauseous. The farmer's dead eyes stared at the fields and a paintbrush, tipped with red, dangled in his chubby hand.

James squatted down and felt for a pulse but the farmer showed no sign of life.

He examined Grimes and saw that his shoes had small deposits of mud and frost on the heels and his jacket appeared lopsided. He couldn't understand why at first, but then noticed that the buttons were fastened in the wrong holes. He chewed his lip and called to Mrs Jepson.

'Is there a telephone nearby?'

'Yes sir, there's a phone box further along this road. It's quite a way, though. Good couple of miles. Is 'e not well?'

'I'm afraid he's dead, Mrs J.'

18

She clamped her hands to her mouth. 'Oh Lord above!' Flustered, she dropped her handbag, patted her coat pockets and pulled out a hanky.

With raised eyebrows, James looked at Grimes' painting of Charn Wood copse. This was a talented artist but what was he doing painting at this hour? He examined the ground, noting a good many footprints around the chair. This was most odd. Why did he leave the kitchen door open? Why didn't he finish his breakfast?

Mrs Jepson dabbed her eyes. 'Poor thing must've 'ad a heart attack.'

James swung round and was quick to hide his own nagging doubts.

'Yes, yes, I s'pose he must have. Listen, Mrs J, we'll skip trying to call someone. We'll drive back to the village and I'll get Dr Jackson out. He'll need to declare the death and whatever else they have to do.'

'But we can't just leave 'im there.'

'I'm afraid we'll have to. I can't lift him, he's twice my size. Let the doctor handle it.'

His cleaner cuddled her handbag and trudged toward the car.

James took one last look around. Something was wrong here. Something didn't look right, didn't feel right. He strode back to the car and opened the door to help his cleaner into the Austin. The cawing of crows echoed through the stillness. The birds settled along the telegraph wires, eager to investigate the motionless man sitting in the chair. James reached into the back seat and pulled out a travel blanket.

'I'll go and cover him up until the Doc arrives.'

Leaving Mrs Jepson to her tears, James covered the farmer with the blanket and closed the side door to the house.

They returned to the village in silence, interrupted only by the odd sniffs from Mrs Jepson. With assurances to James that she was fine, he watched her enter her house. Two minutes later, he pulled up outside the doctor's cottage in the centre of Cavendish.

Dr Jackson's arrival, three years ago, had sparked a good deal of excitement among the ladies of the village. In his early thirties, he had a mass of unruly black, wavy hair, smouldering eyes and a winning smile. As a result, the surgery had become unusually busy with minor ailments afflicting the women in the area. To their constant disappointment, no matter how persuasive certain women were, he remained loyal to his beautiful wife, Helen, and their five-year-old daughter, Natasha.

James hammered on the green panelled door and within a minute Philip answered it. 'Oh, thank God you're in. I need you over at the Grimes' place.'

After James had described the scene to him, Philip made a couple of quick calls, grabbed his black bag and closed the door behind him.

James tugged at his sleeve. 'Philip, do you mind if I ask you something?'

'Fire away,' the doctor replied as he threw his bag and wellingtons into his Morris Minor.

'When you check Grimes over, could you look out for a few things?'

Philip shot him a quizzical look. 'What sort of things?'

James shrugged his shoulders. 'To be honest, I don't know. There was something odd. I don't know what, just something that didn't seem quite right.'

'Well, I'll take a good look and let you know what I find.'

And, as Dr Jackson's car trundled out of sight, James began wondering if he should telephone his long-standing friend, Detective Chief Inspector George Lane. But until he could establish what concerned him about Grimes, he didn't really have anything to tell him.

CHAPTER TWO

He drove slowly through the centre of Cavendish, the image of which he thought deserved a place on the lid of a Fortnum and Mason's biscuit tin, it was so pretty. Children skidded on icy pavements untouched by the sun and two pensioners huddled on a cast-iron bench at the edge of the green, smoking their pipes.

Behind the green stood the small Saxon church of St Nicholas, one of the last to be built under Edward the Confessor nearly a thousand years ago. Along from it was the 16th century Half Moon pub with its low-beamed interior and, next door, the village hall, meeting place for the Cavendish Players and venue for *The Devil Incarnate*.

He winced. What on earth would the new vicar say about this play? It seemed far removed from

Christmas and seasonal worship and goodwill. A Christmas ghost story would have been acceptable, but *The Devil Incarnate?* The previous vicar would have shot them down in flames. If this new chap were to be of the same stock, he'd make them go back to the pantomime and no room for argument, James thought.

Turning onto his drive, James found himself replaying the moment he'd found Alec Grimes. The nagging concerns returned and, as one question emerged, another followed. He parked and wandered, deep in thought, to the front of the house where his gardener was cutting back shrubs from the bay windows. The falling leaves stood no chance of settling, with him on the case, such was his pursuit of the perfect landscape.

A pale green Austin 30 stood on the drive and he looked at it curiously as he trotted up the steps to the front door. No sooner had he stepped into the hall than Beth scurried out from the kitchen.

'The vicar's here,' she whispered.

'I thought you said three o'clock?' he whispered back.

'That's what I thought he said. I've made tea. Glad they're not having dinner, I'd never have been ready.'

Beth helped him slip out of his jacket. 'Did you find Alec Grimes?'

'Yes, dead. Sitting at an easel – most peculiar.'

Beth gave him a look of concern.

'I'll tell you about it later. Come along, darling, you'd better introduce me.'

James hid his surprise when he entered the lounge. He'd been convinced that they would have another ancient vicar at the helm. But Stephen Merryweather was no more than thirty five, a tall, lanky individual with an expression that only a vicar could wear; his was a kindly, pale face that would see no wrong in anyone. He was dressed casually in charcoal grey trousers and a thick blue jumper. Not a dog collar in sight. James held out a hand.

'Reverend, welcome to Cavendish. Settling in all right?'

'Yes, yes, I th-think so. It's v-very nice, isn't it?' the young Reverend replied with an endearing stammer. 'Th-this is my wife, Anne.'

Anne, much shorter than her husband, had chestnut hair that fell around her shoulders and an open, honest face with brown eyes and a button nose. James detected a hint of mischief in her expression. Something told him that this woman had a playfulness about her that would emerge once they got to know one another. James insisted they make themselves at home as Beth wheeled in a tea trolley crammed with mouth-watering delicacies.

The bottom tier held a tea service decorated with delicate cornflowers and poppies. Alongside lay small silver cake forks and a cake slice. The top tier bore an enticing display of home-made cherry scones and a deep Victoria sponge with raspberry jam and butter-cream.

She distributed plates and cotton napkins and invited them all to choose their preferred cake.

'Oh, your Ladyship,' Anne said, 'this looks delicious. Do you do your own baking?'

Beth held her hands up. 'There's one rule I

think we can make clear to you both and that is we don't want you to feel uncomfortable. We may live in the house at the top of the village, but to you, we're James and Beth. And yes, I do my own baking and, I have to say, James does too. The Victoria sponge is his handiwork.'

James waved the compliment aside. 'Yes, the days of the aristocracy lording it over villages are getting to be a thing of the past. Informality is the new concept these days. We used to have a cook but we love cooking ourselves so it seemed a little silly to employ one.'

Anne's shoulders relaxed and Stephen smiled. 'W-well, then, please ditch the 'Reverend' and stick to Stephen and Anne.'

James eased into his armchair. 'Well, Stephen and Anne, let's have tea and cake and get to know one another.'

Beth, delighted to see that everyone had an appetite, played the perfect hostess and made every effort to make Stephen and Anne feel at home.

Over the next hour, James learnt that Stephen had moved to Sussex from Kidlington, near Oxford. Originally a primary school teacher and regular churchgoer, he had found himself drawn more to a religious vocation than a teaching one. After several years of hard study, he'd become a vicar, serving for one year as an army chaplain. Cavendish, James discovered, was his first real parish. Anne had taught at the same school as he had and this was where they'd met. Their two children, Luke, aged eight and Mark, ten, were to join them at the weekend after staying with their grandparents.

'We thought it best to have them out of the way during the move,' Anne said.

Stephen wandered to the French windows and gazed across the extensive grounds.

'J-James, when we were invited to the manor house, I expected ... well, something along the lines of B-Blenheim Palace.'

James chuckled and rose to join him, stirring his tea on the way. 'Yes, most people do. You'll find the original manor house about two miles that way.' He pointed toward the hills of the South Downs. 'You can make out the chimneys through the trees. My grandfather was the last Harrington to live there. He passed it on to my father but not only did he hate the place, he also found it a financial nightmare. Not quite Blenheim, but it has thirty rooms, and there were five of us rattling around like peas in a bucket – my parents, elder brother, younger sister and me – plus a few servants, of course, but a total waste. My elder brother died shortly after he inherited the title so it came to me.'

'And,' Beth added, 'as James said, being the Lord of the Manor isn't what it used to be.'

'That's right. Move with the times and all that. We turned the old family pile into a country hotel and called it Harrington's and it provides steady jobs for several of our villagers. Father designed this little beauty and we've been here ever since. A much smaller affair and more homely.'

Beth chuckled. 'I couldn't imagine living in a stuffy old manor house. That just isn't our thing at all.'

'B-but you still do fêtes and th-things?'

25

'Oh yes,' replied James, leading Stephen back to his chair. 'We've stacks of land so we still host a lot of the village events. We have a vibrant community here so we're never short of festivals and activities. That's most of what my role is, really – apart from running the hotel, of course. Next thing on the agenda is Hallowe'en and Bonfire Night. Oh, and Beth's getting stuck into the play. By the way, you *do* know about the play at the village hall?' He hesitated before announcing: *'The Devil Incarnate.'*

Stephen sighed. 'Y-yes, though I'm not sure what to make of it, or that I should condone it.'

'Only a bit of fun. It's written by one of our villagers although I haven't seen any of it yet.'

Beth invited him to the rehearsals that were due that weekend. 'If you're not comfortable with it, we can compromise I'm sure. After all, the hall does belong to the church, so we mustn't offend, must we?'

'I-I'm sure it'll be fine. Perhaps they could just ch-change the name? It has the sound of menace, as if something u-untoward is going to happen.'

Beth turned to James. 'Oh, speaking of untoward, are you going to tell us about Mr Grimes?'

James couldn't believe he'd forgotten about the farmer. He returned to his chair. 'Gosh, yes. Stephen, you'll need to know about this. You'll probably be arranging the funeral.'

James went through the events of the morning and his audience listened with a mixture of fascination and sadness.

'Was he very old?' Anne asked.

'About fifty, I think. I didn't really know him

very well, always kept himself to himself. Not a true local, so to speak. Moved here about fifteen years ago, but never blended in much.'

Anne frowned. 'Unusual for a farmer to be painting. Farmers around Kidlington were always moaning that they had too much to do.'

'Yes, I thought that.' James reached across for more cake. 'Something else didn't ring true, either.' He eased back in his chair. 'I'm blessed if I can think of what it is, though.'

Beth asked if anyone would like more tea to a resounding chorus of 'Yes!' As she collected the cups and saucers, she turned to James.

'You know, there's probably a perfectly logical explanation.' She glanced at Stephen and Anne. 'James fancies himself as Paul Temple. Sees a mystery to solve in everything. If the deer in the far field walk in a different direction, he needs to know why.'

'Well, A-Anne's a bit like that too,' Stephen added. 'Always reading M-Miss Marple and taking it all v-very seriously.'

James grinned. 'I mistakenly told Beth about a time I'd solved a crime back at Oxford. There was a spate of robberies around our digs and I managed to bag the blighter red-handed.'

'Oh, how wonderful,' Anne said.

'Then I collared someone during my time in the RAF. Some little upstart of a mechanic who was about to sabotage the planes. Turned out he had German heritage and was playing football for the other side.'

'G-good grief,' exclaimed Stephen.

'How wonderful,' Anne repeated gleefully.

Beth wagged a finger at Anne. 'Don't you encourage him. We don't need two sleuths investigating what's probably an innocent death. A heart attack, that's all it'll be.'

James sipped his tea. A heart attack was the most likely reason but indulging in oil painting before feeding the livestock? Leaving your breakfast and the door wide open? But then, he didn't know Grimes at all. Perhaps that's what he did? Perhaps he wasn't a successful farmer. Had he fallen on hard times and given up? His house would certainly back that statement up. But then again, appearances could be deceptive. He might have been one of those men who never spent a penny and hoarded everything under the floorboards.

Anne helped gather the cups and saucers and put them on the tea trolley.

'Oh Beth, I love your nail polish. And what a striking colour.'

She splayed her hands. 'Well, thank you. It's one of my favourites. They have it in Selfridges in London. I can get you some next time I'm in town. It's called Red Rose Velvet and–'

James clicked his fingers. 'That's it! That's what was wrong. I didn't see any of it there.'

Beth, Anne and Stephen stared after him as he dashed across the room. He snatched open the door to the hall.

'Do excuse me, I'm going to put a call through to George.'

Beth gave him an 'Are you serious?' look. 'George Lane?'

'Detective Chief Inspector George Lane, darling.'

He bounded across to the telephone in the hall and, aware of the confusion that had followed his announcement, he called back, 'I don't think there's anything logical or normal about this. In fact, I think this was anything but a normal death.'

CHAPTER THREE

That afternoon, James parked on the grass verge by Grimes' farm. Dusk had fallen and two bored policemen plodded about, shining their torches at nothing in particular.

DCI George Lane's white police car with the single blue light on its roof was parked ahead of him and, further along from that, Philip Jackson was fastening his bag and preparing to leave. Grimes' body had gone but his chair, painting and oils stood in a pile on the ground.

James caught up with Philip. 'Did you find anything?'

Jackson shook his head. 'Nothing too suspicious from what I could see.'

'But you found something.'

The doctor screwed his face up. 'Not really, just a bump. More like a graze on the head. It could've been caused by bumping into the corner of a cupboard or something. It's a heart attack. He'd been suffering with problems for a few months now, heart related and bouts of angina. Not a well man. Nothing untoward here.' He looked past James to DCI Lane who was entering the farmhouse. 'Did you call him in?'

James shuffled on his feet. 'Yes and I'm sure I'll get a flea in my ear for doing so but I remember what it was that didn't seem right.'

Philip threw his wellingtons on the back seat. 'Well, I'm interested to know but I have a patient to see. Are you in the pub tonight?'

'Yes, I'll pop by later – see you there.'

He waved Jackson off and made his way to the farmhouse. His long-time friend, George Lane, was sitting at the wooden dining table in the kitchen, slurping strong tea out of a chipped cup. His large frame swamped the chair supporting him.

George narrowed his eyes at the dull light bulb above, before putting his cup down and shifting his gaze. His voice was gruff.

'Nothing better to do, James?'

James heaved a sigh, pulled out a chair and waited for the inevitable lecture on wasting police time.

'You know I've got better things to do than check out a farmer with a dodgy ticker,' continued George. 'What made you think, for one minute, that there's anything odd about this?'

James looked at his shoes and felt like a naughty schoolboy. He and George were secure in a twenty-five year friendship and nothing would change that. He remembered George as a young constable during their initial meeting when he'd called at the manor to investigate a robbery. Although from different backgrounds, their mutual love of cricket brought them together and both played for the village team. But, where James had sought marriage and children, his friend had opted to marry the job, although he often acted as if he'd entered into a contract with his worst nightmare.

George's chair creaked as he leant back. 'I mean, apart from an unfinished breakfast, there's nothing odd about it.'

'What about the broken plate on the floor, the chair halfway across the kitchen, the–'

'James, he's hardly Mr Houseproud, is he? Have you seen the state of this place? I mean, I know Mrs Jepson comes in once a week, but it's not exactly tidy.'

James admitted he had a point but raised a finger. 'Just hear me out. Those oils and brushes, the ones he was working with.'

'What about 'em?'

James stood up. 'Follow me.'

He heard a groan as George pushed himself up and trudged behind James to where the body had been found. The easel had fallen forward and the paints were piled to one side.

'Have you a light, George? It's getting very gloomy.'

George felt his pockets and brought out a small, metal torch. Aiming the beam downwards, James bent over and studied the shadowy scene, carefully turning over the jumble of paints, brushes and rags.

'George, where's the paintbrush? The one Grimes was holding.'

George shrugged. 'Dunno, might still be with the body. Why?'

'Well, that's what I wanted to show you.' James

31

picked the painting up. 'You see, there's none on there.'

George turned his nose up and squinted at the painting. 'None of what on where?'

'Red paint. Grimes had red paint on his brush. There's none on the painting. There's no red anywhere on this canvas.'

His friend shrugged again, took the torch away from James and began making his way back to his car. 'Well, he was prob'ly just about to paint something red, then, wasn't he?'

James called after him. 'How? There's no red paint there.'

George waved a hand in dismissal. James dropped the painting and scrambled over to him.

'So, are you not doing anything about this?'

'No, I'm not. Jackson's adamant it was a heart attack. He was on medication for heart problems so it's not altogether unusual for someone that age to collapse like that. He may have felt unwell and not had time to get red paint. Believe it or not, I have real crimes to solve. If you come up with something better than an art critique, let me know.' He opened the car door. 'Perhaps he was mixing his paints. Artists do that you know.'

'I'm aware of that, George, but red is a fairly dominant colour.'

'Do you know if he's got any family?'

'Afraid not, I didn't know him at all. But I'll tidy up here; you all right if I lock up?'

'That should be the job of one of my constables...' He noticed James' hopeful expression. 'All right, keep everything locked and we'll start looking for a next of kin. Jackson's registering the death so it's all in hand. See you at your Hallowe'en do. I'll be late – don't finish till ten.'

'Right-ho, but think about the red paint business. Oh, and can I borrow your torch?'

George rolled his eyes and tossed the torch over. He ordered his officers back to the station, eased into his car and, with a curt wave, drove off.

James wandered back to the painting and held it up. He edged closer to the farmhouse to catch the light from the kitchen window. The painting was of the copse at the far end of the top field. He glanced over to Charn Wood but struggled to see any trace of it in the darkness. As far as he could recall, the wood held various shades of green, but no red and he wondered what Grimes had intended to paint.

He retraced his steps to where he'd found Grimes, squatted down and rummaged through the few paints on the ground. Selecting one at a time, he shone the torch on the labels: Cobalt, Cadmium Yellow, Burnt Sienna, Prussian Blue. It made no sense. This was a traditional landscape, not modernist or cubist. Most of the colours here were not on the painting, so why were they there?

The sound of a car door slamming broke his train of thought. He stood up to see a man in his late twenties walking toward him. Dressed in black trousers and a black polo-necked jumper, he held a number of long, rolled-up papers in his hand.

'Alec Grimes about?'

'No, sorry. You a friend?'

'No, mate. Don't know him that well. Why?'

'Well, unfortunately, he died this morning.'

The man started at the news. 'Died? How?'

33

'Heart attack.'

The man scratched his head and appeared to be unsure of what to do next. He looked at James. 'I don't think I caught your name.'

'Don't think I pitched it,' James said as he held his hand out. 'Harrington, Lord James Harrington.' James smiled wryly to himself – even after five years, he still caught himself saying 'Lord James Harrington' rather than 'Lord Harrington'. It had never felt right, to give himself the title that Geoffrey, as his elder brother, had been so proud to bear, although so briefly. He was still the younger son, inheritance or not, in his own mind.

Recognition lit up the young man's face. 'Of course.' He apologised. 'I'm fairly new to the area, but I've seen you around Cavendish. I'm Ian Connell, a builder and architect. I live in the next village along – Loxfield. I work with a firm of property agents and do a bit of building work here and there. Mr Grimes was planning some improvements and I thought I'd pop in with a draft copy of the plans.'

'Improvements? What for?'

'An indoor toilet, plus quite a bit of renovation. He was asking if I could do something inside the house, maybe convert the spare bedroom above the kitchen to a bathroom.'

James studied the young man, who looked a little lost as he took in the scene around him. He waved the plans at him.

'Well, I s'pose I'd better ditch these. No use to him now.' As he turned to go, he called back to James. 'And he never paid me. I spent ages on these. Time's money, you know.'

James watched him walk away. He stroked his chin. It didn't look as if Grimes had two pennies to rub together, let alone enough to pay for improvements.

He watched Connell's car disappear and began tidying away the paints and easel, placing them inside the kitchen. The last thing to pack up was the small wooden chair that Grimes had used; an old chair spattered with oils and smelling faintly of turpentine. As he picked it up, another car arrived – a vintage Citroën with sweeping running boards and huge, bulbous headlights.

'Oh Lord,' he mumbled.

Rose and Lilac Crumb or, as James preferred to call them, the Snoop Sisters, had arrived. Well into their eighties, they had lived together all their lives, never having married. They'd only been residents in Cavendish for about ten years and in the past had moved, rumour had it, whenever they fell out with someone.

James had it on good authority that, in their last village, they'd enjoyed the position of joint treasurers for the Women's Institute. Within a few months, money had disappeared and the sisters were accused of pinching the funds. Although this was never proven, soon after the theft, the sisters treated themselves to front row seats to see *The Mousetrap* in London and accusations flew like daggers to their door.

The sisters subsequently moved to Cavendish and, over the years, had made themselves just as unpopular with their opinions, judgements and criticisms.

James lifted an eyebrow. Did they have some

sort of radar planted in their heads? As soon as anything happened in the village, they seemed to know before anyone else. He guessed that Mrs Jepson had placed a few phone calls and they'd got wind of things.

They hurried across to James, egging each other to go faster and shouting out questions along the way.

'Oh Lord Harrington, what's happened?'

'He did go peacefully, didn't he?'

'Or was he in pain?'

'Has the body gone?'

'No one liked him, you know. Miserable bugger, always has been.'

James listened to their unpleasant ramblings for a couple of minutes. He gathered that, according to the sisters Crumb, Grimes was uneducated, grumpy, lacking social niceties and exceptionally rude. James suppressed a grin – everything they displayed themselves. He had only met the man a couple of times and felt these descriptions were exaggerated. He guessed Grimes came across like that to the Snoop Sisters because he wouldn't tell them anything.

Rose sidled up to him. 'Lord Harrington, are you listening?'

'Mmm?'

'I said, you know he had a part in that *Devil Incarnate* play, don't you? Who's going to take his place?' She huffed. 'Devil Incarnate! Disgusting, having the views of Satan paraded in a church hall.'

Lilac leant forward. 'I heard he wanted nothing to do with it.'

'Really?' James said.

Rose bundled past him. 'John Jepson bullied him into it. Shall we go inside and tidy up? Make it look nice.'

Lilac followed her. 'We could start going through his things. Makes it easier when the house sells.'

The sisters made to pass him but James held up his hands. 'Absolutely not.'

They glared. He drew his shoulders back.

'I'm sorry, ladies, but it's not your place, or mine, to do that. I'll get in touch with the relevant authorities and they can sort it out.'

Rose tried to walk past him, but James blocked the doorway. 'Miss Crumb, I do believe that trespassing is against the law. And, if I may say, it's bad form to go through a person's things without permission of the family.'

The sisters huffed. 'That's what you're doing.'

'DCI Lane has permitted me to tidy up here. You may protest as much as you like but I'm getting onto the right people to do this. This is not your business.'

James willed them to go. He didn't want to be abrupt with two elderly spinsters but, if circumstances dictated, he would be. Although put out, the two sisters turned as one and returned to their car with mutterings about how unfair James was and that, just because he was a Lord, it didn't mean he could dictate to them.

James closed his eyes in relief, retraced his steps and checked that he'd retrieved everything from outside. The beam of the torch caught something. He squatted down to see shards of glazed clay scattered on the ground. He scooped the pieces up and studied them. They appeared to be fragments of hand-made pottery. Another surprise; Grimes must have had a creative side to him – painting, pottery and amateur dramatics, although the latter appeared to be less favoured.

He slipped the pieces into his pocket and returned to the house. Opting to take the painting with him, he locked the door and wandered back to the car.

With the engine running, he sat in the driver's seat with the canvas leaning against the steering wheel. He retrieved a pin from the back of his lapel and switched on the interior light. Feeling the ridges of oil on the canvas, he dug the pin into several areas of paint. With every sharp stab, he examined the pin with increasing concern and his efforts became more determined. Finally, he placed the painting on the passenger seat and turned off the overhead light.

'Well, Detective Chief Inspector Lane,' he said as he put the car in gear. 'You may not agree, old chap, but there's more to this than meets the eye and I intend to prove it to you.'

The Austin's tyres screeched as James spun the car round and accelerated into the distance.

CHAPTER FOUR

That evening, Beth prepared a sumptuous dinner to keep the winter blues at bay: braised beef casserole with feather-light dumplings, Brussels sprouts served with cubes of crispy bacon, together with mashed potatoes creamed with milk and butter.

James devoured every morsel then relaxed in his chair and patted his stomach. Although he prided himself on keeping in good shape, he thought Beth's cooking would be his undoing.

He joined her in the kitchen and wrapped his arms around her waist. 'Anyone ever tell you how lovely you are?'

'Yes, you,' she laughed. 'I didn't do dessert. If you're still hungry we can finish off what's left of this afternoon's cake.'

He released her. 'Thank heavens for that. One more dumpling and you would have had an explosion of Harrington in the dining area.'

She grinned. 'Oh, by the way, Bert rang. He's going to the Half Moon tonight and asked if you were going. I said yes.'

'Oh, jolly good, did he say a time?'

'Around eight. I'll stay here, if that's all right, I have some little jobs I want to get on with.'

'I hope Jackson's still going.'

'Why's that?'

'I wanted to ask him a little more about Grimes.'

Beth wiped her hands on a towel. 'Oh goodness, you're not going to pursue this, are you? You're clutching at straws, if you ask me.'

They went through to the lounge where James refilled their brandy glasses and picked up Grimes' painting. He perched on the edge of the sofa and studied it.

Beth put a hand on his shoulder. 'Now, you're looking at this as if it's a code to decipher. Do you see some sort of hidden message in there?'

He rolled his eyes at Beth and reached into her sewing bag for a pin in order to repeat his stabbing of the canvas. Beth looked on with bemusement. After a few seconds, James held the pin up in triumph and observed Beth frowning with an expression implying that he might have gone slightly mad.

'James, I don't see what you're looking at,' she said, leaning in to examine the pin. 'There's nothing on there.'

'Exactly,' said James.

She pulled her earlobe, none the wiser.

'But don't you see, darling? There's no fresh paint on there.'

'James, I know you fancy yourself as Paul Temple, but this is real life. You've called in two professionals so far. Philip Jackson diagnosed a heart attack and George said there was no case to answer.'

James started to interrupt, but Beth held up her finger to silence him. 'I know you think it's suspicious but, if that's the official cause of death, you can't change that. And the unofficial one? Well, don't you think George would spot a murder if he saw one? He didn't see anything odd, did he?'

He gave her a peck on the cheek. 'Indulge me. Let me play around with it for a day or two.'

With a nod of resignation, she returned to the kitchen. James spent the next hour pondering. No red paint on the canvas; the paintbrush, as far as he could remember, had been bone dry. Grimes had had a bump on his head. That could have been recent, but doubts lingered. There had been a layer of mud and frost on his heels and broken crockery across the floor. The morning, surely, was the one time that a farmer would be in the fields so why would Grimes be painting? The Snoop Sisters had insisted that no one liked him.

He winced. He shouldn't take too much notice of what they said. Medical diagnosis, as Beth had been quick to remind him, was a heart attack. There was no getting over that. Perhaps George and Beth were right – perhaps he was making too much of it.

The brass clock on the bookcase chimed eight.

'Oh Lord,' he mumbled and he leapt up. In the hall, he slipped on his jacket, checked his pockets for gloves and keys and peered round the kitchen door.

'I'm off to meet Bert. D'you want me to come back and get you later?'

'Not tonight,' replied Beth. 'I think I'll finish off here and then listen to the wireless. The BBC is in the middle of an Edgar Wallace mystery and it's getting near the end. You can bring me back some peanuts, though.'

'Right-ho, see you later, then.'

The Half Moon public house overlooked the village green and presented itself, as it had for the last four hundred years, as the hub of Cavendish life. Sleet flurried in the breeze and the orange glow of the pub's lights filtered a welcoming beacon to anyone braving the elements.

The Inn's sign displayed a half moon shining over thatched cottages, with the silhouette of a shepherd walking toward them; seeking a cosy haven from the trials of the working day. James wondered how many weary workers and farm hands had relaxed in the bar over the centuries. He pulled off his gloves, turned the brass knob and walked in.

The noise, heat and ambience were like an invisible hug. The sweet aroma of tobacco, malt and hops was enticing and the constant chatter and laughter gave him a feeling of comfort and belonging.

Above him, horse brasses, leather reins and bent horseshoes were nailed up on ancient oak beams. Sepia photographs of long dead farmers and smocked shepherds holding pewter mugs adorned the walls. A ragged Union Jack hung above a more recent picture of men from the village who had given their lives during the Great War. Toby jugs and ancient, dusty beer bottles lined the shelves and, beneath them, numerous optics offered an excellent choice of spirits.

The taps on the bar tempted the taste buds with beers that, by their names alone, invited customers to taste them: Sussex Mild, Harvey Old Ale, Black Stout, Winter Bitter and the local Old Truman's Christmas beer delivered earlier that week.

Behind the bar stood Donovan Delaney, the landlord, who had taken over the running of the pub five years ago. He'd been a publican in his native Dublin but, on marrying Kate, a Sussex girl, and with a couple of children reaching school-age, they'd moved to Cavendish to be nearer to her family.

Like other newcomers, he'd worked hard to win over the locals, but with Donovan it hadn't taken long. By being open to suggestions and loyal to the popular ales and local breweries, that acceptance had come quickly.

He held up a hand and shouted across to James in a melodic Irish lilt. 'Evening to you, your Lordship. What is it you'll be having?'

James took his cap off and fought his way to the bar. 'Ah, good evening to you, Donovan. A pint of your new Christmas ale, please, and whatever the people with Bert are having. Have one yourself.'

'I don't mind if I do. Your man Bert's in the far corner there. I'll bring it over.'

James placed the money for the drinks on the dented oak bar and wove his way through the throng of villagers with a quick 'Hello' to many on the way. At the back of the bar, a few men were playing darts and he could hear the banging of skittles in the outhouse.

He found Bert in the far booth, by the window looking out onto the village green. His craggy face lit up as he shoved his drinking companions along the wooden bench to make room.

'Oi, oi, Jimmy boy,' he said. 'Take the weight off.'

James shrugged his coat off and plonked himself

43

down next to Bert just as the drinks arrived. Alongside Bert was Graham Porter, the family butcher and an excellent one at that. James loved the vast selections of meat and poultry he stocked and was delighted to learn that he had started keeping pigs and chickens on his smallholding to supply his shop. His latest offering was thickly sliced home-cured gammon which had recently won a county show award.

Next to him were the Doc, Stephen Merryweather and Ian Connell, the builder he'd met at Grimes' farm. Last was Dorothy Forbes, an elderly well-to-do but bossy woman, who insisted on directing the Cavendish Players' dramas. Every few years a brave contender would try to take that mantle from her, but their attempts always failed and to be fair to her, she did do an excellent job.

James felt Bert nudge him.

He whispered. 'Got some nice quality gear come in today. Beth'll be interested – good silky satins, ideal for ball-gowns and what 'ave yer. They're 'alf the price of what you'd pay up town in Bond Street.'

James smirked. He'd known Bert Briggs nearly all his life and, although they came from opposite ends of the social scale, they'd become firm friends. They'd met when they were eight years old when their respective schools were on an outing. James' class, from a small private school in Sussex, had journeyed to the Natural History Museum. Bert's class from Bethnal Green, one of the roughest areas in London's East End, had arrived on the same day. They kept bumping into each other throughout the visit and struck up a friendship.

Two things remained in James' memory of that day. First, Bert never stopped asking questions – he became quite infuriating as he bombarded the teacher and any other passer-by with endless queries about the exhibits, the building and the people. Second, he ribbed James rotten about his upper-crust accent and his 'toff' background and, since they were children, had taken to calling him Jimmy boy – something no other friend or acquaintance had done. James adored Bert's humour, stood in awe of his knowledge and loved to listen to his stories about the East End.

Much to his parents' amusement, James had insisted on keeping in touch and the pair regularly corresponded while at school, although he'd found it difficult to read Bert's untidy scrawl. That untidiness also transmitted itself to his dress sense, from his scuffed hobnail boots to a moth-eaten flat cap perched on the side of his head.

They'd both recently turned forty-five and, whereas James had stayed slim and relatively fit, Bert had become thick-set and turned grey quite early. The lines on his craggy face reminded James of the tight isobars on a weather map. He now lived in the Brighton area, where he spent most days on the markets or at the racecourse.

James watched Bert roll a cigarette and slam the tobacco tin on the table.

'Help yourself. Plenty more where that came from – 'alf the price of shop-bought.'

James observed Stephen's concerned expression. Bert did take a bit of getting used to; everything he sold 'fell off the back of a lorry', but he never asked where things came from. He knew that Bert's childhood had been incredibly hard and he'd resorted to black market activities to help feed the family. His father had left the family home when Bert was small and, with several siblings and an ailing mother, he did what he had to do to keep them fed. As a result, James never enquired about anything Bert did, preferring, instead, to ignore these minor criminal activities, especially considering the occupation of his other close friend, George Lane.

Dorothy rapped her bony knuckles on the table. 'Attention everyone, please! I knew some of my bit-part players would be here tonight. I want to remind you that we start rehearsals for *The Devil Incarnate* this weekend. I expect you all to be there.'

They mumbled that they would be but Stephen shifted uneasily.

'Is the title absolutely n-necessary? It all sounds very evil.'

Bert leant forward. 'You 'ave to 'ave some evil in your life, vicar. Can't 'ave good without evil.'

'W-well, that's true, but–'

'No "buts" me old codger. A good play always 'as some bad in it. A nice conflict, warts an all. But, I bet you a pound to a penny, good'll overcome evil in this one. That 'appens in every story you read.' He met Dorothy's gaze. 'That's right, innit, love?'

Dorothy looked down her nose at him and James had the sense that she didn't particular like Bert. 'You're correct with your assumptions, yes.'

Graham placed his hands on the table. James couldn't imagine him being anything other than a butcher with his huge frame and fiery red hair. 'Does anyone know what it's about?' he asked. 'I'm supposed to be playing a priest or something.' He gently elbowed Stephen. 'You'll have to give me a few tips.'

'Well,' Dorothy said, 'John Jepson's written it. He's not here at the moment, but I'm sure he can explain the storyline in a little more detail. It has something to do with people who come back from the dead. Mud men, I believe he calls them.'

Ian Connell burst out laughing. 'Mud men! Sounds like some sort of horror film.'

James could understand Ian's astonishment. He had to admit it did sound odd.

'Dorothy, have you read this play?' he asked. 'I mean, no disrespect to Mr J but is it, you know, is it any good?'

She pushed her shoulders back as if ready to defend herself, then she shrugged. 'I haven't a clue. It's the first read through this weekend. But Dr Jackson has read a few pages and it seemed well-written, so I'm being guided by him. After all, he's a professional, so I trust him.'

Philip puffed on his pipe nonchalantly and looked a little surprised. 'Mmm, professional in the sense of being a doctor, not a playwright. Don't know if the whole thing is going to be any good. I only read the first Act, but he certainly knows how to write an opening if that's any help.'

Stephen took a sip of stout; his face brightened. 'Well, if we feel it's not right, we can j-join the children and the pantomime.'

He groaned as Bert kicked him under the table. 'Fat chance, vicar. This is the juiciest drama

Cavendish 'as ever put on.'

'Lord Harrington,' Dorothy said, 'Alec Grimes was supposed to be playing a minor part – just a few lines. Would you be able to take that role on? I know you're organising Hallowe'en and Bonfire Night, but...'

James held a palm up. 'Say no more, Dorothy, director of all good plays. Lord H will come to your rescue.'

Bert rolled his eyes as Dorothy zealously thanked him.

Stephen clearly had doubts. 'W-what are the mud men?'

Graham straightened up and making himself big, let out a low moan and groped the air with his fingers.

Dorothy glared at him. 'If you're going to be childish...'

James settled everyone down. 'No, come on, Dorothy. We are genuinely interested.'

She fiddled with her clipboard. 'To be honest, gentlemen, I'm afraid I don't really know. It all sounded rather far-fetched to me. Something about making a man out of mud and it comes to life. What an imagination!'

Everyone stared inquiringly at one another, except for Bert, who swigged the last of his pint down and let out a satisfied sigh at the end of it.

'A golem,' he announced as he waved his glass in the air. 'Donovan, another round over 'ere, mate.'

James frowned. 'A what?'

'Mud men. They're called golems.'

'Golems? D'you mean to say they actually exist?'

48

Bert gestured a 'maybe' or 'maybe not' with his hands. 'Literally, no,' he replied. 'It's a story, a myth. The stories I've 'eard come from Jewish folklore. Now, if the Jews felt they was being persecuted in some way, well, that's when they'd summon up a golem. They make this geezer out of the earth – so they go out somewhere and model a life-size man from mud or clay. Then, they 'ave special prayers and 'ave to summon up the four elements – nature elements, you know, fire, earth, water, wind. Then, the people making the golem circle around the mud man seven times, chanting prayers and pretending to be the elements.'

Bert's audience looked on, enthralled.

Graham folded his arms. 'And what happens when they've done that?'

'Well, then the golem comes to life and seeks out the enemy, or whatever they're asked to do.'

'Y-you mean, it's like a k-killing machine?' Stephen said with a look of alarm.

'Nah, vicar, nothing like that. It's made to protect 'em from their enemies. The blokes who make it will ask it to seek out who's persecuting them – so it goes out and finds 'em. Then it's up to those who are persecuted to decide what to do. I don't fink it ends up as a massacre or nothing.'

Stephen didn't appear convinced. Graham took a swig of beer, while Ian shook his head. Philip, as usual, continued puffing on his pipe, acting as if a visit from a golem were an everyday occurrence.

Dorothy gawped at Bert. 'How on earth do you know all of this?'

'I'm from the East End, love. Lots of Jews up there, so you get to hear lots of stories, 'specially

49

folklore and all that. Most cultures 'ave similar things about people coming back from the dead.' He leant forward. 'It's like all the fertility stuff like the holly parade.'

Graham cocked his head. Bert stared back at him in amazement.

'Well, you've gotta know about that, surely? Villagers go parading holly down the streets during the winter days and that encourages growth and new life. The Morris men have a dance for that. They do it in Cavendish, for God's sake.'

Philip nodded. 'Yes, we do. I've never really known why, though.'

Bert winked at Dorothy. 'I'm not just an 'andsome face, Mrs Forbes. I bet you think there's something pretty special about me now, don't you?'

James pressed his lips together as Bert roared with laughter. He had one of the most disgusting laughs he'd ever heard and this was now resounding loudly through the bar. Those in earshot laughed along with him, even though they'd no idea why they were doing so. Dorothy gathered her bag and papers.

'I've more players to see,' she said, flustered. 'I'll see you at rehearsals. In fact, I'll see you at the Hallowe'en do first.' She scurried away to the sound of muffled laughter.

Once everyone had settled down, James asked Graham if he knew what part Grimes had been supposed to play.

'No idea, James. Bloody glad that Grimes fella isn't in it, though.'

'Oh?'

'I know I shouldn't be like this, him being dead and all, but he owed me money. I got right annoyed when I heard he'd employed Ian here to do some building work. Now, if he could afford that, why couldn't he afford to pay me what he owed? And, more importantly, how am I gonna get that money back?'

'D'you mind me asking how much?' asked James.

'Near on two hundred and fifty quid.'

Philip's pipe fell into his hands. 'Two hundred and fifty pounds!'

'Yeah. He had the option to buy some extra land or something and didn't have the money. He knew I'd had a windfall from an inheritance. He'd agreed to pay it back monthly, but I never got anything from him.'

Bert stubbed out his cigarette. 'Well, I can nip over there and retrieve two 'undred and fifty quid's worth–'

'Bert,' James interrupted. 'Nothing underhand, please. Anyway, I don't think you'd find anything worth that much.' He turned to Graham. 'How long ago was this?'

'About eight months.' A guilty look crossed his face. 'I got that angry with him a couple of weeks ago, I said I'd break his legs if he didn't start paying up.'

Stephen glared and Graham fidgeted.

'I wouldn't, of course. I may look like a giant idiot, but I wouldn't have hurt him. Christ.' He pulled a face. 'Beggin' your pardon, vicar, I mean, I thought it was about time I put the frighteners on, that's all.'

'You're not the only one,' Philip added. 'The Snoop Sisters are doing the rounds after getting the news from Mrs Jepson. They said John Jepson had a run-in with him this morning. Not sure whether that's true, though. Have to take what they say with a pinch of salt.'

'He didn't sound very w-well liked,' said Stephen.

James encouraged the vicar to spill the beans.

'I-I thought I'd try and f-find out a little bit about him – for the funeral. No one seemed to have a good word to say. Well, those that knew him, anyway.'

They sipped their drinks and James lost himself in a daydream. After a while, Bert nudged him.

'All right, Jimmy boy?'

'Ye-s, yes I think so. Bert, what are you doing tomorrow?'

'Ducking and diving, mate. Ducking and diving.'

'Could you spare a couple of hours first thing in the morning?'

'For you, boy, anything.'

'Come for breakfast. Eight o'clock suit?'

'Get Beth to dish up an extra sausage and I'm there.'

Philip leant across the table to catch James' attention. 'What was it you wanted to tell me?'

James suggested they go to the bar where they stood at the far end, away from eavesdroppers.

'Listen, old chap, re this Grimes business. I know you said it was a heart attack and all that, but could you have been wrong?'

Jackson shook his head and studied his pipe. 'I don't think so. It was pretty cut and dried. Why?'

James went through his suspicions and his concerns about Grimes' decision to go out painting at that time. Philip re-lit his pipe and allowed the smoke to dissipate before replying.

'I must admit, I did wonder why he'd been out painting. But, then again, I didn't know him. He always seemed a little strange. Perhaps that's what he did? His house is pretty run-down, so maybe he ran the farm like that as well. What did George have to say?'

'Ah, well, he wanted nothing to do with it.'

'I can't say that surprises me. Perhaps you're looking for something that's not there.' Philip swigged down the last of his beer and placed his glass on the bar. 'Right, I'm down to read Natasha her bedtime story.'

'Give her a peck on the cheek from me,' replied James. He checked his watch and caught Donovan's eye. 'Can I have a couple of packets of peanuts, Donovan?'

Bert joined him at the bar. 'So, what are we up to tomorrow?'

James paid for his peanuts. 'We're searching for clues, Bert.'

And, with that cryptic message, he left Bert at the bar, scratching his head.

CHAPTER FIVE

Bert stabbed his fork into the last piece of fried bread and swept it around his plate to soak up the juices from the bacon and tomatoes.

'That, your very fine Ladyship, was the bee's knees. I'd even go so far as to say that you trumped my old mum on the breakfast front.'

Beth topped up his teacup. 'Well, it's a real pleasure, Bert. I like a man with an appetite and you so enjoy your food.'

'You're not wrong there. You know, you two are getting quite a reputation for cooking around 'ere. I 'ope I'm gonna get some more treats at your 'allowe'en do.'

'Well, Mr Mitchell at the orchard said it's been a good apple harvest this year, so we'll have our usual apple crumbles in the oven.'

'And Jimmy's 'ome-made custard?'

She assured him that home-made custard would be on the menu.

'Well,' James said, getting up from his chair, 'I'm sure that the feast you've devoured will keep you going for the morning at least. Are you going to sit there all day?'

Bert gulped a couple of mouthfuls of tea and pushed his chair back. 'You're in a rush.' He snatched his scruffy jacket and Beth helped him on with it.

James slipped his own coat on and placed a

battered trilby on Bert's head. 'Things to do, old chap. Come on.' He kissed Beth on the cheek. 'Are you here today, darling, or gallivanting off somewhere?'

'I'm with Anne this morning, helping her unpack and settle in. You'll have to get your own snack at lunchtime – unless, of course, you want to call in at the vicarage?'

'How about I pop in and grab the lot of you? Tell Anne not to cook. We'll go to Elsie's café for lunch. Our treat.'

James and Bert made their way out to the garage, where Bert sank into the passenger seat of James' other car – a sleek, bright red, 4-door Jaguar MKVII saloon. The luxurious interior gave off the comforting aroma of old leather and oil. The engine purred under the bonnet as James coaxed her down the drive and onto the open road.

Along the way, James updated Bert on what had happened to Grimes and outlined his own suspicions. Bert took it all in and occasionally appeared surprised. He commented on how flimsy James' notions were but, as he didn't have any plans for the morning, he was happy to play Watson to James' Holmes.

The crisp, winter morning gave the countryside a stark, raw feel – as if all life had gone into hibernation. But life – of the human variety – was definitely thriving. Lights glimmered through steamy windows as the sun strained to warm the frozen earth.

The lingering smell of fried bacon filtered through the air vents every now and again. Children, in buttoned-up duffle coats and polished shoes, dragged their heels to school as mothers hurried them along. Many of their fathers were already making their daily commute to London.

James didn't envy them their journey, especially midwinter. The nearest railway station was five miles away, at Haywards Heath, which meant getting on the bus before boarding the huge locomotives that thundered up to Victoria and London Bridge.

It was washing day for many and, although the temperature had barely risen above freezing, kitchen windows were wide open to free the condensation.

They continued on into the countryside where, in stark contrast to the village, Grimes' house appeared bleak and desolate, as if standing in a lonely vigil for its now departed owner. James parked on the verge and they made their way to the front door.

Bert rubbed his hands together and blew into his palms. Cold, misty air escaped as he spoke. 'What exactly are you 'oping to find 'ere?'

James unlocked the door. 'Humour me, Bert. Something that may stick out as being unusual.'

Bert followed him in and looked around the kitchen. 'Crikey, he weren't exactly house-proud, was he?'

'Mmm, that's what George said.'

The kitchen chair still stood halfway across the floor. The broken crockery remained on the lino. The ornamental robin stood, chipped and faded, staring into space.

Bert opened cupboards and drawers and announced that all was as expected; cutlery, sieves, saucepans along with the staple foods such as bread, flour, oats, eggs and milk. He suggested that he take some of the food. 'It'll be a waste not to,' he said. A tin of Bird's custard powder stood by the side of the cooker alongside a half-eaten apple pie. Bert licked his lips.

'Nice bit o' pie. Looks all right – I think I'll 'ave a piece of that.'

James stared in disbelief. 'Good grief, man, you've only just had breakfast.'

Bert sniffed it and rummaged around in a drawer for a spoon. 'One of your cleaner's specials if I'm not mistaken.' He took a mouthful. 'Not quite up to your standards, though.'

James pulled a face and went through to the back room. The sparseness of it depressed him. Threadbare carpets, curtains in need of a good wash, a shabby armchair and a sunken horsehair sofa. There appeared to be a severe lack of personal mementos anywhere; no photographs, ornaments or anything that would shed light on Alec Grimes, the man.

James slid open the drawers in the sideboard and rummaged through a pile of invoices for animal feed and farming materials and copies of a farming magazine. In another drawer were bank statements. He hesitated. It didn't seem right to examine them; but Grimes did owe Graham money. Perhaps he had some cash tucked away.

He leafed through the statements and furrowed his brow. Grimes had the sum total of fifty-seven pounds, seven shillings and sixpence. Hardly any money was being deposited. He searched the back of the drawer with no success. Did he have a will? If so, where was it? Perhaps the bank had it. He flicked through some other documents but there was no sign of any other accounts.

James viewed his surroundings. Where on earth was Grimes getting the money to have building work done? Connell hadn't been paid and it didn't look as if Grimes had two farthings to rub together. He shivered and scanned the book titles on the shelves.

'Good Lord,' he mumbled, frowning as his fingers drummed their spines. Two shelves appeared to be dedicated to books on the supernatural, with a family bible right at the end. Perhaps that's why John Jepson had been here. Grimes must have been helping him with the play.

'Oi, oi,' Bert shouted from the kitchen.

James found his friend holding up the doormat. Beneath it was a pentagram crudely chalked on the lino.

'Oh dear. I must say that ties in with the books in the back room: a couple of dozen titles on what looks like devil worship and black magic.'

Bert frowned and James waved him in to the back room where Bert folded back the rug by the door frame. James peered over Bert's shoulder to see another pentagram carved into the floorboards. 'How extraordinary.'

Bert replaced the rug and shrugged. 'So 'e was into black magic. It don't prove anything. Lots of things go on behind closed doors, mate. A village looks quaint from the outside, but on the inside? Well, it's the same as everywhere else.'

James heaved a sigh. 'This is frustrating.' They wandered back to the kitchen and he looked at the dresser. 'That's odd.'

'What?'

'There's some more of these pottery pieces. There were some of these on the ground where he died.'

'So he broke a bowl. 'ardly murder.' Bert squatted down and reached in between the dresser and a small cupboard. He pulled out a dinner knife coated in dried egg yolk.

James glanced across at the table and studied the now dried-up, half-eaten breakfast with a fork by the side of it. A solitary fly feasted on the grease.

'Well, now, what on earth was he doing throwing a knife over here?' James remarked.

'How d'you know he threw it?' Bert opened the cupboard above and picked up the brown sauce on the shelf. 'He prob'ly popped over 'ere for sauce and dropped it. Or, he was beginning to feel unwell and things went flying.' He waved the knife at James. 'Not everything's got a sinister twist, you know.'

James clenched his jaw and Bert, chuckling, slapped him on the back and placed the knife in his hand.

'There's nothing 'ere. You've got a dry paint-brush, some books on devil worship and a couple of pentagrams. John Jepson's into the same thing by the sounds of it. Don't mean he's gonna get struck down, does it? And Jackson's a good doc. He's not gonna sign off a death certificate if there's something dodgy.' Bert swung round and faced James. 'Hey, you don't think it's our new vicar, do you?'

James' frustration turned to laughter. 'I can't imagine such an unassuming chap doing anything untoward, can you?'

'They're always the worst. You know what it's like when the neighbours get interviewed about a murderer. Always such a quiet bloke, they say. Never 'ad a bad word about anyone.' He peered through the window. 'What's 'appening with the animals?'

'They're being looked after by the farmer along the road, but I suppose they'll be sold off.'

'Graham might get 'is dosh back if he can prove he's owed it.'

'Perhaps,' James said putting the dirty knife on the wooden drainer. He threw a tea towel to Bert. 'Come on, help me out with these plates and I'll run you to where you need to be. I'll wash, you wipe.'

After dropping Bert off, he collected Beth and the Merryweathers and chauffeured them to Elsie's, a small café on the outskirts of Charnley, the next village along from Cavendish. The converted cottage had become a firm favourite and he and Beth had often popped in to have lunch.

Settling into cushioned bay-window seats, they ordered a sherry aperitif and Anne asked which dishes were the best.

'Oh Anne, everything on Elsie's menu is divine,' said Beth. 'From the cheese on toast to the steamed pudding desserts. You can't go wrong and it's all made on the day in that tiny kitchen at the back. Whatever you choose, you're going to enjoy it.'

James sipped his cream sherry. 'Well, I'm going for devilled kidneys and mashed potatoes.'

The waitress, dressed in black with a pristine white cotton apron, jotted the order down. Beth handed her the menu.

'I'll have the lemon sole with fresh peas and a slice of bread and butter on the side.'

Anne took Stephen's menu from him. 'We're both having the same – herb sausages with onion gravy and mashed potatoes.'

James ordered another sherry for Stephen who insisted that that would be his last.

'B-best be careful. Need to write a ser-sermon today.'

'Don't worry, the old herb sausies will soak it all up. Reminds me of our twins – do you re-member, darling? They always loved sausages. Still do – have them every day if they could.'

'Oh yes, I meant to ask,' Anne said. 'How old are your boys?'

'Twenty. They're both at Oxford, studying. Well, *supposedly* studying!'

Beth explained that James was convinced, after their last visit, that Oxford had turned into an enormous social club. Hardly any studying went on and the twins flitted from one social gathering to the next.

'W-what do they want to do?' asked Stephen.

'Well,' said James, 'Harry wants to take over here and help run Harrington's. I think he sees my job as a life of old Riley – which, on the surface, it may appear to be, but the engine room has to stay well-oiled. Oliver's keen to teach. He's pretty musical, plays the piano and whatnot. Wouldn't surprise me if he ended up teaching music, something in that line.'

'They're both admirable ambitions,' Anne said.

Beth beamed proudly. 'We think so, and you can probably speak with Oliver about your teaching experience. You'll meet them when they get home for Christmas. And, I expect to meet your two this weekend. Will they be here in time for Hallowe'en?'

'Ooh yes. I've already told them about that and they're getting really quite excited.'

'Remind me, how old are they?'

'Luke is eight and Mark is coming up for ten.'

James and Beth both remarked on what nice ages those were and, as they discussed the adventures and toys available to children nowadays, the waitress delivered their meals.

James salivated at the smell of his lightly-spiced lamb kidneys lapped with thick mushroom gravy. Stephen's and Anne's sausages, made by a local Charnley butcher, had a hint of mixed herbs with sage and onion, while Beth's succulent and delicate sole had been freshly caught that morning off the coast at Brighton.

Halfway through her meal, Anne took a break and leant toward James. 'I heard you went back to Mr Grimes' farm today.'

'Yes; didn't find anything to convince Bert of my little theory, but I did find one or two oddities of interest.'

Beth frowned. 'What do you mean – oddities?'

'Well, a stack of books on devil worship and pentagrams under the carpets, for starters. Broken crockery and his breakfast knife lying on the floor.'

'H-heavens,' said Stephen. 'That does s-sound somewhat alarming.'

'Yes, struck me as a little odd, but Bert seemed to think we all have little secrets going on behind the curtains. Not that Grimes had any curtains to speak of.'

Anne agreed. 'Kidlington, where we were before, is only a small village but the gossip! Much of it had no foundation; just people with too much time on their hands.'

Beth understood completely. 'The more people know about each other, the more they gossip. And, let's face it, it is a very human trait to be nosy about people.'

Stephen's face paled. 'Oh, Lord, what on earth do you talk about if y-you're giving a funeral service for someone who d-dabbled in the dark arts? Perhaps I sh-should ring the Bishop for some advice?'

James loaded his fork with kidney. 'Good idea. You may have to call the old Bish, get his thoughts. I s'pose Grimes is due a Christian burial, the same as everyone else. I mean, forgive and forget and all that.'

Stephen's concern became the topic of conversation until the owner of the restaurant, Elsie Taylor, waddled over to them. James and Beth were convinced that Elsie tasted all of the meals before they were served – her whole body was built for comfort rather than speed.

At thirty-five, she had not married, her single passion being food – cooking it, eating it and sharing the finished article with her customers. She'd tied her wiry blonde hair back into a pony tail and her face glowed from the heat of the kitchen. She fanned herself with a spare menu.

'Good afternoon. Lovely to see you again.'

'Ah, Elsie,' said James. 'Fine fodder as always. These kidneys are by far the best I've had. By the way, this is Stephen and Anne Merryweather. Stephen's the new vicar at Cavendish.'

She wiped her palms on her apron. 'Oh, that's nice. I'm pleased to meet you. Hope you're enjoying your food.'

'I-it's really very good,' replied Stephen. 'I can s-see why James brought us here.'

'Special occasion is it, or is his Lordship showing me off?'

'Bit of both, really, Else,' James replied. 'Just settling the vicar in and this is the best place for good food – apart from the manor, that is,' he winked at her. 'Poor thing's hardly got his feet under the table and he's got a funeral to do.'

'Oh, I'm sorry to hear that. Anyone I know?'

Beth continued. 'You may do. Alec Grimes, a farmer on the road to Cavendish – do you know him?'

Elsie frowned and repeated the name a couple of times. After a while, the name resonated. 'Oh yes, I know. He's the one that took that farm on a few years back. Not a local man.'

'That's the one,' said Beth. 'Unfortunately, no one seems to have known him well. The farmhouse is a little run down but there doesn't seem to be anyone to inherit. I guess the whole thing will have to go to auction.'

'Oh, but his son will have that, surely?' Elsie replied.

James almost choked on his potatoes. 'His son? Alec Grimes has a son? Are you sure?'

'Oh yes, although I don't think anyone saw much of him,' Elsie said, as her finger and thumb squeezed her bottom lip. 'Now, what was his name?' She called over to a lady who was getting ready to leave with her husband. 'Mrs Thorp, you remember Alec Grimes, that farmer on the Cavendish road? You know, the one who bought the farm off Ted Basinger. He had a son, didn't he? Can you remember his name?'

Mrs Thorp didn't hesitate. 'Keith,' she replied as she buttoned up her coat. 'Moved to Scotland.'

Elsie thanked her and returned her attention to James. 'That's it, Keith. Had a right falling out with his dad. That's when he moved to Scotland. Hasn't been back since, as far as I know.'

'Well,' Beth said, 'that's a surprise but how awful they fell out.'

Anne put her hand on Stephen's arm. 'Somebody ought to contact him. He'll want to be at the funeral. I mean, even if they've argued, he might feel dreadful if he didn't attend.'

Stephen, his mouth full of sausage, mumbled in agreement.

James leaned forward. 'Elsie, old thing. Seeing as you seem to have all the gossip, do you know what Keith and his dad fell out about?'

'No, I'm afraid not, your Lordship,' replied Elsie. 'I wouldn't have known he had a son, to be honest. It's only because we've got someone in the village that did know him quite well, so I

65

would hear of him being spoken about. That was Mrs Keates, down the road here. She's at number seven. She worked alongside Keith for a while. May still be in touch, though I doubt it. He didn't seem to be the socialising type, especially with older people. But she seemed to know him better than most.' She smoothed her apron down. 'Anyway, I'd best get on. Enjoy the rest of your meal.'

'Well, well,' James said. 'I wonder whether Keith has come back? That's a lead to pursue.'

Beth gave James a despairing look. 'You're not going to start with the Sherlock Holmes act again? Why don't you listen to the experts? It was a heart attack.'

'Oh, I don't know,' Anne said, her eyes sparkling. 'I like a good mystery.'

James grinned at her with equal enthusiasm. 'Yes, me too. It's only for this afternoon, Beth. I've got too much on, what with Hallowe'en and Bonfire Night coming up. Won't hurt to ask around, though. Anyway, she may have a contact for Keith.'

'W-what if she hasn't? It doesn't sound like he's the sort to stay in touch,' Stephen said with some concern.

'Then I'll toddle over to George and ask him to do a search through official channels,' replied James. He turned to Beth. 'Satisfied?'

Beth attempted to look annoyed but gave in. They rounded lunch off by treating themselves to portions of steaming treacle sponge pudding before venturing outside.

James dropped Stephen and Anne at the vicarage with a promise to let them know about

66

Keith's whereabouts as soon as he had the details.

Beth declared she'd walk back to their house, as she wanted to call in and see Dorothy about the play and what was required for the costumes. She was involved with the sewing club and Bert's offer of material would, she said, come in very handy.

James wasn't so sure that purchasing anything from Bert was a good idea. He was certain that, at some stage, his friendships with Bert and George would clash and did his best to avoid discussions of buying and selling when the two were together. He kissed Beth goodbye and strolled toward the car. In the distance, he heard several youngsters singing.

'Please to remember, the fifth of November,
Gunpowder, treason and plot.
I see no reason, why gunpowder treason,
Should ever be forgot.'

James waited for the source of the singing to appear and finally observed a group of children approaching, led by young Tommy and Sue Hawkins, whose father ran the local library. They proudly displayed their life-size Guy Fawkes in a beaten-up old pram. He sported a homespun red wool beard, a trilby hat and a grotesque cardboard mask across his eyes and nose. His torn trousers and jumper were filled with rolled-up newspaper and straw and he flopped about lethargically as the pram rattled over uneven pavements.

The Bonfire Night celebrations had been a part of the Cavendish community for over two hundred years and every generation of children, including his own, looked forward to the festivities. He was almost grateful to Guy Fawkes for having tried to blow up the Houses of Parliament all those years ago. Without it, the Harrington tradition of hosting the Bonfire Night party would never have existed. The children sprinted across to him.

'Penny for the guy, your Lordship?' Susan asked angelically.

James felt in his pocket and brought out some change. 'For you, Susan, two shillings.'

Her eyes were like saucers as the coins gleamed in her hand.

'Thank you.'

James ruffled Tommy's hair. 'Vicar and his wife are back. I'm sure if you knock on their door, they'll give you a couple of coppers.'

'Brilliant,' Tommy said. 'Have we got lots of fireworks, Lord?'

James chuckled. 'More than we need, Tommy, don't worry your socks about that. Bonfire's growing and getting all set to burn. We just need the guy here to stick on top of it and we'll be set. When are you bringing him over?'

'Monday lunchtime. Mr Chrichton's letting us come over between lessons. We're missing out on PE, but that's all right. Building a bonfire's much more fun.'

The other children shouted in agreement.

'I'm missing netball,' Susan added with a twinge of regret. 'But that's all right, too.'

'Jolly good. You collected much?'

The children yelled across one another and, in between interruptions, James learned that they'd collected over five pounds and all of the money would be going toward the staging of the pantomime. The first night would be performed solely for the old people who lived in the residential home outside the village. James reminded them that what they were doing was a splendid thing and that the elderly folk would no doubt enjoy it.

He squatted down next to Susan and explained that the vicar's two boys would be arriving in the next couple of days and that he was putting her in charge of making them welcome.

'They're going to be here for Hallowe'en, so make sure they become a part of your little gang, won't you?'

Susan promised with every ounce of sincerity. The trust of a real Lord and the reward of an extra shilling encouraged her to do just that. The children raced down the vicarage path in a rampage. James chuckled at their excited shrieks of 'Penny for the guy'. That'll shake Stephen from his sherry-induced slumber, he thought. 'Right,' he muttered as he unlocked the car door. 'Let's call on Mrs Keates.'

CHAPTER SIX

Storm clouds gathered as James negotiated his Jaguar through the narrow country lanes to Charnley. The ancient woodland between the two villages hadn't changed for centuries and, with no other cars on the road, he could imagine the scene, during the English Civil War, of Cavaliers and leather-clad Roundheads cantering among the sturdy oaks while, deep in the forest, blacksmiths fired up their forges.

Heavy black clouds rolled over the Downs and raindrops the size of marbles splattered on the windscreen. James switched the wipers on and concentrated on the road.

Like Cavendish, Charnley welcomed visitors into its cosy, quaint environment. The pub and church were at the heart of the community by the village green but with the awful weather he found the streets empty except for one lady scurrying toward her house, fighting with her umbrella all the way.

He slowed down and squinted through the foggy windows to locate the house on the High Street. The windscreen continued to mist up and he rubbed it furiously, careful not to veer off the road at the same time. Eventually, number seven came into view.

Mrs Keates lived in a two-up, two-down Victorian terrace house that opened straight onto the street. It had small sash windows; the woodwork was painted a glorious canary yellow and recently, too. The wooden front door provided a delightfully sunny aspect on such a dismal day and James imagined that someone with a particularly jolly disposition lived there.

He leapt out of the car, pulled his collar up and ran to the door. Standing as close as possible to the house, he rapped on the iron knocker and was happy to see he didn't have to wait long. The door opened a fraction and a round-faced, middle-aged lady peered tentatively at him.

'Yes?'

'Ah, Mrs Keates?'

'Yes.'

'Mrs Keates, I'm Lord James Harrington from the next village, Cavendish. I wonder if–'

The door swung open and Mrs Keates more or less yanked him into the long, polished hallway.

She chuckled with embarrassment.

'Oh I'm so sorry, your Lordship, making you stand out in the rain. I didn't recognise you with your collar up.'

James smiled to himself. He didn't like to rely on his title. Sometimes, however, it did come in handy. He folded his coat collar down.

'Quite all right. Didn't expect you to just invite me in.'

'I must admit, I wasn't expecting anyone today, especially yourself.' She laughed again and wiped her hands on a towel. 'Would you like some tea? Or my 'usband's got a nice whisky. I could do you a hot toddy, warm you up from the cold.'

James' eyes brightened as he rubbed his hands together. 'What a splendid suggestion, Mrs Keates.'

Mrs Keates asked if he minded coming through to the kitchen. 'I've quite a bit of baking on at the moment.'

James didn't need asking twice. The aroma coming from the back of the house prompted him to fall in with her suggestion. He followed the doughy smell of bread and baking into a tiny square kitchen at the back of the house.

He put Mrs Keates at about fifty years of age; quite a buxom woman, with curly salt and pepper hair and a round, squashed face, with rosy cheeks and a jovial countenance.

The kitchen was in a state of chaos. He surveyed the floury work surfaces and the cakes in their various stages of production.

'Dashed good display of sponges, Mrs Keates.'

'We're having a party at the village hall tonight. A ninetieth birthday, so we thought we'd spoil him. I seem to be the one who always cooks the cakes. Seem to have a knack for 'em.'

James sniffed a new batch of fairy cakes. 'You certainly do, Mrs Keates. Can I be cheeky and pinch one?'

'Of course! Take a couple home with you if you like. I've got to get started on the soul cake next.'

'Soul cake? Haven't had one of those in years.'

'Oh yes, you know, for Hallowe'en. Always have a soul cake on All Souls.'

James tucked into his fluffy, iced fairy cake with hundreds and thousands sprinkled on the top. He closed his eyes as the light, vanilla sponge melted in his mouth.

'I say,' he said after swallowing the rest of the cake whole. 'You wouldn't fancy doing some of these for our Bonfire Night, would you? I know it's short notice and all, but–'

'I'd be happy to. That's on the fifth, isn't it? The Tuesday. Or are you doing it at the weekend?'

'No, no, always do it on the fifth. I could come and pick you and hubby up. We're having quite a feast and a whole hoard of fireworks.'

Mrs Keates agreed that it would be lovely and she speedily accepted his invitation. She let her tea brew and began preparing a hot toddy for James.

He watched as she poured malt whisky into the

glass, added a spoonful of honey and topped it up with hot water. She squeezed some lemon juice into it, added a pinch of cloves and gave it a stir. He gave a mock bow as he accepted the dram from her. She invited him to sit down and asked, for the umpteenth time, whether he was sure he was comfortable sitting in the kitchen.

'The kitchen is fine, Mrs Keates. Elsie Taylor told me where you lived. She said you knew Alec Grimes' son, Keith.'

She looked at him in astonishment as she plonked herself down and wrapped her hand around her teacup. 'Now that's a name I haven't heard in a few years. What d'you want to know about 'im for? Beggin' your pardon – that must have sounded quite rude. It's none of my business, of course.'

James waved aside her concerns and took her through what had happened to Alec Grimes, but didn't reveal his suspicions. He was, he told her, trying to contact Keith so that he could attend the funeral.

'Well, we worked together at the sweet factory just outside of Brighton,' she explained. 'I was on the lollipop line and he had sherbet fountains. I felt sorry for him, really. Didn't seem to have any friends to speak of, and he was stuck out on that farm, which he didn't like at all.'

'Oh, why's that?'

'Hated it, he did. I mean, that farm came under the Cavendish parish, but it was quite a way from the village. He seemed to be more of a city boy. Didn't like farming or the countryside; he wanted some life, girls, music. You know what they're like these days. All that rock 'n' roll nonsense.'

'So what did Alec think of that?'

'Now I never met him, but I do know they didn't get on. They had big arguments about the farm. Alec wanted to keep it in the family and Keith wanted nothing to do with it. I remember Keith came into work once with a black eye and split lip.'

James' eyes grew wide and Mrs Keates rested her hands on the table as she thought about it.

'I said to him, Keith, what have you done? And he came straight out with it. He said his dad had hit him. Not for the first time either, from what I gather.'

'How strange. I mean, it's not as if it was an old family farm.'

'Wasn't just that,' she said softly. 'There was the other stuff as well.'

James leant in and whispered. 'What other stuff?'

'Supernatural business, I've heard.' His jaw dropped. Mrs Keates pulled her chin in with a 'What do you think of that?' look and lowered her voice further. 'Some say he was very religious – although, from what I gather, no one saw him in church, if at all. Others say he was a wizard or something, dabbling in the dark arts. Now that makes more sense, don't it, if he don't go to church?'

James chose to remain quiet as she continued telling him what she supposed about a man she'd never met. Clearly she was influenced by what others had told her and, on probing further, those others hadn't met Alec either. This was like listening to the Snoop Sisters all over again. James decided he wouldn't get much more from her.

'Do you know whereabouts in Scotland he moved to?'

'Oh, now you're asking. Such a long time ago. Now, he spoke about Edinburgh and Glasgow.' She got up and rinsed her hands. 'I said to him, whatever do you want to move all the way up there? Said he wanted to get as far away from his dad as possible.' She grabbed a cloth and wiped the table. 'D'you want a top-up?'

'No thanks, I'd best–'

'Glasgow it was,' Mrs Keates blurted out. 'I remember now, because he spoke about getting work at the shipyards.'

James congratulated her on remembering the details and decided that he really ought to get going. 'You've been an absolute peach, Mrs Keates. Sorry to bundle in unannounced, but thank you for the cake and the hot toddy. Pity you haven't got some soul cake: haven't had that in years. Think it died out in Cavendish.'

'Well, I'm making a couple,' she replied. 'I can always make another one.'

James held his hands up. 'No, no, I mustn't impose further. I'm sure my wife has a recipe somewhere. Ought to get her to revive the tradition.' He made his way down the narrow hallway to the front door. 'Well, cheerio Mrs Keates. Thanks for your help and I'll be in touch about Bonfire Night. If not me, it'll be my wife.'

'Ooh, that'll be lovely. I shall look forward to it.'

Instead of returning straight home, James decided to pop in to Lewes and visit George.

75

He never needed much of an excuse to visit the old town; its history lured him at every opportunity. Dating back to the fifth century, Lewes had started as a Saxon settlement. After the Norman Conquest in 1066, a stone castle and priory were added and, later still, Franciscan monks had arrived in the area. Now, the town was full of small shops and winding streets with architecture dating back through the centuries.

He could see the preparations for Bonfire Night were well under way. Lewes always began its preparations earlier than anywhere else as it had become a popular place to celebrate Bonfire Night. Most towns and villages across England, including Cavendish, had an effigy of Guy Fawkes – but not Lewes. James recalled the history lesson from school as if it were yesterday.

Way back in the 16th century, seventeen Protestants were burnt at the stake in Lewes during the Catholic reign of Queen Mary. And, this coming Tuesday, seventeen burning crosses would be paraded through the town to remember them. Besides the parade, barrels of burning tar would be thrown in the river. It was certainly a spectacle worth witnessing.

James had attended one of these evenings years ago and, although it had been great fun, he wondered how on earth someone hadn't been seriously hurt.

He trotted up the steps of the police station and asked for George. The desk sergeant told him to take a seat, and put a call through to the main office. After a few minutes, the door to the inner sanctum opened and George's gruff voice beckoned him in. He stood a couple of inches taller than James and his brown hair, combed back off his forehead was still mainly brown with flecks of grey. His pale blue eyes were bright.

'Fancy a cuppa? I'm gasping.'

'That would be lovely,' replied James. 'You all right? You look a bit flustered.'

After ordering tea from a young policewoman, George continued speaking as he led James down the wood-panelled corridor.

'Got some old dear who's lost her cat. Thinks half the force should be out looking for it.'

He showed James through to a small office that looked over a busy and industrious area. Papers were piled high on top of grey filing cabinets and uniformed police bustled in and out. A woman police constable brought in two chipped mugs of tea; her face lit up when James took the trouble to thank her. George eyes went heavenward.

'You've made her day. No one thanks anyone for anything around here. Too busy.'

James quietly sang the words to Gilbert and Sullivan's 'A Policeman's Lot is Not a Happy One', but stopped when George glared.

'If you've come here to prattle on about Alec Grimes, you can drink your tea and go. I'm too busy for amateurs.'

'Too busy looking for cats, I suppose,' James said sardonically.

George couldn't help but smirk and leant back in his chair, waiting for James to elaborate. James cradled his mug.

'I took a look around Grimes' house this morning, with Bert.'

'Why?' George frowned. 'And how did you get in?'

James took a bunch of keys out of his pocket and jangled them. 'I told you I'd tidy up, so I had to take the keys. Anyway, the Snoop Sisters, you know, Rose and Lilac Crumb, were doing their level best to get in on the act, so I locked everything up so nothing would be disturbed; just in case it does turn out to be a crime scene.'

James chose to ignore his friend's raised eyebrows.

'Anyway, I've found out quite a lot that leads me to think that this may have been foul play.' George gave him an uninterested nod. 'First thing is, no one seems to have liked him. A couple of people argued with him during these last two or three weeks. He owes people money and his son has had nothing to do with him for ages.'

George looked blank. 'James, not many people like me. I argue with folk and my brother owes me a fiver. It doesn't make me a murderer.'

James held up a finger. 'And he was a witch, or wizard ... well, someone who practises black magic. His house is full of books on devil worship. And there are pentagrams on the floor.' He felt pretty pleased with himself.

With a resigned look, George placed a hand on a beige folder on his desk. 'The report I've got says he died of a heart attack. Two medical opinions can't be wrong.'

'What about the bump on the head?'

'It's a bump. Nothing else.'

'What about the paint?'

'James, we spoke about this. Just because there's

78

no red paint doesn't mean there wasn't going to be red paint. There's nothing to indicate foul play.'

'Do you think it's a recent painting?'

'Well, of course! Why would he be working on it if it wasn't recent?'

'Hah!' James said, loudly enough to alert the uniformed staff close by. George twisted in his chair and looked through the glass petition. 'Get on with your work.' He returned his attention to James and asked him to explain exactly what 'Hah!' meant. James leant forward with a degree of excitement.

'I have that painting at home and I stuck a pin in it several times at various places in the canvas.'

'And that proves what?'

'That he hadn't worked on that painting in weeks. The paint was bone dry. Oils take ages to dry, weeks sometimes. It may be dry on the surface but, underneath, the oils stay sticky. Every colour on that canvas is dry. And the painting is signed. Why sign a painting you haven't finished?'

'Right, I admit that's a little strange,' said George, 'but I'll ask you again. What does it prove?'

James slumped back in his chair. 'Nothing I suppose. You've got to agree that it's a little odd. I mean, why sit yourself out there with a finished painting? And leave a perfectly good breakfast half-eaten? A farmer too, at that time in the morning. Come on, George, it screams suspicion.'

'Much as I'd love something a little more exciting than a missing cat, I'm not creating a murder enquiry just because you're bored. It was

79

a heart attack.'

James let out a frustrated sigh.

'However,' George added, 'I have to say that snippets do appear odd, so I'll ask around.' He wagged a finger at him. 'But don't go running around advertising the fact. I haven't got too much on at the moment, so I'll take another look at the reports and what you've told me. But that's all I'm doing and I'll thank you to leave it alone. And keep your hands off. Your fingerprints are probably all over the property now. If this does turn out to be something odd, you will have messed things up.'

James swallowed hard. He hadn't thought of that. But he made a silent vow to continue with his own investigation albeit with more care.

'Well, I appreciate you giving it some thought,' he said. 'In the meantime, I wonder if there's something you could do as a matter of urgency? This son of Alec's – young Keith Grimes. The vicar wants to contact him about the funeral. We know he's estranged and all that, but it wouldn't be right to go ahead and not let him know, would it? So, we wondered whether you could track him down.'

George opened up his notepad and scrawled down the details then made a couple of phone calls. Placing the receiver back on its cradle, he leant on the desk and linked his fingers.

'Right, I've got someone onto that. If we find him, I'll let you know what the son says, or if he's coming down. When's the funeral?'

'Not sure, but if you give the vicar his details I'm sure the two can sort it out between them.'

James rubbed his chin. 'Tell me, George, d'you know much about Hallowe'en? You know, black magic and all that?'

George groaned. 'Bloody Hallowe'en. And Bonfire Night. The only thing I know is that we get some right idiots setting off fireworks.'

James chuckled at him and slid his chair back. 'Thanks for the tea, old man. Are you involved in this play we're putting on, *The Devil Incarnate?*'

George groaned again and confirmed that he was. He'd wanted to help do the lighting or something backstage, but that awful woman, Dorothy Forbes, had insisted he don the greasepaint and tread the boards. At least, George said with some relief, he'd managed to land a small part with only a couple of lines. James acknowledged his feelings.

'Mmm, that's what she's saddled me with. I've taken over the part that Grimes was supposed to be playing. You're at rehearsals this weekend?'

George grunted and James took that as a yes. For someone in such a senior position, he wondered how George managed to land himself with things he didn't want to do. Although, in all fairness, Dorothy was a fierce personality and excellent at manipulating people. He said goodbye to George and saw himself out.

On the drive home, his thoughts turned to Alec Grimes. No matter what argument George put up, that painting had been finished months ago. And why be in such a rush to button your coat up the wrong way? And why were the heels on his shoes encrusted with mud? He'd forgotten to mention that! It's as if he'd been dragged to his seat. Seeing a clear road ahead, James put his foot down. Determination set in. It was time to dig deep and get the proof that George needed.

CHAPTER SEVEN

James closed his front door on the bitter weather and wiped his shoes on the doormat. Beth came through from the kitchen.

'I wondered where you'd disappeared to.'

She helped him slip out of his coat and he rubbed his hands together.

'Darling, is the water hot? If it is, I'm going up for a bath. I've been in and out of this damned weather all day and I feel chilled to my bones.'

'The immersion heater's been on so go and run your bath. I'll bring you a nice warm drink. What do you fancy?'

'I'll have a small Cognac, thanks. Won't be long, I've lots to tell you. Are we on our own for dinner, or do we have guests?'

'Much as I love company, I'm pleased to say that we're on our own tonight.'

'Splendid,' replied James. 'We have the evening to do as we please.' He trotted up the wide staircase and straight to the bathroom, a large airy room with polished navy blue and white tiling and primrose yellow accessories.

He turned the taps full on, then filtered bath salts and oil into the water and swirled the ingredients around the tub. Padding across the tiles to the corner-shelf, he turned a small wireless on and was greeted by the mellow voice of Danny Kaye singing 'Ballin' the Jack'. James hummed along in the background, quietly shuffling the steps that accompanied the lyrics. The mirror steamed up and the walls dripped with condensation as James slid into the tub and sank down until only his head appeared above the foaming bubbles. Beth popped in with his Cognac and set it down on the table behind him.

'I'm doing toad-in-the-hole, so it'll be a little while,' she said. 'Take your time. You can tell me everything once you've relaxed.' She kissed his forehead and closed the door behind her.

James rested his head back and pondered the origins of toad-in-the-hole. How had sausages baked in batter ended up being given such a ridiculous name? His stomach growled and it was then that he realised how hungry he was, even more so when Beth was cooking.

Like most girls, she had learnt most of her cooking skills from her mother, who had attended a cookery school before she'd married. Although Beth could turn out some excellent Cordon Bleu cuisine, she was equally at home producing normal everyday dishes. Toad-in-the-hole was one of his favourite meals and he hoped that she was going to serve it with onion gravy.

He sipped his Cognac as Connie Francis, Frank Sinatra and Pat Boone serenaded him. The drink sent a fiery glow to his stomach and banished any chills that remained. Beth's warning shout announcing that dinner would be ready in ten minutes made him stir, albeit reluctantly.

Dressed in dark wool trousers, a powder blue sweater and feeling warm and reinvigorated, he trotted down the stairs and through to the dining room where Beth had set the plates down.

'There you go,' she said. 'Gravy's on the side.'

James flicked out his napkin then leant in to smell the meaty sausages encased in crispy Yorkshire pudding batter, with peas to the side. In a separate dish, Beth had whipped up fresh mashed potatoes and, the gravy, he was pleased to see, included fried onions and mushrooms.

In no time at all, he'd loaded his plate and began to tuck in with relish. Beth gazed at him in amusement. 'I guess I won't get anything from you until the meal is over.'

'Oh, gosh, sorry darling,' James said with his mouth full. 'I'm being terribly rude. If you weren't such a damned good cook, I wouldn't go at it like a ravenous dog.'

He allowed himself another mouthful of sausage and onions then updated Beth on his afternoon with Mrs Keates, his discussion with George and the likely whereabouts of Keith Grimes.

Beth expressed a keen interest and commented on how tragic it was that Keith would never have the opportunity to make up with his father. James waved a fork at her.

'Don't feel too sorry for him, darling. He may well have killed him.'

'Oh, don't you think you're taking this a little too seriously? Why would he want to kill him? I know they didn't like each other, but it sounds like he had his own life up there and never came back.'

'But how do you know? He may be skulking around here and up to no good. Anyway, who's to say what went on between them? For all we know, they may have made up and were still in contact.'

'But then, surely you would have found some correspondence or something. Grimes doesn't have a telephone, does he? And it sounds like that farmhouse was bare.'

James had to agree. 'Yes, you're quite right. That house had nothing in it. It's as if he'd erased his entire history. Quite distressing, really. You wonder what must have led him to do that. He must have been married, had a sweetheart and all. But all I found – where I looked, anyway – was just invoices and old magazines. No photographs or family mementos. Couldn't even find an address book.'

Beth tilted her head. 'Not much to show for your life, is it? Something happened in his past that made him that way. I wonder what it could have been?'

They continued to dissect life and discuss what people leave behind when they shuffled off this mortal coil and agreed that, when push came to shove, you truly did go out of this world the same way that you came in – with nothing.

He finished the last morsel of dinner and sat back. 'By the way, how much do you know about Hallowe'en? You know, the superstition side? Black magic and all that?'

Beth frowned and said she didn't really know anything except the normal games people played. 'That reminds me, don't forget you need to make your apple crumbles for the Hallowe'en party. You make such a nice recipe and everyone enjoys it.'

'Absolutely,' replied James. 'The Harrington special will be available on the night. Oh, by the way, I talked Mrs Keates into doing some baking for us on Bonfire Night. She's baking a soul cake for their Hallowe'en do. Have you still got your recipe?'

'Why yes! I haven't made that in an age. But, do you know,' Beth added, 'I think it may be time to revive it.'

'Good show, darling. It'll be a night to remember.'

Beth pushed her chair back and perused the recipe books on the shelf beside her. 'You know, if you want to know about Hallowe'en, you could do worse than speak with Professor Wilkins. He runs the local historical society. He must know something about the local customs here, or at least have some literature. Then there's Charlie Hawkins at the library. I'll bet there are some good books in the reference section. Why do you want to know?'

'Oh, just curious, what with all this business with Grimes. I know you think I may be taking this too far, but my inquisitive nature is not allowing me to drop this.'

'Well, sweetie, all I'll say is be careful. It's all very well listening to Paul Temple and reading Maigret, but that's fiction. The real world is different and that's why we have a police force.'

James grinned at his wife's lecture and assured her that he would tread carefully. She gave him a stern look.

'I hope you do. And Wilkins is around. I saw him in the village earlier. I know he's not the most approachable man in the world, but I think he is the most knowledgeable one.'

James helped her clear away the plates and followed her into the kitchen. His mind buzzed with plans for the imminent village functions, but Grimes' death remained a fixture, too.

He wanted to pursue this matter of Grimes' death, but his official duties were a priority. The role of Lord of the Manor was, in most parts of the country, an extinct one. James' determination to keep the tradition alive was welcomed and embraced by the villagers. But, with this ever-changing and evolving world, he knew his son would inherit a different lifestyle to the one he enjoyed currently.

Harrington's was certainly the way forward for their family. He imagined his ancestors would be turning in their graves if they could see the number of strangers who spent their leisure time at the old manor. They could, however, still be proud of the annual traditions, including Hallowe'en this coming Thursday. He'd planned to open up the large, grassy field to the side of the house and, although it had rained that day, the forecast had promised a return to dry, frosty evenings.

While Beth stacked away the dinner plates, he flicked through the handwritten recipes that she kept stored in a blue folder. He knew the one he wanted.

The paper had been folded and unfolded over the years and looked tired and frayed. Grease marks had made parts of it translucent over time, but that added to the sentiment and the ultimate joy of making his beloved grandmother's apple crumble. For some reason, he felt that typing it out on fresh paper would spoil the dish itself.

Beth hummed 'Three Coins in a Fountain' as she washed the work surface and James checked the cupboards to ensure he had the ingredients. Butter, flour, brown sugar, cinnamon and cloves. All present and correct.

They expected around forty villagers for Hallowe'en. The cold weather kept many of the elderly from attending but it was really a night for the children. By contrast, Bonfire Night saw the numbers triple. Indeed, the whole village turned out for that. Even if it snowed, the older residents stood close enough to the bonfire to keep warm.

'Oh, by the way,' said Beth, 'Mr Mitchell from the orchard, popped by with a basket of apples for the apple-bobbing. We have so many. I hope you have ideas for how to use them all.'

'Did he leave some half-barrels as well? If not, we'll have to find some large buckets.'

'Yes, he left three. They're out the back by the barn. What are you planning?'

James leaned on the kitchen surface. 'We'll have apple-bobbing and also snap-apple. That's the one where you hang the apples from pieces of string and try and bite them without using your hands. We've got Bob Tanner's little folk band and the Morris dancers to do some seasonal steps. I'm clearing some of the field so we can have a ceilidh so I hope this rain does disappear. Now, if we've lots of apples, perhaps we could have that game where you have to pass an apple to each other from under your chin.'

'Oh, that's great fun,' replied Beth. 'We used to

do that at Christmas, do you remember? That's a real hoot.'

'And, if you're going to make some soul cakes, we should re-introduce souling. I thought it had died out but clearly Charnley still celebrate it.'

Beth's forehead furrowed. 'You'll have to remind me what that is.'

James held the door open for her as they wandered through to the living room. 'From what I can remember, people make house calls and beg for soul cakes. The person receiving the cake promises to pray for the deceased relatives of the person giving the cake. I'll get something set up here. And we'll have to have different people to give out the cakes.' James winked her. 'We don't want everyone praying for *your* dead ancestors, do we?'

Beth hit him playfully. 'And what about cabbage night? Is that still going ahead? I mean, it's on the same night.'

She had introduced the Boston tradition of playing pranks on Halloween the previous year and it had proved to be a great success with the youngsters.

'Absolutely, I don't think the children would forgive us if we didn't do it.'

Her eyes sparkled. 'Those children are going to be so excited. It'll certainly be a noisy evening.'

'Yes, well that's one thing I do know about Hallowe'en. It's the night the dead are said to return; so the more noise you can make the better. It scares away evil spirits.'

They chuckled as James pulled her toward him. 'You know, John Jepson's play is all about bringing people back from the dead. You never know, the ghost of Alec Grimes may pay us a visit.'

Beth rubbed goose bumps from her arms and playfully slapped his chest. 'Don't you spook me, James.'

He grinned and assured her he would keep her safe from any evil intentions. He leant forward and gave her a kiss.

'It would be odd if something happened, though, wouldn't it?' He crossed over to the cocktail cabinet, grabbed the Cognac and two glasses. 'Come on, let's listen to the wireless; part two of Paul Temple's on. I might get some designs on how to go about tackling this Grimes business.'

CHAPTER EIGHT

Bob Tanner and his folk band, the Taverners, tuned their fiddles and guitars on the makeshift stage and discussed the songs and dances for the Hallowe'en ceilidh. With some input from Beth, they'd decided to give a little variety to the evening with a selection of Irish reels, Morris tunes and a string of chorus songs that everyone would know and join in with.

They began practising a few jigs while James carefully wove the last of the Chinese lanterns amongst the long parade of cherry trees that lined the field. He unravelled the wire to an extension and pushed the plug down firmly. The twinkling lamps sprang to life among the bare branches.

'Oh, that's perfect,' Beth said. 'Better than last

year, I'd say.'

He stood back and had to agree. 'That looks rather jolly, doesn't it?' He adjusted the lantern above him. 'I did wonder if we'd seen the last of these.'

The lanterns were a family heirloom from the thirties and had begun to look tired and frayed. Over the decades, haphazard repairs ensured their continued use and, in some ways, added to their appeal. Although James spoke about replacing them, Beth insisted they be mended and displayed. Each paper lantern shone a colourful beacon in the clear, winter air. Golden yellows, fiery orange, azure blue and emerald green flickered in the stillness and immediately turned the cold, grassy field into a welcoming hub.

Bert stood up from lighting some logs for a campfire. Although the hog roast would provide heat, the night air would be too chilly without some further warmth across the other side of the field. Flickers of flame took hold and lapped around the base and he blew gently to encourage them.

Beth put her hands on her hips. 'You're doing a wonderful job, Bert.'

He grinned. 'I'll put a rope fence around so people don't fall into it.'

The enormous hog roast, delivered by Graham Porter earlier in the evening, stood on a spit at the entrance to the field. It had been cooking for over an hour and James had followed Graham's instructions about turning the meat. He did so now and licked his lips as fatty juices dripped onto the spitting flames. The salted skin from the

91

hog had already turned crisp and brown and would provide a wonderful crackling.

The sweet smell of Bramley apples, cinnamon and warm bread wafted out of the kitchen and this, coupled with the aroma of fresh pork, served to increase his hunger pangs.

Anne stood in the kitchen, buttering bread rolls and slicing sage and onion stuffing to serve with the hog roast. A typical vicar's wife, she'd immersed herself in the social scene immediately, contributing even in the smallest way to village events. But, unlike her predecessor, she wasn't teetotal and loved a drink with everyone else. James found what he was looking for and poured her a large glass of sweet sherry.

'Oh I shouldn't really,' she said, snatching the glass with a cheeky grin. 'Luke and Mark have arrived and Stephen's getting them dressed, so they'll probably look a complete mess. He has no sense when it comes to dressing children.' She peered through the window at the clear skies. 'The perfect weather for Hallowe'en.'

'It certainly is, and thank you for what you've done. Beth's overjoyed to have your help and your company. You're a lot more fun than the Reverend Culver's wife, your predecessor. They were a lovely couple but rather set in their ways and I think their age was catching up with them.'

Beth, making minor adjustments to the lanterns, shouted across, 'We're grateful to you and Bert. We could never have done this on our own. The ladies of the WI normally help but a lot of them had other plans.'

Anne, no longer overawed by mixing with a Lord

and Lady, continued buttering and shouted back. 'It's the least I can do. How're we doing for time?'

'It's coming up to a quarter to seven,' Beth replied as she made her way to the kitchen.

James checked his own watch. Soon, the villagers would arrive and all the planning, cooking and organising would have been worth it.

The children had probably finished their cabbage night antics and would soon be arriving with their parents.

The first batch of apple crumbles browned on a low gas in the oven. It was heartening to see how such a simple dish could be so popular. With Beth's encouragement, he'd discovered a natural talent for baking and, now, at any of the village festivities, he happily contributed something from Grandma's recipe book. Winter, of course, meant making good use of the Bramley cooking apple.

Earlier in the day, Bert had helped lay some willow matting on the grass for the ceilidh and attached paper bunting around the stage, which consisted of upturned tea-chests and old wooden chairs. To one side of the dance floor stood barrels of water for the apple-bobbing contests and apples, secured on string, hung from the trees for snap-apple.

The school children had shown their skills with some creative pumpkin carving. Beth scurried around placing candles inside them while Bert followed close on her heels with matches to light them. Haunting pumpkin faces gazed across the field in ghoulish glee. James made his customary walk around the field; no matter how many times he hosted these events, a slight worry always lurked in his stomach before the villagers arrived. He so wanted everyone to enjoy themselves.

At seven o'clock, the villagers began to arrive and many of the children raced to signal which pumpkins they'd helped carve. Then they spotted the apple-bobbing and yelled at the tops of their voices for their parents to come and see.

The Taverners had now warmed up and the small troupe of Morris men was now in place to start dancing. They had bells attached to their shoes, which rang out as they leapt to the accompaniment of jigs and reels.

Although they were more traditionally associated with Bonfire Night, Beth couldn't resist handing out sparklers to all of the children as they filed in.

James loved the inner child inside her and her own exuberance helped make these evenings a success.

By seven-thirty, the evening was in full swing. Villagers chatted and laughed, children whooped and giggled, the band played non-stop and although Graham normally commandeered the hog roast, James had wrestled that pleasure from him. There was something about roasting a hog that made him feel as if he were back in the Dark Ages and he wondered if some of his ancestors had done this all those years ago. He was brought back to the present by two unexpected voices.

'Hello Dad!'

He blinked in surprise to see Harry and Oliver standing either side of Beth. The twins were not identical; Harry had inherited Beth's dark colouring and deep brown eyes, while Oliver had his father's fairer tone. They stood taller than James and had become more muscular since joining the rowing team in Oxford.

James let go of the carving knife he'd slid into the hog. 'Well I never! What are you doing here?'

Oliver shook hands with him. 'Got a lift down from a friend. He's visiting his cousin in Brighton, so we bundled in and told him to make a quick detour.'

Harry skirted around to James and pulled out the carving knife. 'Anyway, you always get to do the good jobs. If I'm going to help out here when I leave Oxford I need to learn how to distribute the old hog.'

'Looks like a natural butcher,' Graham Porter chipped in as he held out an open roll. 'Shove a pile of that pork in here, Harry. I'll have some of that stuffing and apple sauce too.'

Harry loaded three slices of hog roast into Graham's roll and squashed a layer of stuffing and sauce on top. Graham sank his teeth in and pulled off a strip of crackling to take with him. Harry told James that he'd serve the rest of the queue.

Stephen and Anne beckoned for James and Beth to join them.

'James, Beth,' said Anne. 'These are our boys, Luke and Mark.'

James and Beth made a huge fuss of welcoming the two youngsters, who seemed completely over-whelmed by the noise and activities going on around them. They were similar in looks with their shiny black hair and brown eyes. Both had a few freckles over their cheeks and looked smart in grey shorts, knee-high socks and thick blue sweaters.

Anne tightened the scarves around their necks and instructed them to keep their gloves on.

James gazed around the field until he saw the person he sought. He waved Susan Hawkins over; she dragged her brother, Tommy, with her.

'Susan, this is Luke and Mark,' he said, squatting down to her level. 'They're the Reverend and Mrs Merryweather's boys. Now, they're going to be a little shy with all these strangers, so why don't you and Tommy introduce them to everyone and make them welcome?'

Susan, taking her duties seriously, ordered her brother to follow her lead. Both she and Tommy led their two new friends away.

'You'll have to excuse me,' Beth said, 'more villagers arriving. I'd better keep up with the hostess role until everyone's here.'

James led Stephen and Anne over to the spit.

'Got a surprise myself, tonight,' he said. 'Harry and Oli blagged a lift for the weekend. Boys, this is our new vicar, Stephen Merryweather, and his wife, Anne.'

Harry gave them a warm welcome. 'Crikey, you're a lot younger than the other Rev. Are you going to be giving us some good old triple S's?'

'S-some what?'

'Seriously Super Sermons,' Oliver explained. 'The old vicar used to do Seriously Sleepy Sermons. But you look a lot more twentieth century than the antique we had before. Harry and I will try to get to one of your services when we've more time. We're back at Oxford tomorrow, I'm afraid.'

'Quite all right. I-I'll provide a warm welcome when you d-do come,' replied Stephen.

'Oliver!' Beth called. 'Could you help with the apple crumbles?'

'Ah ha, duty calls.' Oliver saluted Stephen and Anne and strode off toward the house.

With the evening in full swing, James and Beth began to relax and mingled with the villagers. In between the traditional Hallowe'en games, the children played chase, hide and seek, and found a long piece of damp rope to skip with. The band belted out dance melodies, Scottish reels and Folk tunes, while Bob Tanner called out the steps to those who didn't have a clue what to do and, judging by the hilarity on the dance floor, that covered everyone.

James winced as he overheard one boy relate his cabbage night adventures earlier in the evening. 'Yeah, we smeared golden syrup over everyone's car handles,' he crowed. The surrounding children giggled. Bert planted a glass of warm cider in his hand.

'Little bleeders,' he said. 'Glued a peacock feather to my hat. Only put it down for five minutes.'

James did his best not to laugh but failed miserably. 'I can't exactly imagine you being an angel as a child.'

'Too right I weren't,' Bert's eyes twinkled. 'Got a good turnout tonight, Jimmy boy.' He gestured to the far end of the field. 'I didn't know Ian Connell had kids. Is he married?'

'No, no, he's not. They're not his children. I believe Philip said they were cousins, or niece and nephew or something. They're staying for the weekend to attend our little gathering.'

'Seems to spend more time in this village than

his own. Mind you, 'e *is* living in Loxfield. I think I'd spend more time 'ere if I lived at Loxfield.'

'Yes, never seems a terribly welcoming sort of place. I only met Ian the other day. The morning that Grimes died, as a matter of fact. He'd gone over to meet him with the design for the work he wanted.'

'Poor geezer. Must take ages to draw up plans like that. He's just finished doing some work for the Professor.'

'Really? What's he had done?'

'Repaired the roof on the museum and put in some new glass displays. Done a good job, too, from what I 'ear. You might wanna give him a shout for the patio work you want done.'

'He certainly seems to have made himself at home here. Nice that he joins in our little shindigs. Wonder how much Grimes owed him for those plans?'

'Not enough to murder him,' Bert said with a smile. 'I'm off to get some apple crumble before it disappears.'

Across the field, he spotted Dorothy Forbes with her husband and grandchildren talking with Philip Jackson and his family. No doubt the single ladies would be a little put out that the doctor had brought his wife, James mused. Beth sidled up to him.

'Everyone seems to be having a good time,' she said, 'and the apple crumble is another roaring success.'

He snaked his arm around her waist and kissed the top of her head. 'Yes, it's all going pretty well, isn't it? Any hiccups your end?'

'No, I'm mingling in the places you're not and vice versa. Mrs Jepson and her husband aren't here yet, though. They normally arrive dead on seven.'

'Oh, I think they're coming with Peter Mitchell,' said James. 'He's going to pick them up. He'd promised to drop off some apples to a grocer so he said he'd pick them up on the way back.' He gave her a squeeze. 'Good of Oli and Harry to pop down.'

'What a lovely surprise and the children so adore them.'

James agreed as he watched the twins wrestling with a group of young boys. He sipped his cider. 'Best circulate again. I'll go clockwise and catch up with you across the field.'

'Oh James, did you know that Keith Grimes' old teacher is here?'

'Really? Who's that?'

'Our primary school head, Mr Chrichton. He was at the grammar school in Haywards Heath when Keith was there. Remembers him very well, I'm told.' Leaving that snippet of information with him, Beth wandered off toward Philip and Helen.

James scanned the crowd for Mr Chrichton, but couldn't see him. As the evening went on, the light from the fire faded a little and the darkness made recognition impossible from any distance. He tossed a few more logs on to build it back up again before meandering across to the trestle table with the apple crumbles on it. Graham was helping himself to a portion and spooning custard into his bowl.

'Having a nice time, Graham?'

'Right good, thanks. The kids are loving it, of course. Nice to be able to do something for 'em. Times are a bit hard at the moment.'

'Really? I thought you said you'd inherited a sum of money?'

'Oh, I have' he replied. 'It's just all tied up at the moment. I put a load into building the business up and starting the smallholding. It'll be good in the long term but I wonder if I should've kept some by. You know, rainy day money. Of course, if Alec had paid me back, it would've been easier. I s'pose that money's gone forever.'

'Well, not necessarily,' said James. 'There's his son, Keith. Perhaps you'd best have a chat with him. You may be able to sort something out once they lay their hands on the will.'

'Crikey!' said Graham. 'I'd forgotten all about him. Is he here?'

'No, we're trying to track him down. I'd certainly have a chat with him when he does arrive.'

'Don't you worry, I will. I rue the day I ever agreed to that deal. Cheating git. Sorry, I know he's dead an' all, but it annoyed me no end, him not paying me back. Not a penny. I wonder if he was ever gonna pay me? Good job Ian didn't get involved. He'd have done all that building work and never got paid.'

The pair jumped as Ian suddenly appeared next to them. 'Oh, I would've got it,' he said as he helped himself to apple crumble. 'I've always got my money. One way or another, even if it's a barter agreement of some sort. Nice crumble.' He wandered off.

100

James glimpsed Mr Chrichton making a beeline for the hog roast. He excused himself and went across to speak with him.

'Mr Chrichton?'

'Lord Harrington. Thank you so much for inviting me.'

He was a tall, thick-set man with a pleasant demeanour. He'd never married or had a family which James thought was a shame as he seemed so at home with children and they always loved being around him.

Chrichton continued, 'The children enjoyed doing the pumpkins this year.'

'Yes, they did a splendid job, didn't they? I was going to ask the Cubs and Brownies to do it, but I understand they were on an adventure trip last week.'

'That's right, a big adventure with the Scouts and Guides.'

'I'm sure they had a wonderful time.' James steered him to one side. 'Mr Chrichton, may I pick your brains?'

'Well, of course.'

'Do you remember Keith Grimes?'

'Keith Grimes? Yes, yes I do. I heard about his dad. Is Keith coming home for the funeral?'

'We're trying to track him down at the moment. I understand he didn't get on with his father.'

Mr Chrichton grimaced. 'I only met Alec Grimes once and I could have killed him there and then. Sorry, that sounds very melodramatic, but he was what I'd call a very uncaring man. He never came to any parents' evenings, or sports days – nothing. Keith was only at my school for about a year. I understand that Mrs Grimes died young. That's what I heard, anyway and it was well before Alec moved here. I suppose he was struggling. But the way he treated Keith ... well, it was criminal.'

James frowned and asked him to explain what he meant.

'Your Lordship–'

'Please, call me James.'

'James, I know when a child is being mistreated or bullied, and I would bet my life on it that Keith was beaten regularly.'

'Good Lord!'

'Keith never said a word to me about it, but he always had a fearful look if you asked him about any bruises he had. I tried going round there to sort it out. That was the one time I met Alec. Asked him to tell me what was going on with Keith and to admit it if he was beating him. Well, he came at me with a pitchfork, threatening all sorts of things.' He sipped his cider. 'I don't mind telling you, I feared for Keith Grimes that night. I wish I hadn't gone round because I'm sure I made it worse. I'm sure he took it out on the boy.'

'Nasty piece of work.'

'The worst. I don't blame Keith for leaving when he did. If he'd have stayed I reckon there would have been murder in that house.' He waved to Stephen. 'Excuse me. Just want to catch the vicar about the Christmas festivities at the school.'

'Of course,' James replied, stepping aside.

Donovan Delaney, who had overheard the conversation, got James' attention. 'Speak to yer man, Pete Mitchell – someone said that him and Keith were in the same class at school.'

'Really?' replied James. 'From what I'm hearing, I can't see Keith pitching up at the funeral.'

'Did you know that I put Alec in hospital once?' said Donovan smugly. 'Knocked him out cold so I did. Out for two days with concussion, and I don't mind telling you, I'd do it again, so I would.'

James gawped at Donovan and, at the back of his mind, could well believe it. Donovan was not a small man and he couldn't imagine trying to pick a fight with him. The big Irishman put his hands in his trouser pockets, looking almost pleased with himself.

'Very insulting to the wife, so he was,' he continued. 'In my pub as well. I told him, you don't be doing that here. You walk out now or get carried out later. Started raising a fist, telling me I was irresponsible serving alcohol. I ask you, what else am I supposed to serve in a pub? Told him to take a hike. He wouldn't go, so I punched him and down he went.'

Donovan's son, Josh, ran up and tugged at his sleeve, demanding a turn at apple-bobbing.

Donovan let himself be dragged away but shouted back to James, 'Won't be many people sad to see him buried.'

James looked on, a little bewildered by the information coming at him but quickly snapped out of his daydream after Beth grabbed him for a dance.

As a change to the jaunty reels, the band launched into Glenn Miller's 'In the Mood' and he and Beth jived and bopped to the swing classic.

103

He drew her close as they swirled with the rhythm and beat. When the final note rang out, they joined the villagers to give the band a generous round of applause.

James kissed her gently and whispered 'I love you' as the band launched into another reel.

As the evening continued, the men hovered in a group around the diminishing hog roast where Harry held court. The women chatted, exchanged news, and planned their involvement in the forthcoming play, children raced around the field, excited to be staying up past their bedtime.

Villagers mingled, people came and went, and the band played on without a break.

Stephen, swallowing the last of his soul cake, wandered across to James, who was watching Donovan give piggyback rides to the children. He spotted Bert and waved him over.

'I say, you wouldn't believe the bad press Alec Grimes has with the people here,' he told them. 'He sounds a rotten egg. Did you know that Delaney put him in hospital?'

Stephen gaped.

'Get away,' Bert said. 'What for?'

James led them to a less crowded area, where he was quickly interrupted by the orchard grower, Pete Mitchell.

'Sorry I'm late, your Lordship.'

'That's all right, old chap. There's plenty of food left. Just take yourself–'

'Something funny's going on,' Mitchell said with an anxious look.

'What do you mean something funny?'

'Well, first, I went to pick up Mr and Mrs Jepson, but there was no one in. The house is in darkness. I tried round the back and nothing. Looks like the whole place has been battened down for the winter. Second, earlier this evening, I had to swing by the other side of the village to make an apple delivery and I went by Grimes' farm.'

James listened to what Mitchell had to say and asked the others to wait while he searched for Beth. He finally spotted her bent over double in a line of people, trying to pass an apple from under her chin to under her neighbour's chin.

'Hey sweetie,' she mumbled, desperately trying to keep her apple safe. 'Are you having a good time?'

'I'm having a wonderful time, darling,' said James leaning over her. 'But I'm afraid I've got to pop out for half an hour.'

'What for?'

'Mitchell's just shown his face. The Jepsons are missing and he saw a torchlight being flashed about over at the Grimes place. We're going up there to take a look.'

Having passed her apple on, Beth stood up with a concerned look. 'Who's we?'

'Bert and Stephen are coming with me.'

'You be careful. Why don't you call George?'

'Because he'll think I'm wasting his time. I don't want to go to him unless I have something conclusive.'

Beth pulled him close. 'The slightest hint of anything untoward, you go straight to the nearest phone box and call him. Promise?'

'Promise, although he should be here shortly. Keep the party going, darling. I'll be back before you know it.'

He nudged Oliver. 'Get a drink for Mitchell, will you, sport? He's only just arrived.'

As he motioned for Bert and Stephen to go through the back gate to the garage, he was more than mindful of the worried expression he'd seen on Beth's face.

CHAPTER NINE

The darker side of Hallowe'en seemed to descend as James drove through the village and on towards Grimes' farm. The noise and jollity of the party had faded soon after they'd driven off and the myths surrounding this devilish night took on a reality as the spindly branches of trees and shrubs cast eerie shadows across the road. Those villagers who hadn't taken advantage of their hospitality were staying huddled round their hearths, snug in their living rooms or perhaps had already retired to their beds.

Mitchell had arrived at the party just after ten o'clock and had been agitated from the start. James knew the man well enough to know that he wasn't someone to overplay his part so his behaviour did signify that something was seriously amiss. Now James' head was full of questions:

Where on earth had the Jepsons gone? They never missed the Hallowe'en celebrations, yet now they'd disappeared.

Mr J had visited Grimes the morning he'd died.

And Mrs J had confirmed that some sort of altercation had taken place. Was it more than just a social visit? Had he killed Grimes and realised what a fix he'd put himself in? Perhaps Mrs J had found out and rushed to her husband's side?

He grimaced. God no, that really didn't sound like Mrs J. But then, how well did he really know his cleaner? How well did he really know anyone in the village?

Bert, sitting alongside him, searched his pockets and brought out a tin of Old Virginia and some cigarette papers. He began rolling a cigarette and offered the tobacco around.

'Anyone else?'

James and Stephen declined.

The vicar leant forward from the back seat. 'You don't think this is something s-sinister, do you?'

Bert struck a match and lit the tip of his roll-up. 'Prob'ly poachers or something. In fact, I'll bet you 'alf a crown it's poachers. Season's on a roll for rabbit. A lot of 'em about at the moment and they know no one's on the Grimes farm.' He grinned at James. 'C'mon Sherlock, what's your take on all this?'

James concentrated on the shadowy road ahead. He knew how Bert felt about his claims of foul play.

'I don't have one, to be honest. You may well be right, Bert. In which case, I will give you half a crown with interest. The fact that you're here, though, proves you're as interested as I am.'

'Just making sure you don't get up to no mischief.'

'Actually, the thing that I find more concerning

is the mysterious flight of the Jepsons. Where d'you think they've migrated to? They never go anywhere.'

Bert rubbed his chin. 'Now that, my friend, is a mystery. P'haps we should be snooping around their place instead of 'ere.'

James pulled onto the verge.

Bert peered into the darkness. 'I'll tell you something for nothing,' he said. 'This 'ouse don't look like a welcome in the hillside at the best of times, but it looks bloody depressing when it's as black as my mum's coal cellar.'

James leant across Bert and opened the glove compartment. He took out a couple of small torches.

'Only two torches, I'm afraid.'

Bert dug deep in his pocket and brought out his own. James immediately wondered if his friend ever carried out any burglaries. He certainly gave the impression that he'd be well-prepared for such things. He passed his spare torch to Stephen.

'H-have you got any w-wellingtons?'

The groans that followed this question confirmed to James that they hadn't thought things through. The farmhouse was positioned on land within a natural dip and rain from the previous day would have settled. Although it was a crisp night, with all the activity that had taken place, the ground would be sticky.

Switching their torches on, they trod through gooey mud before reaching the uneven paved area by the kitchen door. Bert put his nose up to the window.

'No life in 'ere.' He shone his torch along the

wall. 'I'll take a look round the side.'

'I say,' said James, 'Mitchell said it looked as if the lights were coming from near the copse rather than in the house. D'you think we should toddle over?'

'Blimey, you stupid or something? I ain't trundling over there – it's as dark as a miner's armpit.'

James grimaced at Bert's analogy.

'W-we could always come back in the morning,' Stephen added, hope in his voice. 'You know, l-look for footprints.'

Bert spread his palms out. 'How're yer gonna know who's been where? Looks like the world and 'is wife's been stomping round 'ere with 'obnails on.'

James tried the kitchen door. Locked. He looked toward the copse although it was impossible to see it in the darkness. But if someone was prowling around with a torch, they would surely see it. Bert was right. It was pitch black and there was no sign of life. He felt in his pocket, took out a key and nudged Stephen.

'Why don't you stay here? I'll take a quick look inside. Shout if you see anything.'

Stephen was clearly relieved not to be too involved but didn't appear overly excited about standing there either.

James went into the kitchen and shivered. The lack of heating had left the farmhouse cold, damp and uninviting. He flipped the light switch to discover the electrics were switched off.

The torch provided a dim tunnel of light into the recesses of each room. He lifted the carpets and mats to take a second look at the pentagrams. He scanned the books again and the fact that it was dark, and Hallowe'en, made him shudder. He moved quickly, slammed doors and trotted up the stairs loudly, in a subconscious attempt to calm his nerves.

But every room in the house lay empty, just as James had left it a few days ago. If someone had been there, they hadn't inflicted any damage or given the impression of searching for anything. But then, Peter Mitchell hadn't specifically mentioned the farmhouse, more the grounds surrounding it.

A muffled groan broke his thoughts. James stood still, cocked an ear and turned slowly. Was that inside or out? He caught his breath. There it was again. Outside. He crept down the stairs, tiptoed through the kitchen and out of the side door, where he collided with Bert.

'Did you hear groaning?' James said.

Bert answered him with a frown.

'What d'you think it was?'

'Search me,' said Bert. 'I was out front. Where's the vicar?'

James shone his torch from side to side. 'I don't know. I left him here. You don't think that was him, do you?'

Bert felt inside his jacket and, to James' astonishment, brought out a small cosh. 'Let's try the back. Turn your torch off.'

Their shoes squelched in the wet mud as they crept along the side wall. James pulled a face as icy water seeped into his socks. He whispered to Bert. 'Whose idea was it to come out here?'

'Yours.' At the corner, Bert stopped him. They

peered around the wall to the back of the house.

They heard another subdued groan. Bert grabbed James. 'That's the vicar.'

James switched his torch back on and eased along the wall. They came to an abrupt halt.

'Stephen!' He rushed to where Stephen lay sprawling on the ground, clutching his head. 'What on earth happened?'

'I-I'm not sure. Just thought I-I'd walk about and someone hit me over the head.' He stared at the cosh and then at Bert.

'Oi, it weren't me, yer dopey git.'

Stephen took his hand away from the back of his head and looked at it. He swallowed hard. 'Oh, look. B-blood.'

'Sit still, old chap.' James stood up, found his car keys and tossed them to Bert. 'There's a phone box on the corner, further up the road here. Take my car and ring for an ambulance. Tell them to get the police down here, too. George will probably be at ours by now. Call Beth and see if he's there. Have you got enough change?'

'Yeah, I'm on me way. Sit tight vicar.' Bert thrust the wooden cosh into James' hand. 'You don't wanna be roaming around 'ere in the black of night without some protection.'

'Did you have that with you at the party?'

Bert avoided his gaze and shuffled on his feet as James glared at him.

'What on earth were you expecting to happen?'

Bert jutted his chin at Stephen. 'Well, 'im being attacked weren't expected.'

James conceded that it wasn't and, on hearing Stephen groan again, decided not to pursue the

111

matter. Bert scurried out of sight and he heard the Jaguar pull away from the farm. He helped Stephen to his feet and the vicar leant against the wall with his eyes closed.

'I say, Stephen, are you all right? Let's get you into the kitchen. I'm sure there are some drinks of some sort in there.'

'Th-that would be nice.'

'Go easy. Here, put your arm around my shoulder and I'll take your weight.'

With Stephen draped against him, James tottered back to the kitchen and settled his vicar on a wooden chair. He searched the cupboards for refreshments and finally managed to find a bottle of ginger beer. It fizzed as he opened it and Stephen gratefully swigged half the bottle in one go.

James told him to rest easy and wandered outside. He shone the torch back and forth, up and down the path and into the mud. There seemed to be plenty of footprints, but who did they all belong to? So many people had trampled about here lately.

He popped his head in.

'I'm taking a look round the back,' he said to Stephen. 'I'll be two seconds – shout if you need anything.'

Stephen shakily said that he was fine. He placed his arms on the table, then leant forward to rest his head on them.

James pulled the door to and retraced his steps to where Stephen had fallen. The torch's beam shone across the damp grass. Goosebumps erupted on his arms as the night air crept into his bones.

The light skipped over an uneven area, a bump that didn't seem quite natural. He quickly redirected the torch and slowly took in every area of the elevated mound.

Then he gave a startled gasp.

'Good Lord,' he mumbled.

He stepped onto the grass. Before him lay a life-sized golem, moulded from the earth. It stared eerily at him through the gloom as if ready to rise from the dead.

James gazed through the glass and into the ward at the cottage hospital. He spotted Stephen on the left-hand side, in the furthest of five beds. Anne was by his bedside, her hand tenderly holding his. He wondered how welcome he would be. The poor man had only been in the village five minutes and he'd nearly got him killed. He took a deep breath and passed through the swing doors. The ward sister marched over.

'Lord Harrington! Can I help you?'

James, dressed in a silky smooth camel coat, took his felt hat off and did his best to offer her the full Harrington charm. He found it worked well for the most part and he hoped it would on this occasion.

'Ah, hello Sister. That's our vicar over there in the far corner. He came in last night – got knocked over the head.'

'The Reverend Merryweather?' she replied. 'Oh yes, he said you might be coming in. Visiting hours are nearly finished, your Lordship, so you'll have to make it quick. I can't make exceptions.'

'And quite right too, Sister. I'll just toddle

113

across and see how the invalid is.'

He sauntered through the ward, nodding to other patients and offering a quick hello. The clinical smell of the hospital was not in itself unpleasant but one he didn't like, all the same.

When he reached them, he saw that Stephen was propped up by pillows, with a crepe bandage around his head. A tuft of hair poked out giving him an almost comical look. James gave him a cheery hello and pecked Anne on the cheek. Anne made to get up, but James gently pushed her back and stood behind her.

'Stephen, how are you, old man?'

The vicar sighed. 'Wh-what a way to start my role.'

'This'll give you something to chat about on Sunday,' replied James. 'I say, you *will* be out by Sunday, won't you?'

Anne held her husband's hand. 'Of course. He's coming out today, aren't you?'

Stephen confirmed to James that he would be out later that morning. The doctors had carried out a thorough check and when he'd been prodded, poked and blinded by shining lights, they had announced that this was a simple case of concussion.

'Any stitches?'

'Only three, th-thank the Lord. The doctor's due round at t-twelve. He's supposed to be letting me go after that.'

James pulled a chair up next to Anne. 'It's a rum do, isn't it. Can you remember anything much about last night? Who it was that clobbered you, I mean.'

'A-absolutely nothing. It was so dark and who-ever it was ... well, they were behind me. Didn't hear a th-thing.'

Anne turned to James with a worried look. 'You don't think someone was trying to murder him, do you?'

'Absolutely not!' James exclaimed. 'I think we may have been disturbing something though, don't you? Damned if I know what. Have the police been to see you?'

Stephen explained that they'd asked him one or two questions, but he'd been so groggy they'd left him alone. But, he confirmed, they would like to see him once he was up and about.

Anne blew her nose and wiped a tear from her eye.

James patted her hand. 'Don't you worry, it'll be perfectly fine. Stephen here was just in the wrong place at the wrong time. Could have been any one of us. Anyway, look, he's all right now and I promise I won't take him out to play again. I feel just awful getting him to come with us.'

Anne thanked James and explained that it just wasn't how she'd expected their first couple of weeks in the village to go. James empathised with her. Bert was right about village life. It didn't matter where you lived – one never truly knew what went on behind closed doors.

The ward sister approached, reminding every-one that visiting times were coming to an end.

'Anne, I'll give you a lift back. You say goodbye to hubby and I'll wait downstairs. Stephen, get the hospital to call when you're ready and I'll come and get you.'

As James turned to go, he bumped straight into George, who fixed him with an irritating sneer.

'If I didn't know you better,' he said, 'I'd have said you'd arranged this bloody attack just to get me interested in this blasted death.'

'Steady on, George.'

'I want a word – with all of you,' he said, rolling his trilby in his hand. 'And Bert. And Mitchell. And anyone else who can shed some light on what the hell's going on.'

The ward sister bristled. 'Gentlemen! Kindly continue this discussion away from my patients.'

James gave her a quick smile. 'I'm so sorry, Sister.' He pulled George toward him. 'George, for goodness sake, calm down. How about I get everyone gathered at my place this afternoon and you come over for a spot of tea? Still some crumble left over from last night.' He looked back over his shoulder, winked at Anne and steered George away. 'Where were you, by the way? I thought you were coming to our little shindig – you missed Harry and Oliver.'

'I was on my way,' George replied gruffly, 'until some idiot told me a vicar had been attacked and I had to put my social life on hold. Christ, you can be bloody irritating, James. Why couldn't you have waited until I'd arrived before gallivanting off?'

James grimaced as he followed him out of the hospital and into the car park.

'Yes, hindsight's a wonderful thing, isn't it?' He held open George's car door. 'Still, at least you're taking an interest in the Grimes case now.'

George glared as he got in the car and slammed

the door shut. He wound the window down. 'There wasn't a case until you poked your nose in.'

He shoved the gear stick into first and drove off.

James leant on the door of his Jaguar until Anne appeared. He helped her into the car and slipped into the driver's seat.

'Anne, do you want to collect your boys and come and have lunch with us? It's the least we can do bearing in mind what's happened.'

'I'd like that very much, thank you.' She turned to James. 'Is your Inspector friend going to investigate this? I do hope so.'

'He's coming round this afternoon to have a chat.' James' mind suddenly conjured up the images of the pentagrams and the life-sized golem. 'I just hope it's not anything too unsavoury.'

CHAPTER TEN

That afternoon, James, dressed in dark grey flannels and a loose black polo neck sweater, stoked the fire with the poker while pondering how George's visit would go. Orange flames flickered around the logs and projected a fierce heat.

After he'd enjoyed a light lunch of poached eggs on toast, word came through that Stephen was ready to leave the hospital so James returned to chauffeur him back to the house. The hospital doctor, Stephen advised, had told him to take things easy for a few days. Beth, mindful that Anne would be busy tending to her husband more than usual, insisted they all stay on and have dinner that evening.

'I want to spoil you rotten after everything that happened yesterday,' she said.

'You've really no need,' Anne said. 'None of this was your fault and please don't ever think that we blame you. You really have been such wonderful friends to us from the moment we arrived.'

'But you've only been here a few days and you've experienced such an awful attack. I can't remember the last time anything like this happened in the village. And as for James taking on this detection business, well—'

'Oh, but it *is* exciting, isn't it?' Anne looked a little guilty. 'I mean, I'm completely shocked at what happened to Stephen, but what a story to tell the grandchildren!'

Beth laughed. 'Anne, your children haven't even reached the big school yet! I know you get a kick out of James' sleuthing but, as I keep telling him, this is real life, not fiction.'

On learning that they were staying for dinner, Luke and Mark jumped up and down with excitement.

'Can we have some left over apple crumble?' asked Mark.

'I just want the apple crumble,' added Luke. 'It can be my *whole* dinner!'

James assured them that crumbles would be served but that they had to have a main course too. Anne chivvied them out onto the patio with an order to get some fresh air.

Comfortably ensconced on the sofa, Stephen, with a heavily bandaged head, gratefully sipped hot tea, while the two boys played football at the back of the house.

'Luke, Mark,' Anne shouted to them. 'Don't kick that ball near these windows. If you break anything, it'll come out of your pocket money. And you won't get crumble.' The punishment of no crumble sent the boys scrambling further away.

Beth set a plate of lemon shortcake on the coffee table. 'Don't worry, Anne. It's not a leather ball – it's just a soft one that James found in the garage.'

The doorbell rang and James smoothed his hair back. 'This will be our visitors. I'll go, darling. Perhaps we'd best get some more tea.'

Anne jumped up to help Beth prepare more refreshments. As they disappeared into the kitchen, James invited Bert through to the lounge; he was quickly followed by Pete Mitchell and George. He manoeuvred armchairs to ensure they were relatively close to one another. Beth and Anne served fresh tea and distributed shortbread and cherry scones.

James made himself comfortable in his much-loved wingback chair. Stephen and Anne remained on the sofa, while Bert and Pete Mitchell took a couple of armchairs opposite them. Beth lounged on a small velvet couch with her stocking feet tucked underneath her.

George cut an authoritative pose in the middle of the room and James almost laughed.

'You look as if you're about to sum up a crime scene, old chap. Take the weight off and sit down. You know we're willing to help where we can, so have some tea and fire away.'

George did as he was told and settled on the end of the sofa. He rummaged around in his pockets, pulled out a notebook and pencil and stared at James.

'Right. First. Just because I'm here doesn't mean that I think there's anything funny going on. This may have been some idiot playing about on Hallowe'en.'

Anne glared at him. 'I don't call attacking the local vicar playing about, Inspector.'

George's eyes flashed with annoyance.

'Detective Chief Inspector, Mrs Merryweather.'

Anne flinched. 'Oh. Sorry. Well, anyway, this isn't playing a game is it?'

George gave her a 'you'd be surprised' look as he found a blank page and licked the tip of his pencil.

'Right, now before you cut me down in flames, I'm not suggesting that anyone in this room is to blame; but, it makes sense to ask you some questions. Some may be a little intrusive, but I've got to get the facts down. Beth, James, when did your party begin last night?'

Beth put her cup down. 'Well, we were here all afternoon getting food ready and also put up the lanterns and candles. You know, fixing the place up to look good. James was sorting out the games and getting the apple desserts going, setting up the hog roast, that sort of thing.'

'Anne was here too,' added James, 'buttering the rolls. Bert was helping me out in the field. He was getting a small bonfire built to provide some heat.'

Anne leant forward. 'Stephen was still at home

120

getting the children ready.'

'And what time did people start arriving?' asked George.

Beth searched her memory. 'I guess around seven. That's the time we said it would start and people pretty much stuck to that.'

'And who arrived first?'

'Actually, darling,' said James, 'it was before seven. Bob Tanner and his folk band were here and set themselves up on the stage.'

'Oh, that's right. Yes, they were here about six. And the Morris men were here too.'

'Right,' replied George. 'So apart from those people you've just named, no one else was at your place before seven?'

Beth's face paled. 'Oh George, you don't think it was one of our guests, do you?'

George sighed impatiently. 'I don't know, Beth. But I have to start somewhere. The vicar is new and the few villagers that have met him so far were here. And, if this has got something to do with Grimes' death – and I'm not saying it has – then, yes, I do think it's quite close to home.'

'So you're not ruling out a link to Grimes?' said James with a hint of sarcasm.

George's lips tightened. 'As I've said, James, I'm not ruling it out. But I have to consider the possibility because of where Reverend Merryweather was attacked. If the Grimes death is suspicious, then I have to look at family, friends, acquaintances. Nine times out of ten, it's a member of the family or an acquaintance that's involved.'

James leant back in his chair and reluctantly appreciated his friend's point although he hated the thought of any villager being involved in such an unsavoury incident.

'Well, I think Dorothy Forbes was one of the first through the gate,' he said. 'People seemed to pitch up all together, really. Once the children had finished doing their cabbage night thing, they toddled off to get the parents and then come here. But I think just about everyone was here by eight, half past eight at the latest.'

George scratched his head. 'I know that you invite the whole village, but not everyone comes to these affairs. Can you give me a list of those people who did attend?'

James grimaced and glanced hopefully at Beth who confirmed that she would see to it.

'And what about leaving?' continued George. 'Did you see anyone leave early?'

The group looked at one another blankly and Beth gave a helpless shake of the head. 'I don't think anyone took much notice. It was dark. The lanterns only give out so much light. People came and went through the side gate – we don't have any formalities so they would have come and gone as they pleased.'

'Right, so could anyone have left for a half hour and come back again without being missed?'

James stirred his tea thoughtfully. 'Yes, yes I suppose if they'd wanted to. Anyone could have.'

George turned. 'Bert, anything to add to that?'

Bert screwed his face up and shrugged. 'Not really, mate. I 'ad a chat with most people last night, but I couldn't tell you when I did or if they were there all night. Anyone could've sneaked out and been back without being missed.'

'The o-only people with a c-cast iron alibi are in the band,' said Stephen. 'Th-they never stopped playing.'

'And us, of course,' Anne added.

George heaved a sigh. 'But no one can vouch for anyone all of the time – apart from Bob Tanner.' Anne avoided his eye contact. 'Well ... no, I suppose not.'

George read through his notes, then focussed his attention on Mitchell.

'Mr Mitchell, perhaps you'd better go through what you saw on your way to the party. Try not to leave anything out.'

Pete Mitchell cleared his throat and put his cup down. He'd arrived straight from the orchard and, excusing his unkempt clothing, insisted on leaving his muddy walking shoes on the front step. He then asked them to excuse his grubby socks.

As he was clearly an outdoor man, his rugged face made him look a little older than his twenty-six years and it creased with worry as he thought about what to say. His hand rubbed the stubble on his chin and he fidgeted in his chair.

'Right, well,' he began, 'I came round here early yesterday afternoon – to drop the apples off like. I didn't stop coz I'd got quite a bit to do at the orchard, what with my wife being at her sister's. She's just getting over the flu and her sister offered to look after her, you know, convalescent sort of thing. Anyway, I says that I'd see 'em later, like; that I'd pick up Mr and Mrs Jepson on the way. That's right. I 'ad to drop some apples off at a shop, but I said I'd pick the Jepsons up on the way.'

'And what time did this all happen?' asked George.

'Ah, right. Well, let's see. I'd arranged to pick Mr and Mrs Jepson up at about eight-thirty, I think. So, I must've left the orchard at eight. I knew I'd be early, but I didn't think it'd matter. But there weren't anyone there. At the Jepsons' house, I mean, which I thought was a bit odd. Anyway, I thought I'd go and drop the apples off with the shopkeeper and come back. I had to go down past Grimes' farm to get back to the village.'

'What shop are we talking about?'

'The little grocer down Blandon Lane. Always takes a stock of cookers off me.'

'Cookers?'

'Yeah, apples. Cooking apples.'

George waited for him to continue.

'Right. Well, I got to where Grimes' farm is and just looked across. Don't know why, but anyway, that's when I saw lights. Like torch lights in the distance.'

'In the distance?'

Mitchell shuffled his feet. 'Yeah, well, it looked like in the distance. I mean, it weren't in the house.'

James leant forward. 'But it could have been near the house?'

'Well, yes, I suppose so. Well ... I'm not sure. At first, I thought it was further back, like, near the copse.'

'Th-that's what you s-said last night, when you arrived,' Stephen added.

George took out his pipe and carefully filled the bowl with tobacco. 'So, you don't know if this

124

light was by the farm or half a mile away in the copse?'

'Not really,' replied Mitchell. He looked across at everyone apologetically. 'Sorry, but after a night's sleep it don't seem so clear.'

'And you said torch lights, not a torch light?'

Mitchell sat up in surprise. 'Oh, did I? Well, I'm not sure that it was lights, now. I think it was prob'ly just the one.'

'But you're not sure exactly where?'

Mitchell grimaced and looked at James, who felt obliged to pitch in.

'It was dark, George, and he did only drive by.'

George studied everyone in the room. Beth took advantage of the silence that followed to offer more tea and cake. Everyone seemed relieved to have an interlude in the proceedings.

Mitchell fidgeted uneasily as he rolled his cap in his hands. George lit his pipe.

James watched as Beth and Anne organised tea, then got up to stretch his legs. 'Mitchell, old chap, did you go back to see if the Jepsons were home?'

'Yeah, yeah, I did,' he replied, 'and they still weren't there. I knocked on the front door about four times. Then I went down the little alleyway, the one that takes you to the back of the house, and knocked on the window but there was nothing. No lights on, upstairs or down. Then I thought perhaps they'd already left and come to you.'

James worriedly looked across at George and wandered to the French windows to watch the boys playing. This wasn't good, especially if Mr

Jepson had argued with Grimes the morning he'd died. And now he and Mrs Jepson had upped sticks and gone. George joined James at the window.

'What are you thinking, James?'

James said nothing. George had yet to find out about the argument between Jepson and Grimes and he decided to keep quiet about it until he had time to think or at least speak to his cleaner. He couldn't believe the Jepsons would be mixed up in this. George, unfortunately, had a built-in sixth sense. His eyes narrowed.

'Is there anything you're holding back?'

James gave him an indignant look. George lowered his voice and aimed the tip of his pipe at him.

'Because if there is, you need to let me know. If you want me to investigate this, and you've been badgering me to do so, then you've got to be straight with me. And, if this does turn out to be more serious than I've let on, you've got to accept that someone you know might be involved.'

James' mouth went dry as George continued.

'That's the problem when you go poking your nose in. Things jump out and you're thrown a surprise that you didn't expect. And then you wish you hadn't meddled.'

James composed himself and turned to face him. 'If I have something that I feel is important to you, George, I'll let you know. I promise.'

George grunted in exasperation and returned to his seat. James wandered across to the fireplace and leant on the mantelpiece as George continued questioning Mitchell.

'So, what time did you get to the Jepsons', that second time?'

'Must've been about nine, nine-fifteen.'

'How far are they from here?'

Mitchell shrugged. 'About five minutes, I s'pose, by car.'

'But you didn't get here until ten? What were you doing in between?'

A long silence followed. James watched Mitchell; he shifted under George's unswerving gaze and swallowed hard.

'I went back to Grimes' farm.'

James studied Mitchell as he explained that he'd returned to see if the lights were still there and they were.

He caught Bert's eye; he was clearly thinking the same as him. Last night, Mitchell hadn't mentioned going back to the farm. It was the other side of the village. Why would he go back? Why had he changed his story? He returned to his armchair. 'I say, Mitchell, did you know Grimes at all?'

'Not really. He had some of my apples, but I never really talked with him much.'

'Did he pay you?'

George stole a glance at James. 'What's that?'

'It's just that Grimes seemed a little short of the old readies and he doesn't – or, rather, he didn't – seem to pay up for things.'

Mitchell tensed and looked at the floor. 'He didn't pay me for the last lot, no. It weren't much but, well, we have to make a living like, don't we?'

George scribbled more notes on his pad.

James picked up his teacup. 'This mud man,

golem thing. Do you think that's relevant, George?'

'Not sure how,' replied George. 'What are you thinking?'

'Well, the pentagrams on the floor at Grimes' place, the devil worship stuff, the play that's going on, the vicar here getting coshed – it all denotes some sort of supernatural theme, don't you think? And why go to all the bother of making a golem?'

'I'll have a look into it, James. Remember, I'm not even sure that this is linked to the Grimes death. It's easy to see how it would tie in, but I'm not sure why at the moment.' George turned his attention to Stephen.

'Do you have any enemies in the village, Reverend?'

Stephen stared in horror. 'Me? No. Y-you don't think this was planned, do you?'

'George,' Beth interrupted, 'you can't be serious! He's only just moved here and no one knew he would be going to the farm.'

'Where were you before you came here?'

'K-Kidlington, near Oxford. I-I used to be a teacher there. Anne did too.'

Bert kicked his shoes off. 'No one would wanna hurt 'im, George. Wouldn't say boo to a goose.'

'You know him?'

'Not well, no. But I know people and 'e's no trouble. Blimey, he even wants to rename the local play so it don't offend. He's as quiet as the proverbial church mouse.'

'This play, *The Devil Incarnate*,' continued George. 'That's all to do with the supernatural, isn't it? Stephen's a vicar – perhaps he's annoyed someone by getting involved and wanting to change it.'

James frowned at George. 'Involved with what? It's just the local play. Unless there's some sort of witches' coven going on that we don't know about. Anyway, he didn't know Grimes, so how could the two be linked?'

'I'm not saying it is,' replied George. 'You're the one that suggested this was linked – not me. Now you're not sure?'

'Fair comment,' James said as he munched on a scone. 'But why would an amateur play be so emotive?'

Beth held a hand up. 'That's an easy one. The supernatural link. Whether you're for it, as Grimes was, or against it, as is Stephen, there's a common link. If someone feels that strongly about something they can sometimes act irrationally. And, if there is some sort of devil worship thing going on, well, I don't know much about it, but I can't imagine them being nice people.'

George scratched his head and put his pipe down. 'People have killed for less. And where are Mr and Mrs Jepson?'

James made to steer George off the subject, but Bert had already caught his friend's attention.

'Ah, now that's the rub,' he said. 'Now 'e was round at Grimes the morning he died. Had an argument with him, by all accounts and quite a heated one too.'

Bert appeared pleased to have been of some help but James silently cursed him. George caught the look and eased himself out of his chair.

'Right, I think I've got enough for the time

being. I'm off.'

James leapt up. 'Is that it? No more questions?'

George confirmed that he really needed to do some rooting about to see if there was a case. 'Don't forget, James,' he said. 'Bert mentioned that he thought it might have been poachers and that *is* the most logical answer.'

'But why mould a golem?' asked James. 'And why attack Stephen?'

'Well, you've got me there, but it could be two different incidents – kids messing about on Hallowe'en and poachers getting riled,' replied George. 'Look, I 'aven't got all the answers, but I've known several innocent bystanders get attacked because they've interrupted the nightly wanderings of poachers; and there is poaching in that area. Anyway, I'll dig around, see what I can find out.'

George bade goodbye to everyone and requested they make themselves available for more questioning if need be. James followed him through to the hall.

'By the way, James, don't forget to give me that list of people who came here last night. Soon as you can.'

'Of course. I'll run it over tomorrow.'

The inspector jabbed a finger at him. 'And I don't need any prompting or interference from you. I'd like two and two to equal four, not seven.'

James held his hands up. 'You know where I am.'

'And don't keep anything back,' continued George. 'I clocked the look you gave Bert when he mentioned the Jepsons.'

James apologised and stressed that he just couldn't see Jepson murdering anyone.

'You'd be surprised what people are capable of.' Stephen popped out from the lounge.

'Inspector – sorry, D-Detective Chief Inspector. Have you found Keith Grimes?'

'No, not yet. I'll follow up on that and let you know what I find out. When's the funeral?'

'This coming Wednesday.'

'Right you are. Leave it with me.'

Stephen returned to the lounge as James swung open the front door.

'George, are you looking at the body again?'

'Already on to that. Our doctor's taking another look and we've taken fingerprints at the farmhouse. You in church on Sunday?' George suddenly looked surprised. 'Crikey, that's the day after tomorrow, isn't it?'

'Yes, it's a busy few days,' replied James. 'We've got rehearsals for this play on Sunday evening, the funeral on Wednesday and, of course, we've Bonfire Night to round everything off.' He frowned at George. 'You're not usually at church.'

'Oh, I will be on Sunday,' said George. 'I'll be sitting at the back watching. I'm sure the news about the vicar will have spread like wildfire. They'll all be there, gawping. Can learn a lot from people-watching.' He placed his trilby on his head and trotted down the steps to his car. 'Cheerio.'

James deliberated as he closed the door. George always said that it was normally a family member to blame when a serious crime took place. Although his friend would not agree to a crime having occurred, James felt more convinced than ever. He wondered whether Keith Grimes had already arrived in Cavendish.

CHAPTER ELEVEN

After a delicious evening meal of roast beef and horseradish sauce, James drove the Merryweathers home and returned to relax in front of the fire.

The varnished walnut clock rang a gentle chime announcing a quarter to ten. Benny Goodman's 'Stomping at the Savoy' provided a rhythmic beat and, over a glass of port, he and Beth discussed the possibility of Keith Grimes having arrived in Cavendish. Beth contemplated the possibility as she manoeuvred James' arm over her shoulders so she could snuggle into him.

'But why kill him?' said Beth. 'I mean, he hasn't been living down here for, what, ten years? With no contact with his father. Why suddenly come down to kill him?'

'Maybe there *has* been contact. Perhaps Keith has fallen on hard times and needs to raise some cash? The farm, admittedly, is run-down, but there's the livestock, the house. It'll be worth something.'

'I suppose so,' replied Beth. 'Specially the land. I think that *would* be worth something, particularly to developers. Oh dear, you don't think we're going to go the same way as Crawley, do you?'

James assured her that he didn't think so. Crawley, like Cavendish, had existed as a small hamlet for hundreds of years and had now been transformed into a New Town for Londoners to move to. They'd already built thousands of houses with local shopping parades, a library and schools. The locals, of course, opposed all of the proposed plans and many villagers despaired of what they viewed as unwanted destruction of their tiny community.

'I'd be surprised if they built two new towns in the same county,' he replied. 'Anyway, they'd earmarked Crawley for that little venture just after the war. Cavendish is too far off the beaten track. I mean, we're not even near the railway. Crawley is bang in the middle of the main London to Brighton commuter service. You could be right about the land, though. There's money in land deals.' James sipped his port. 'I wonder if Grimes made a will? I didn't see anything in his bureau. Didn't see any letters, come to think of it. I'll have to remember to ask George in the morning.'

Beth caught her breath. 'I nearly forgot. I'm supposed to be doing a list of guests from last night.' Her eyes pleaded. 'Will you help, sweetie?'

'Of course. Let's do it now.'

James found some paper and took out his fountain pen. Between them, they jotted down the names as they sprang to mind and, after a couple of minutes, Peter Mitchell's name cropped up.

'Mmm...' Beth reached across to tidy up the magazines. 'What did you make of Mr Mitchell this afternoon? When he mentioned going back to the farm?'

James swivelled round. 'Yes, that was a little odd, wasn't it? You know, he said nothing to me about going back there. In fact, I'm damned sure he said he'd come straight from the Jepsons' place. I

133

mean, Grimes' farm is in the other direction, so why trundle all the way over there just to return here?'

'He didn't make eye contact then, either,' said Beth. 'Most of the time he spoke, he looked at George and occasionally caught your eye. But when he got talking about that second visit, he looked down at the carpet. That's a sure sign he wasn't telling the truth. Do you think he went back?'

'I must admit – that part of his story didn't ring true. And he did look pretty damned shifty. Wonder what George made of it? But, if he didn't go back to the farm, where the devil did he go? It doesn't take half an hour to get from Mrs J's to here, it's five minutes in a car.'

'Perhaps he got his timings wrong?'

'No. No, I don't think he did.'

Beth shrugged and they carried on with the list. As a final check, they telephoned Donovan and were delighted to hear that Bert was on the premises. They went through the list with him and Bert recalled a couple more names to add.

Satisfied that everyone was accounted for, James suggested they turn in for the night. 'It's been an eventful few days and I could do with a good sleep to recharge the batteries. I do hope Stephen will be all right for Sunday.'

Beth circled the room, turning off the wall-lights as James secured the fire-guard and opened the lounge door for her.

'I'm looking forward to hearing his first performance,' he said as they climbed the stairs. 'Wonder what he's going to talk about?'

'Well, one thing's for certain,' replied Beth. 'He has plenty of material to play with.'

The church pews filled quickly as villagers, local farmers and inquisitive onlookers descended from Cavendish and surrounding areas. John 'Beaky' Brownlee trod lightly on the organ pedals and the timeless classic, 'All Things Bright and Beautiful', played softly in the background to welcome parishioners.

Adults, who in their childhood had ridiculed Brownlee's long hook-nose, had taken to calling him Beaky and the name had stuck with the new generation of village children. Now retired, he continued playing in the church and delighted in teaching the organ to several younger villagers, who were eager to take up the mantle when Beaky became too old to play.

James and Beth took their places at the front. Every so often he checked to see who had arrived and waved to several members of the congregation as they filed in. Rose and Lilac Crumb pushed their way into the third row.

He leant in towards Beth. 'Full house. Even the Snoop Sisters are here.'

'Maybe they queued overnight,' said Beth. 'It's certainly brought people out of the woodwork.'

James agreed. Everyone who'd enjoyed their Hallowe'en party was there, although some were not regular churchgoers. Their children fidgeted awkwardly, much to the annoyance of their parents. He grinned. Harry and Oliver had behaved in exactly the same way, especially with the old vicar. He hadn't been the most inspiring orator in the world and, James admitted to himself, even he had felt bored listening to him. He hoped Stephen would provide a more motivating and inspirational sermon.

Bert suddenly obscured his vision and told him to budge up along the pew. James stared incredulously.

'What on earth are you doing here?'

'The same as most of these old codgers,' replied Bert. 'Nosing about.'

James and Beth exchanged grins. Stephen, who had been at the entrance with Anne, welcoming his parishioners, finally walked to the altar with a beaming smile for everyone. His long, black cassock exaggerated his height. He'd taken the bandage off his head and certainly looked a lot brighter than he had on Friday.

On reaching the pulpit, he gazed at his new audience. A hush descended. Footsteps echoed at the back and, as one, everyone turned. DCI George Lane had the grace to look embarrassed as he took his place at the end of the last pew.

James settled back and listened to Stephen introduce himself and tell the congregation a little about his background and how he had found his spiritual path. He had, James thought, a likeable manner; his intonation varied and he even included a little humour here and there which, along with his minor stutter, quickly endeared him to the parishioners.

'I-I suspect that my arrival has brought you here *en masse,* so to speak, because of my small mishap.'

A murmur passed around the congregation.

He chuckled. 'P-perhaps I need to do this every week to guarantee a good crowd.'

The parishioners relaxed and laughed with him.

'W-well, I have to say, it wasn't the welcome I expected, but I believe these things come along for a reason. I-I'm not exactly sure what the reason is at the moment but, being in the profession I'm in, I must f-forgive whoever did this. He, or she, will I'm sure come to a time in their lives when they will look back on this incident with either regret or r-relish. Indeed, perhaps this did not come to *me* for a reason, but to my attacker. A man, or woman, who c-could well be sitting here this very morning.'

The villagers shifted uneasily.

'O-our gracious Lord watches over us and we are here to learn from every aspect of our lives,' continued Stephen. 'The triumphs, the disasters, the high and l-lows, the gloomy, the funny. All emotions touch us, all acquaintances rub off on us, all human nature affects us, consciously and s-subconsciously. The Lord certainly does move in mysterious ways, but he does so for a reason. To teach us something. My attacker, in our eyes, is a criminal, am I right?'

The villagers quickly murmured in agreement, but stopped as Stephen held his hand up.

'B-but is he? What if it transpired he was a poor man seeking food and money for his starving child? A child that may die if he does not provide for it. Then we w-would feel sorry for him. Indeed, if we knew he needed help, we would provide food and shelter for him.'

The congregation agreed again.

'S-so, the lesson for me, for *us*, is forgiveness. Until we hear all sides of the story, w-we cannot judge, just understand. So, I would ask that we do not make judgements about people and their actions. Even if the reason is c-criminal, we must look to what leads that person to act in such a way. Jesus was a great mediator in such circumstances. Where people c-cast their opinions and pointed their fingers, he sought to understand and forgive.'

He scanned his congregation. 'So, from having said that I am not sure why this incident c-came along, I-I appear to have surmised that the lesson is to forgive, and not to allow the intrusion of spiteful or evil thoughts.'

Stephen's voice became more assertive as he stepped down from the pulpit and began wandering up and down the front of the church, something that neither James, nor the congregation, had witnessed before. But, as James watched, he thought it took away the barrier that a vicar stood behind. Stephen's message became more direct and personal.

'Now, I must come to the story of A-Alec Grimes,' he continued. 'In my efforts to find out about Mr Grimes, I have heard many unfavourable remarks and opinions.' His gaze settled briefly on Rose and Lilac. 'Some from people who never knew him, never met him, or met him just the once.' His eyes scanned the congregation. 'S-some, I'm sure, were true, some untrue, and many, I believe, exaggerated. Yet, are we so perfect?'

Stephen closed his bible and strode up and down the nave.

'Remember the message in Matthew, seven. Do not j-judge, and you will not be judged. If you judge others, so you will yourselves be judged, and whatever you deal out to others will be dealt to you. Why look at the speck of sawdust in your brother's eye with n-never a thought for the plank in your own? How can you say, "let me take the speck out of your eye", when all the time there is a plank in your own. F-first take the plank out of your own eye, and then you will see clearly to take the speck out of your brother's.'

And so went Stephen's first sermon – delivered with empathy, passion and purpose. A far cry, James whispered to Beth, from the last vicar's style.

An hour later, members of the congregation filed out of the church, full of conversation. While happily exchanging pleasantries with the Reverend Merryweather and his family, they made sincere promises to return the following Sunday. Even the children had seemed to enjoy the service. George wandered down the church, hat in hand, to James, who remained seated on his pew, chatting with Bert.

'More snoopers than normal, James.'

'Most definitely. Any clues where you were sitting?'

George rolled his trilby in his hand. 'Not really. It's always worth a shot. The police always pitch up at weddings and funerals, but I've never gleaned anything from it. I live in hope. Any thoughts since yesterday?'

James shook his head. 'None at the moment, but I'll keep poking around. You on duty today?'

George grunted that he was on the late shift and buttoned up his coat. 'Right, I'll be off. You let me know if you find anything out. And Bert, no funny business on my shift.'

As George strode out of the church, Bert got up and buttoned his own coat. 'Right, I can take a hint. I've got some stuff to move, so I'd best get it sorted early. What are you doing now?'

'I thought I'd pop by Pete Mitchell's place and see if I can fathom out why he lied yesterday,' replied James.

'You be careful, Jimmy boy. By the way, I've got some satin for Beth. I was up the market first thing. I'll bring it to rehearsals later.'

James grinned as he watched his friend scamper off to embark on some dodgy deals. He took a deep breath and stretched out his legs. The church had emptied completely and he remained seated as Stephen approached him.

'How's the head?'

'N-not too bad, actually. Anne dosed me up with p-plenty of painkillers.' He sat down next to James. 'D-d'you think it went all right?'

'I think it went more than all right,' James said. 'A very timely sermon under the circumstances and an audience riveted to your every word. I believe, young Stephen, you will have quite a crowd at your Sunday sermons.'

'Yes, well, I-I did have something written about moving into a new area, but that seemed rather tame after the e-events on Thursday.'

'Nothing like a bit of blood and gore to get the

public in.' James got up and patted him on the back. 'Let's hope you fill the place every week.'

'B-by the way, James, I forgot to thank you for the Hallowe'en party. Not just for looking after me after that commotion, but the actual party. The boys loved it.'

'Yes, it's always a good night and I hope that you'll be here for many more. And now, of course, I've got Tuesday's Bonfire Night to get organised.'

Stephen's face lit up. 'Ah yes, Anne and Beth are at the vicarage now sorting out the c-catering and who's doing what.'

'Good show. Remind them that Mrs Keates is doing some baking for us. Might be a good idea to get in touch with her today.'

'I-I'll let them know. Perhaps we could pop across to her now? I'm free for an hour or two.'

'Sorry, Stephen,' said James, 'but I'm off to see Pete Mitchell. Why don't you run the girls there yourself? Elsie's will be open – she does a mean cream tea on Sunday. She opens between twelve and four and has the wireless on. Whatever she charges goes to their local church fund. It's a pleasant way to pass an hour on a Sunday.'

Stephen thought this a good idea and suggested that perhaps they should do something similar after the Sunday service in Cavendish. James made his way out of the church. Pete Mitchell was pacing up and down on the gravel, twisting his cap in his hands. When he saw James he dashed over to him.

'You don't think that detective thinks I 'ad anything to do with this Grimes business, do you?' he asked nervously.

141

'Well, no, at least, I don't think so,' replied James. 'Would you have reason to be involved?'

'No! It's just that I get in a real state when police interrogate me.'

James assured him that George had simply been asking routine questions to get an understanding of what had happened. 'There's certainly no interrogation going on,' he added. 'Have you been in a similar situation before, then?'

Pete's eyes shifted left, then right. 'No, no, it's just that the police are always so suspicious.'

James put an arm around Pete's shoulder, steered him out of the churchyard and onto the high street. 'I'm sure everything will be fine. I'm a good friend of DCI Lane, so I'll get a handle on what he's thinking.'

Mitchell relaxed. 'If you could, I'd be grateful. I'd best get going. Can't stop working on a Sunday, not this time of the year.'

James ignored the remark and continued talking. 'You went to school with Keith Grimes, didn't you?'

Mitchell continued folding his cap. 'Yeah, I did. Only for the last year, like. I mean, they're not a Cavendish family. Keith changed schools a few times from what I can gather. Came to our one for the last year.'

'What did you make of him?'

'Never knew 'im, really. Kept himself to himself. Real loner, like.' Pete put his cap on. 'Wouldn't surprise me if he did it – you know, killed 'is old man. They always say it's the quiet ones, the loners, who do these things.'

'What makes you think he was murdered?'

Mitchell looked like a frightened rabbit. 'But ... I thought...'

'Oh, you may be right,' replied James. 'At the moment it's just a heart attack.'

Mitchell detached himself from James and said he had to go.

'I say!' James pulled him back. 'There is one thing, Mitchell.'

'What's that?'

'Well, you never said anything to me about going back to Grimes' farm on Thursday night, but you told George that you did. Is that true?'

An uncomfortable silence followed and James could see Mitchell turning the question over in his head. He eventually shrugged.

'Must've slipped my mind like, you know, with everything that's been going on. Look, I've gotta go, things to do.' He scampered off and unlocked his van in double-quick time. The van's tyres squealed as he drove off.

James watched the vehicle disappear around the bend and muttered, 'You, young man, are hiding something.'

CHAPTER TWELVE

Later that evening, James followed Beth and Anne into the village hall, which was in a state of organised chaos.

There was a tremendous buzz of activity as members of the Cavendish Players busied themselves in different areas of the building, under the watchful eye of Dorothy Forbes.

Behind the stage he could hear hammering and sawing and, on the stage itself, Ian Connell balanced precariously on a paint-stained step ladder to adjust the main spotlights. Young boys in shorts slid across the recently polished floor and a few volunteers from the Women's Institute had gathered behind a long trestle table to dispense cups of tea from a large silver urn.

Dorothy strode across the wooden floor in her stout shoes. She wore a calf-length tweed skirt and twinset. She peered, sternly, over spectacles perched on the end of her nose. James awaited her instructions.

'Ah, Lord Harrington,' she bellowed, clipboard in hand. 'Your group is over here. Lady Harrington and Mrs Merryweather, I believe you're costumes.' She checked the notes on her clipboard. 'Yes, costumes. If you go to the back of the stage, through to the green room, we have sewing machines set up. Excuse the mess, the men are designing hills for the scenery.' She marched off.

Beth grinned at James. 'No rest for the wicked.' She linked arms with Anne. 'We best not dawdle or we'll get detention.'

She and Anne chuckled like naughty schoolgirls and went in search of their fellow costume makers.

James took a cursory look around to locate his particular group. He spotted Graham Porter with Bert where, he surmised from the subtle handshake and whispering, that a deal of some sort was being finalised. Like many of Bert's business

144

ventures, James could never quite establish the legalities of it all and would prefer not to know. He strolled across.

'Evening, Graham, Bert.'

'Wotcha, Jimmy boy,' Bert said, waving a brown paper package at him. 'I'm off to the green room – got the material 'ere for the costumes. Got it from a mate in Petticoat Lane – good price, too, even cheaper than the stall price.'

Petticoat Lane was the big Sunday morning market in the East End of London and he knew Bert would have been up before sunrise to be there when it opened. This was obviously where he'd been before the service that morning. The market was always heaving with people wanting to purchase all manner of goods, from fabrics and foreign delicacies to circus monkeys and parrots.

Graham led James to a quieter corner. 'Tell me, James, is it true that you've found one of them golem things up at the farmhouse?'

'Yes, I have to say it was rather eerie – certainly didn't expect it. Seems old Grimes was delving into black magic.'

'I hope that's not where all my money went.'

'Well, you'd like to think not, wouldn't you? Graham, what exactly was the arrangement that you had with him?'

They unfolded a couple of rickety wooden chairs. Graham appeared a little embarrassed and took a deep breath. 'He came to me saying that he'd got the opportunity to buy the copse. You know, Charn Wood, the area up at the top of the field, and some of the land behind it as well. It'd come up for sale.'

'That was the subject of the painting I found him with. Did that land not belong to him, then?'

'Grimes had the run of the field to the side, but the copse and beyond it I think was something to do with the farmer down the road, or spare land or something. He said he wanted to use it for something. Tch, prob'ly some sort of ritual gathering! He told me he'd raised most of the money, had some sort of policy mature but was short by two hundred and fifty quid. He was nice about it – said he'd pay me interest on it and we worked out a monthly payment. We shook hands on it and we were both happy.' Graham pursed his lips. 'Unfortunately, I didn't put anything in writing straight away. I said I'd get it written up and he told me he'd sign it once it was done. I got a paper drawn up but every time I went round there he was either too busy or didn't answer the door. I never got a payment from him – not one. My own fault, I know. I should have got Mr Bateson to do something legal for me.'

'But he went ahead and bought the copse?'

'As far as I know, yes.'

'So what happened when he didn't pay you? Did you confront him?'

Graham's heavy bulk shifted awkwardly. 'After three months I went round there, told him it wasn't on. I mean, we had a gentleman's agreement and all that. He laughed at me. Bloody laughed! I couldn't believe it.' He leant forward. 'I grabbed him by the collar and pushed him up against the wall. I said that if I didn't get a payment by the end of the month, I'd kill him. Then I punched him, winded him like, in the stomach.

He told me I'd get the money but I'd have to wait.

'I'm regretting I said it now of course. I mean, George Lane is gonna have me down as suspect number one.'

James crossed his legs and told him it was likely. 'He'll certainly want to question you, I'm sure. But you probably have an alibi, don't you?'

'Not really. I was at the shop the day he died, but Sarah had gone early. She fancied a trip into Brighton, the kids were at school, so I was on my own, just pottering about like. I could've put the closed sign up and gone anywhere. I didn't though – 'ad too much to do. And I was at your Hallowe'en do on Thursday, but I don't stick to Sarah like glue. We were talking to different people and your boys were entertaining the kids for most of the evening.'

Graham looked James straight in the eye. 'I could've skipped out and knocked out the vicar, but I didn't, I swear to you,' he said, becoming agitated. 'Why would I want to harm Stephen? I don't even know him but he seems a nice bloke. I've got no reason to–'

James patted his knee and assured him he had nothing to worry about. Dorothy's no-nonsense request that they join her in the middle of the hall did not go unheard or unheeded. Graham mooched across to her, his shoulders heavy with the burden of what might be.

James stacked the two chairs against the wall as he wondered how many people had threatened to kill Grimes. He liked to think that George would dismiss Graham from his enquiries, but doubts nagged at him – mainly because George was

147

adamant that a local was responsible. If it was someone local, it would be an acquaintance or friend.

But Graham had been in the village for years. He'd become the quintessential village butcher; the farmer's friend because he paid extra for the best meat; the housewife's favourite because of his jovial and open nature. He had a clumsy charm about him but was that charm hiding something? As he watched Graham's sorry demeanour, he hoped not.

'Chop chop, no dilly-dallying!' Dorothy said.

James stood alongside Graham, giving him a reassuring squeeze on the arm. Philip Jackson, Bert and Donovan Delaney joined them.

'Lord Harrington, where is Inspector Lane?' Dorothy said with a reproachful look.

James managed an apologetic smile. 'He's on shift until ten this evening – is that a problem?'

'It will be if he doesn't attend rehearsals,' she replied. 'Do make sure he gets to the next one and please go through this scene with him. It's the only one he's in.'

James assured her that he would. Dorothy distributed their scripts and ordered them to stand in a circle.

'Right, chop, chop. Dr Jackson, we'll begin with you – do try to sound menacing. That's what this scene is about. You are the people who are summoning up the mud man.'

Philip Jackson took a couple of puffs of his pipe and held up his script. 'What is it you want from me?'

'To ward away the evil that has brought disease

to our people,' Graham answered.

Bert sniggered but, on seeing Dorothy's glare, quickly stopped.

'Then you must make a human image of clay. Make this image and give prayers to the elements and you will achieve success in killing the evil that has spread among you.'

After a short silence, James realised that all eyes were on him. He quickly studied his script. 'Oh, sorry, er ... an image of clay?'

'Tch, tch,' Dorothy said with exasperation. 'Lord Harrington, it would be far better if you could sound a little less ... well...'

James tilted his head quizzically. Bert nudged him.

'What she means is, don't sound like a bleedin' toff.'

James grinned at Bert. 'Sorry, Dorothy.' He cleared his throat and started again in an edgier tone. 'An image of clay?'

'But what're we to do with it?' Donovan Delaney demanded, impressing everyone with his hard-nosed characterisation.

'You will need to capture the four elements. Earth, water, fire and air,' said Philip. He turned to Bert. 'You will bring the element of earth.'

Dorothy instructed Bert to hold up an imaginary piece of mud. 'You'll have the real thing on the night,' she explained.

'You,' Philip moved on to Donovan, 'will embody the furnace of fire. You,' he said again, stabbing his finger at James, 'will breathe air into the clay. And you,' he pointed at the space where George should be, 'must bring a ladle of pure water. On the fourth hour after midnight, we will meet on the high bank where the loam pits are found. Here, we will fashion the golem and order him to banish all evil from our community.'

'Stop just there' said Dorothy. 'Very good. Philip, you do sound menacing, but try to keep in character. You slipped a little on occasion. Maintain the deep and rich resonance of your voice. Right, gentleman, carry on.'

Dorothy turned on her heel and strode off to the next group. Philip relit his pipe and waited until she was out of earshot. 'Did she used to be a headmistress or something?'

James patted him on the back and said that as far as he could remember she'd always been a housewife and a mother, albeit a fierce one. Jackson likened her to a frustrated dictator.

Ian Connell trotted down the steps from the stage and wandered across to James. 'It feels wrong doing this when one of those things was found up at the farm.'

'Yes, I s'pose it does,' replied James. 'But it's too late to change things now. I say, Ian, if you don't mind my asking, what was it that you were doing for Grimes?'

Ian scratched the back of his head. 'Inside toilet. Re-do the plumbing upstairs then renovate the kitchen. If there was any money left over, extend the lounge by a couple of feet.'

'That's an extensive piece of work. Do you still have the plans?'

Ian said he did.

'Could I pop round and take a peek?'

'What for?'

150

'Have some plans of my own to put to you.'

Ian fished out a card from his jacket pocket. 'My address is on there. I'm in the office all day tomorrow, so you can pop in when you like. I'll let my secretary know you're coming – we'll have the kettle on.'

Stephen tapped James on the shoulder as Ian disappeared. 'H-hello, how's it going?'

'Yes, good thanks. Dorothy's a little put out about George not pitching in, but we can't help that. Any news on Keith Grimes?'

'Nothing. The police have c-called at his flat but there's no one in. The neighbours haven't seen him for a few days.'

James put his hands in his pockets. 'Well, that's all very odd, don't you think? Keith Grimes must be here, in Cavendish. Where else would he be?'

The vicar proposed that Keith could, perhaps, just be on holiday. 'H-have you forgotten my sermon already?' he said knowingly. 'Don't be so quick to judge your fellow man.'

Beth tugged James' sleeve. 'Dorothy has a couple of suggestions about changing the script, but Mr Jepson's not here. Do we have any news on where they may be?'

'Oh lord, I'd forgotten all about them. No, they've disappeared completely. Not a dicky bird.'

Stephen rubbed his forehead wearily. 'Oh dear, y-you don't think Mr Jepson had something to do with this, do you? I mean, I don't know the man but it all seems rather unsavoury. And he's your cleaner's husband. That p-puts you in a tricky position. And the subject of this play's too close for comfort.'

151

James held up his script. 'I'm hoping this is simply an overactive imagination.'

'I-I feel as if there's a huge "but" at the end of that sentence.'

James pulled a face and admitted he had difficulty keeping that line of thought going. 'The facts of the matter are that he's written a play about a golem. He knows all about devil worship; he was the last person to see Grimes alive; he's argued with him and now he's disappeared, along with his wife. If his wife is anything to go by, it's exceptionally out of character.' He met Stephen's gaze. 'So yes, although it pains me to say it, I do think he has something to do with it. And he's not doing himself any favours by running off.'

To James' relief, the rest of the evening passed pleasantly and little else was mentioned about Grimes' death or Stephen's blow to the head.

Rehearsals always created a great deal of laughter as the villagers contributed to the play as best they could. They stood patiently to be measured for costumes while panels of wood were being slowly transformed into hills and cottages, and the Women's Institute ladies continued steadily supplying drinks.

People in small groups repeated their lines over and over, many promising Dorothy they'd have them memorised by the next rehearsal. Although they knew they'd never be a match for Gregory Peck or Grace Kelly, they did their best and that's all anyone could ask.

At just after quarter past ten, George Lane plodded into the hall. He took off his hat and mumbled his apologies to Dorothy, who responded with an icy stare.

'It's a good job you don't have many lines to learn – three at the most,' Dorothy said. 'Lord Harrington will go through the scene with you. But, please, do make sure you're here for the next rehearsal.'

George, normally a bulldog of a man, did as all others in Dorothy's presence and vowed that he would, most definitely, do his best to get there on time. James laughed.

'So, Detective Chief Inspector Lane, are our streets safe from robbers and murderers tonight?'

George mumbled that they were and then pulled him to one side. 'I won't be pursuing the Grimes death, though.'

James frowned. 'Why on earth not?'

'The medical reports agree with Philip. It was a heart attack. No evidence of foul play.'

'What about the knock on the head?'

'It's recent, but not conclusive and not something that would kill a man. Could've happened during a fall.'

'But what about the golem and Stephen being coshed?'

'I had a word with the boss,' replied George. 'We've got a couple of major crimes that have taken place. They're outside our jurisdiction, but the Met needs some officers, so we're ditching what isn't important.'

James laughed in disbelief. 'Not important. Stephen could have died. There's already been one death.'

'Look, where Grimes is concerned, we've taken fingerprints, blood samples and logged the details.

I've a constable tying up all the loose ends. But, if it's a heart attack, it's going to be difficult to prove anything more sinister happened. Stephen's case is an assault, probably poachers, and we'll continue to look into that officially. I've got the local bobby on the beat looking into that. But, you've gotta be honest, James, there's not much evidence.'

'And the golem?' said James.

'Practical joke – youngsters having a laugh,' replied George. 'It's not a secret that this play's about a mud man. I mean, word gets around. There were poachers in the area, because one of my officers picked 'em up. They swear blind they weren't anywhere near the farm, but unless I get a good witness, I can't charge 'em. Unofficially, I'll make a few more enquiries about Grimes, but I can't spend a lot of time on it, boss's orders.'

George made a beeline for the WI refreshment table. James grudgingly bowed to George's decision and remained diplomatic with his own opinion. He began to question himself. Was he seeing things that just weren't there? Had he been listening to too many episodes of Paul Temple? He intended, nonetheless, to keep on investigating until Bonfire Night. That gave him until Tuesday at the latest. If no leads cropped up, he'd ditch his enquiries altogether.

'That leaves me with two days,' he mused. 'Two days to find some sort of evidence.'

CHAPTER THIRTEEN

The following morning, James made himself comfortable in his study. He swivelled gently, back and forth in his Captain's chair, while contemplating the menu for Harrington's country hotel that Didier, his French chef, had provided.

He studied the suggestions: his love of good food and wine made this a pleasure rather than a chore. And, each time, he found himself praising his talented chef for his innovativeness and flair. Didier's short and portly frame appeared to grow several inches whenever he received such acclaim. He always went on to do his best to source only the finest ingredients.

Launching the business back in the 1930s had, initially, been a struggle. Hitler's influence had been spreading through Europe and James had wondered if opening a fine hotel at that time would prove a disaster. Thankfully, the spectacular opening night had captured well-to-do guests. Calling in a few favours from friends, James was able to obtain the services of the up and coming Joe Loss Orchestra which generated publicity he had never thought possible.

When war broke out, the thought of closing down was not an option. He and Beth decided to help with the war effort, offering the house up to be used as a military hospital for wounded servicemen. James, during this time, served as an engineer in the RAF and observed, first-hand, the horrendous injuries inflicted on the men fighting at the front. It felt right to give something back to the brave young men who were risking life and limb for their country.

With the war a distant memory, the house was, once again, a thriving getaway for the wealthy. Recommendations spread by reviews and word of mouth and they now welcomed guests from across the globe.

To ensure continued custom, he and Beth had introduced a number of country pursuits for their guests including shooting, walking and fishing. James regularly spent time on the banks of the River Ouse, honing his fishing skills, occasionally surprising Beth with a couple of fresh trout for dinner.

His stomach rumbled as he examined Didier's latest menu. Appetisers included home-made duck pâté, fresh prawns wrapped in smoked salmon with a dill sauce and, lastly, pea soup. The entrées consisted of Sussex beef or home-cured pork served with honey-glazed parsnips, crisp roast potatoes, cabbage, sautéed carrots and red wine gravy.

If this failed to quell hunger pangs, guests could complete their meal with a choice of apple pie sprinkled with brown sugar and cinnamon smothered with a good helping of creamy vanilla custard, or lemon tart served with a dollop of double cream. He pulled the phone toward him and dialled the kitchen direct. Chef answered immediately.

'As usual, Didier, you have selected the perfect

menu. But are you depriving our guests of a fish course?'

'*Oui, oui, attendez,*' Didier replied. 'My apologies, Lord 'arrington, but I was unsure whether the fish would be available. I 'ave been offered local trout. I can serve this with a lobster and crab mashed potato.'

'That sounds delicious. Listen, I think Beth and I may have to sample some of this. Can you book us in on Wednesday, say seven o'clock? Reserve a table of four, but it may just be the two of us.'

'*Oui, oui,* it is my pleasure, always.'

With the menu agreed, James spent the next couple of hours ensconced in the study, poring over accounts, bookings and plans for the '58 season. For inspiration, he'd collected a number of brochures showing similar country houses in various locations around the world.

Always wanting to keep one step ahead of the competition, he examined them closely. One particular hotel advertised a grand patio overlooking the Bay of Naples. On it stood wicker chairs and sofas with bright yellow cushions and huge navy parasols.

They didn't have the Bay of Naples as a backdrop; however, they did have the South Downs and distant sea views. These last couple of days he'd wondered about asking Ian Connell to draw up some plans for an extended summer patio. It could run the length of the house and would be perfect for dining alfresco.

He gazed out of the window. Dining outside on a summer's evening – what a splendid thought. He made a mental note to call in and speak with Ian.

157

There was a knock on the door and he turned to see Charlie Hawkins, the librarian, standing there. He had a briefcase in one hand and gestured 'hello' with the other. His hair flopped over his eyes and his wide, honest-as-the-day-is-long smile prompted James to leap up.

'Charlie, how lovely to see you. Come in, come in.'

'Beth said I could come straight through,' he said. 'Is that all right, or are you busy?'

'Nothing that can't wait. What brings you here?'

'Tommy and Susan, actually. They're at your far field over there with the rest of the school, doing the last of the bonfire. Mr Chrichton's given 'em a long lunch as a treat.'

James looked across to the field where he saw numerous schoolchildren chucking heaps of wood onto the growing bonfire. 'Should be a cracking night. Do you want a drink or something?'

As if on cue, Beth pushed the door open and came in with a tray which bore freshly brewed breakfast tea and two toasted crumpets dripping with butter. She placed the tray on the small coffee table by the window.

'Have them while they're hot,' she said. 'Anne and I are doing some sewing in the lounge – for the costumes. Shout if you need anything.'

She closed the door and James invited Charlie to join him in the armchairs by the large bay window.

'Get stuck in, Charlie.'

'Don't mind if I do,' he replied with a twinkle in his eye. 'Blimey, no shortage of butter in these, is there?'

James pushed a cup and saucer toward him. 'Mmm, Beth tends not to do things in halves. If you're to have a crumpet, it is to be the best crumpet ever tasted.'

Charlie licked his lips and took a sip of tea. He reached down, opened up his leather briefcase and brought out two large, hardback books with images of pentagrams, witches and satanic rituals emblazoned on the front.

'I got wind that you were interested in finding out about this devil worship stuff,' he said. 'Would these be useful?'

James took the books from him and flicked through pages of pictures and diagrams. 'Excellent. Do you want my library card?'

'Nah, don't bother,' replied Charlie. 'These are from the reference library, so I shouldn't really be taking them out. But, as it's you, I don't mind. Providing I get 'em back, of course. This is to do with Grimes, isn't it? You're playing detective, is that right?'

James grimaced. 'Oh, Lord, who told you that?'

'Anne. Right excited she was – says you're just like Lord Peter Wimsey.'

James roared with laughter but quickly squashed the notion of being a hard-hitting investigator. 'I'm really just taking an interest. Anne tends to get a little carried away. It's endearing, but a tad exaggerated.'

James reached back and carefully placed the books on his desk, assuring Charlie that he'd take good care of them. He had a lot of time for young Hawkins, a widower from South London, who'd lost his wife to pneumonia just three years previously. He knew it must be hard bringing up Tommy and Susan, his two children, but he seemed to do a grand job and had relatives, friends and most of the village to help out when needed.

'Anyway,' James said, 'I'm not sure that I'm going to look into this much further. You know, initially, I was convinced there was foul play with Grimes, but it seems it was a heart attack. Had it confirmed last night.'

Charlie pushed the last piece of his crumpet into his mouth.

'Well,' he said, swallowing another swig of tea, 'I'll take 'em back if–'

'No, I'll hang on to them for a couple more days,' said James. 'I'm intrigued to see why Grimes was so interested in such a subject. What possesses a man to favour that type of thing?'

'Takes all sorts to make this world,' replied Charlie.

They watched the children loading more timber onto the bonfire. James grinned. They were throwing anything remotely flammable onto it – old rickety chairs, table legs, broken branches and small sticks from the hedgerows. Mr Chrichton tossed them as high as he could. What had been a small pile of twigs was slowly being transformed into a mountain which stood at least ten feet tall already.

'By the way,' James said, turning back to Charlie, 'I wanted to thank you for the other night. Well, not you really, rather Tommy and Susan. They made the vicar's kiddies feel at home.'

'Thanks, they're little blighters most of the time, but their hearts are in the right place.

Although I understand there was some blackmail involved by a certain Lord of the Manor.'

'Nothing underhand, old man, all for the sake of goodwill.' James glanced back at the books on the desk. 'I say, Charlie, did you know Grimes at all? It appears he could have been a rotten egg.'

Charlie was quick to agree. He delved into the pocket of his jacket and brought out a notebook.

'I made a note of this because I thought it'd interest you. He didn't come into the library much but, when he did, he borrowed books on religion, the supernatural and devil worship. Nothing else. I must admit, I didn't get on with him.'

The comment piqued James' interest and he invited Charlie to continue.

'I mean, I know most farmers in this area and, yes, they're all busy and can't always spare the time to chat, but they'd always pass the time of day with me. But Grimes? He was a moody sod. Never engaged with me at all and I'm sure that a lot of my reference books went missing whenever he came in.'

'I have the key to his house. If you want me to take a look, I will. He's got stacks of books in his living room. It should be pretty obvious if it's a library book. To be honest, if his son doesn't want them, you may as well take his books for the library. It's a way of paying back any fines.'

'Is that Keith you're talking about?'

'Yes, d'you know him?'

'I know of him,' replied Charlie. 'Heard he got knocked about a bit.'

'Where did you hear that from?'

'Oh, only the other night. Mr Crichton spoke

161

about it at the Hallowe'en do. I think you'd been talking to him about it. Quite emotional he was. Sounds like he was pretty mad with Grimes – almost had a bust-up with him about how he treated Keith and the other kids.'

James frowned. 'Other kids?'

'He seemed to hate kids. Well, that's the impression I got. He walloped Delaney's son a few months ago.'

'Really?'

'Yeah. And not just a clip round the ear, a proper slap. Donovan put him straight.'

James sank back in his chair. That was the second incident where Donovan was concerned. First Grimes insulted his wife and now he'd hit the son. And Donovan wouldn't have stood for that.

'Mind you,' Charlie added, 'if someone hit one of my kids, I'd 'ave something to say about it. I mean, if they do wrong, you do something about it yourself, don't you? Well, either you or a teacher. Maybe a copper, but no one else.'

James agreed and the two continued talking about children and families in general. Having come to a natural pause, James decided it was time to visit Ian Connell. They wandered through to the hall, where James helped Charlie put his trench coat on. He felt the pockets of his own jacket, brought out Ian's card and waved it at Charlie.

'I'm popping round to Ian Connell's. Best give him a quick call first, make sure he's in. D'you need a lift?'

Charlie bent down and picked something up from the floor.

'You dropped this. Must have come out of your pocket.' He examined the pottery piece and turned it over in his hand. 'Where'd you get this?'

James peered at it. 'Oh, over at Grimes' farm. There were quite a few fragments lying around. I don't know why I kept them.'

'You got any more?'

James fished around in the pockets and handed Charlie several small fragments. 'Looks like it's all from the same thing,' he added. 'Probably a broken jug or something. There seemed to be some broken crockery in the kitchen when I was there.'

Charlie uttered an emphatic 'No'. 'This is old. I don't mean Victorian old, I mean *old*.'

James studied the pieces. 'How do you define "old"?'

'See this glazing?' said Charlie, pointing to one of the shards. 'Here, on the rim? That's something you normally find on jugs and bowls from 'undreds of years ago. I only know because we've got a few books on pottery at the library. You flick through 'em now and again and, funnily enough, some of it sinks in.' He laughed at himself. 'You should go and see Professor Wilkins, over at the Historical Society. He'll probably let you know what this is.'

'Yes, Beth suggested I speak to him about the devil worship stuff. Seems he's the man to talk to.' James took the pieces from him.

'Good luck with that,' Charlie added. 'Get him on a good day. He got the hump with me when I corrected him on some historical fact the other day.'

James assured Charlie that he could handle Wilkins and, once the librarian had gone, he examined the pottery more closely.

CHAPTER FOURTEEN

The village of Loxfield, seven miles north of Cavendish, had grown rapidly due to its proximity to a branch line that fed the main commuter links to London. Unfortunately, the influx of new residents had made a negative impact on the community and the village had rapidly lost its charm.

James saw that the bigger the metropolis, the less community spirit there seemed to be and, having collided accidentally with a couple of people on the main thoroughfare, this philosophy had proved him right. Neither gave nor accepted an apology, but chose to glare accusingly before striding on.

Such attitudes saddened him and he blamed it solely on the village expanding too quickly. The shops and cottages he passed appeared tired and in need of repair. Residents appeared to take no pride in the village; indeed, the encroaching grey clouds further dampened his mood and he took a dislike to the place.

Ian's office stood at the end of the high street. James looked at the sign above the window: *Sutherland Property Agents and Auctioneers*. This same title appeared on a polished brass plate screwed to the wall beside the door. Underneath, in brackets, he read 'Residential Builder and Architect, Ian Connell'.

The bell above the door rang an irritating jangle as he entered and three staff showed little desire to greet him. Finally, one young lady decided to show him a degree of courtesy, although it took her some time to summon the energy to get up.

'Can I help you?'

'Ah yes – I'm looking for Ian Connell.'

Ian's voice shouted, unseen, from the back of the office. 'Lord Harrington, I'll be two seconds. D'you want tea, or something a little stronger?'

James gave the young woman a curt thank you and moved on. Ian's 'office' turned out to be a desk at the back of Sutherland's – quite a small one, at that. He looked in the direction of the whistling kettle and saw Ian through a small arch with a tea caddy in one hand and a bottle of whisky in the other.

'Well, as it's gone midday and it's rather damp out there, I'll go with a tot,' James said, brightening. 'Just a small one, though.'

Ian, dressed in a wool jacket and open neck shirt, reached up for two glasses and opened the bottle.

'Sorry about the office – it needs a splash of paint, I know.'

'Oh, I don't know,' James said unconvincingly. He poked his head through the arch and realised Ian wasn't the only one there. A young blonde woman stood a couple of feet away; seeing James, she broke into a smile as she held out her hand. She spoke with a soft, Scottish lilt.

'Good afternoon, Lord Harrington,' she said. 'I'm Ian's secretary, Diana.'

'Ah, hello Diana.' He looked at Ian. 'I must admit, I was expecting more of an office, not a shop. Is all of this yours?'

Ian shook his head vigorously. 'I wish. No, it belongs to a Miss Sutherland. It's a family firm and I managed to get dibs on this space here.'

'Well, good for you. Business booming?'

Diana acknowledged that it was and made to steer him through to the back office. She was a stunning woman with a glowing complexion, clear blue eyes and long, ash-blonde hair pinned up in a loose bun. He wondered if she'd ever been a model. She certainly had the legs for it; long legs, with slender feet in black stiletto shoes.

'Tell me, Diana, do I detect an Inverness accent?'

She tilted her head. 'Not many people can pinpoint an accent.'

James explained that he found the further north one went in Scotland, the softer the accent. 'What brought you down here?'

She perched on the corner of Ian's desk and crossed her legs. 'My family are landowners in Scotland but I'm an independent girl and wanted to come to the city and be a secretary. I worked in London for two years but the countryside beckoned. So, I managed to get a job here in the agency, but I also help Ian out.' She held up some property details. 'I particularly love property. Valuing and auctioning means I get to see houses and that means looking at things I love.'

'Ah, yes, and women love to see what other

people do with their homes, don't they?' replied James. 'My wife is the same.'

'Exactly, and women tend to get what they want.'

James raised his glass to her, thinking that she could probably get the Crown Jewels if she asked nicely.

Ian sat down at his desk and invited James to do the same. 'Diana and I met about two years ago. I'd finished learning my trade and wanted somewhere to work from. She was already here and negotiated rent on a desk. Been here ever since.' He winked at Diana. 'She does all my paperwork and accounts, a few letters and some filing.' He ran a finger down her back and James realised that Diana was more than just a secretary. He took a deep breath.

'Ian,' James said, 'is this a convenient time?' The young man straightened up and Diana reached for her coat and bag.

'Don't you boys mind me,' she said, raising her hand. 'I have customers to see. Nice meeting you, Lord Harrington.'

James rose from his chair, feeling obliged to kiss her hand. 'And you. Why don't you get Ian to bring you along to our Bonfire Night?'

She gave him a smouldering look, then assured James that she would do her best to come along. She slipped on her jacket and James watched her walk away, mesmerised by her swaying hips.

'I say, Ian, you've got a peach of a girl there.'

Connell said nothing, but the smugness confirmed his comment. But James wondered why someone like her settled for being a secretary. He had the feeling she could do whatever she wanted to do.

Ian reached down and brought up a long roll of papers. Unfolding them across his desk, James saw that these were the plans for Grimes' farm. He examined the documents slowly, impressed by the detail.

'I say! You certainly know your stuff.'

'Yeah, I like to think I do,' said Ian. 'I trained as an architect, then a surveyor. But, to be honest, I decided it wasn't for me. I like to get my hands dirty, so I turned into a jack of all trades. Brickie, plumber, carpenter – the works.' He nodded at the plans. 'This is a sideline, really, if I've not got much work on.'

'Well, you've certainly slotted plenty of experience into your years,' replied James. 'You can't be more than thirty.'

Ian agreed, explaining that he couldn't really settle properly when he left school, and that's why it took a while to find out what he really wanted to do.

'So, where are you from originally?'

'Plymouth. Dad was in the Royal Marines – got killed during the war. Mum died last year.'

'Oh, I am sorry.'

Ian shrugged and waved away his condolences. 'It's in the past and, to be honest, I never got on with 'em.'

'Oh?'

Ian winced. 'They wanted me to follow him, you know, into the Marines. The Connells have a lot of military history – all the sons are expected to join up. But I told 'em I wouldn't, that it weren't for me. Couldn't stand the discipline at home, so I certainly didn't want it in the forces. Decided to do my exams and leave home. Went back for the funerals, you know, to show my face, but not been back since. Moved here when I met Diana and decided to stick with her. Property's a cash-earner and she's something pretty special, don't you think? Can't go wrong, can I?'

James understood perfectly. A nice set-up, good business, beautiful girlfriend, just what every man wants. But he did feel that Ian's tone reflected a touch of egotism. Diana's appeal seemed to lie in how ornamental she was; he hoped Ian went for personality as well as looks. But, he had to admit, Ian knew his stuff where drawing up plans were concerned. He put his glass down.

'Listen, Ian, the reason I'm here is personal. I'm impressed with these drawings and I understand you did some work over at the museum. I took a look at it as I came past and you appear to have done a good job. Anyway, I'm toying with the idea of putting in an extensive patio over at Harrington's. Would you be free to take a look and provide a quote?'

Ian's eyes lit up. 'Yeah, I'd love to. Sounds right up my street. I'd pencilled in work on the Grimes place but as that's fallen through, I'm more or less free for the next few days.'

'Yes, shame about that. Looks like you took your time over those plans too.'

Ian looked at his drawings with a little irritation. He explained that it had cost him time and money that he knew he couldn't get back. 'Still, when the house goes to auction, I'll put a bid in,' he said.

'There's a lot of potential in a house like that – do it up into something nice and sell it on.'

James stared at him. 'Is the house going to auction?'

'Well, I'm guessing that's what's gonna happen. Sutherland's have the authority to auction that property. Not quite sure why – must be something they agreed with Grimes. I mean, he hasn't got any family, has he?'

'Well, yes, he has,' replied James. 'He's got a son, Keith.'

Ian's eyebrows knitted together. 'What?'

'We're trying to track him down for the funeral, but he's disappeared off the face of the earth.'

'Oh. Right. Grimes never mentioned a son to me. I thought he was a one-man band.'

James said it had apparently been a strained relationship. 'Not unlike your own family.'

'Mmm, surprising how many fathers and sons there are like that. It's not all happy families everywhere you go, is it?'

James stood up. 'Listen, I won't take up any more of your day. Let's arrange a time for you to come over and discuss everything.' He reached into his inside pocket. 'Blast! I haven't brought my diary.'

'Doesn't matter,' replied Ian. 'Call me later when you get home – I'm in all day. And thanks. I appreciate you thinking of me for the work – it means a lot. If I get you on my books as a client, it gives me some credibility. Sorry, hope you don't mind me saying that.'

'Not at all – if you do a good job, I'm happy to recommend you.' He tapped the desk. 'Did you know anything about the land Grimes had bought?'

Ian shook his head. 'I don't personally but he probably did it through here seeing as Sutherland's is up to auction the place. You'd need to ask the girls in the main office.'

James felt in his pocket for his car keys. His fingers stroked a piece of glazed pottery.

'By the way,' he said. 'When you were up at Grimes' place, did he show you any old pottery?'

'Pottery? No, he never showed me anything. It was all I could do to get in the house. Why?'

James assured him it was nothing and waved goodbye. A few minutes later, he located a telephone box and dialled Beth who answered within a few seconds.

'Darling,' he began, 'do we have guests round for dinner tonight or anything planned?'

'Not unless you've arranged something since you left,' replied Beth.

'Well, I'm going to swing by and ask Professor Wilkins if he'll pop up for a drink later.'

'What, that old grump from the historical society?'

James smirked and said that Wilkins was not old and was only an occasional grump.

'I'll prepare an early dinner and make sure we're all straight before he visits,' she said. 'Could he come round about eight o'clock?'

James confirmed that this suited very well and hung up. He walked toward the Jaguar, quietly thrilled at the thought of an alfresco area at the hotel. Ian, he was sure, would do a good job and it would attract a number of guests during the summer months.

He thought about Ian and Diana. They made a handsome couple, but they were a little too showy for James. He checked his watch. It was early afternoon. He ran his tongue over his lip wondering what to do next and stopped in his tracks. The library books: he could track them down. With a spurt of energy, he jumped in his car, fired up the engine and sped off in the direction of Cavendish. Fifteen minutes later, he'd pulled up by Grimes' farm.

Unlocking the front door, he peered into the kitchen and crept inside. He felt foolish for being so clandestine; however, after the incident with Stephen, his imagination had leapt into overdrive.

James went straight through to the lounge where he took the books down and laid them on the table. Opening the larger, hardback books, he let out a 'Tut'. Each one had a library reference sticker inside stating 'This book is the property of Cavendish Reference Library and Must Not Be Removed'. There were ten in total, nine of which related to religion, witchcraft and devil worship. The tenth, however, jolted him out of his musings. He drew up a chair and slid the book toward him.

'Roman Artefacts of Sussex.'

Leafing through the pages, his gaze took in maps, drawings and photos of mosaics, villas, jewels and pottery.

After a few minutes, he bundled the books together and transferred them all to his car.

Before driving off, he studied the pottery pieces again, rolling them in his fingers and holding them up, as if they were going to provide some insight. Instinct told him this was an important find. His obsession with Grimes and devil worship had been side-tracked. In its place, a new train of thought.

CHAPTER FIFTEEN

After a smooth shave and a soak in a steaming bath, James splashed his face with Givenchy cologne. He wandered through to the bedroom that overlooked the back of the house. They'd recently decorated the room and James was pleased with the polished oak floor and the large, square patterned rugs that added contrast to the pastel interior. Beth had chosen the palest of green walls and dark yew wardrobes alongside deep, brass-handled chests of drawers. James had secretly had his doubts at first but, he had to admit, the room had been transformed and remained a warm haven for slumber.

He chose to dress a little more formally than usual, as the Professor always appeared in a suit and tie no matter what the occasion. He slid the hangers along the rail, wondering what would be most suitable. After some deliberation, he settled on charcoal flannel trousers, a white shirt, v-neck maroon sweater and a plain maroon tie.

Smoothing his hair back, he trotted down the stairs and headed straight for the kitchen.

'Hello, darling,' he said. 'You're obviously thinking along the same lines as me.'

173

Beth looked down at her striking dark red skirt suit accessorised with diamond and pearl jewellery.

'I changed three times before I got to this. I didn't change this much when we went to the Lord Mayor's banquet.'

He helped store the cooking utensils.

'Dinner was splendid, as normal.'

Beth examined the well-thumbed recipe book. 'The way to a man's heart,' she said, laughing. 'It's no wonder your granddad didn't stray from the family home with these recipes. Your granny should have been a professional cook.'

'Well, you know, she did her part during the Great War. Managed to concoct all manner of delicious meals when she volunteered to help the wounded.'

Beth linked arms with him as they walked through to the living room and made themselves comfortable on the sofa. She reached across and switched on the wireless.

'You know, I was thinking – if Alec Grimes did die of a heart attack, none of this is as sinister as you think. I mean, is it worth speaking to the Professor?'

James tilted his head. 'To be honest, I'm not entirely sure. It certainly seems like I'm chasing something that's not there, doesn't it? But, I set Bonfire Night as my deadline so I may as well play the game.'

'But you can't deny science. A heart attack's a heart attack.'

He held a hand up in defence. 'I'm not denying science. Anyway, there's nothing wrong with delving in a little deeper, that's why I've invited the old Prof around. And I am genuinely interested in these pottery pieces. Well, more intrigued, I suppose.'

'Well, I hope he's not here all evening. The man's a delectable dish, but he's abrupt, almost rudeness personified.'

James agreed. 'Perhaps he needs a good woman,' he said, taking her hand in his.

'A good talking to, I'd say,' she replied. 'I hope Harry and Oliver never turn into grouches.'

'That's hardly likely,' said James. 'Certainly not while you've got life inside you.'

They went on to discuss the day's events and ended up on the subject of Ian and his secretary.

'I must say, she's a stunning girl,' added James. 'The sort of person you'd see playing glamorous roles in Hollywood. You know the sort, more like Rita Hayworth. Ian rents the office space from Sutherland's. I think Diana must know them – she managed to get him a good rate, anyway. And, she's more than a secretary, too. Ian more or less said as much. She is a beautiful woman – high cheekbones, slender legs, beautiful smile...'

Beth playfully poked him in the ribs. 'Hey, don't you plan on eloping with her.'

He laughed. 'Not my type, darling and to be honest, I couldn't quite make her out.' He took a sip of sherry. 'Anyway, enough of her. I looked at the plans Ian did for the Grimes place. Damned good – very detailed and he knows his stuff, so I've asked him to pop round to discuss the patio at Harrington's.'

'Oh, that's marvellous. I think it'll look perfect

on a summer's day.'

'Me too. He's going to call in and go through it with us. Anyway, enough of me – I forgot to ask, how did you and Anne get on with the costumes?'

Beth spoke of her day with great enthusiasm. After he and Charlie had left, she and Anne had been joined by several villagers. They'd ensconced themselves in the lounge for two hours and continued sewing the whole time. Between them, they'd finished the outfits belonging to the leading parts and had made a start on a few of those for actors in the minor roles.

'Anne, I've discovered, is a mean seamstress,' added Beth. 'She taught us all a thing or two about stitching and hemming. Oh, and Stephen popped in. When the ladies left, he, Anne and I went to Elsie's for afternoon tea. I think you've hooked him on her tea and scones.'

'Well, I can think of worse places to go. We'll have to take them up to the manor one evening for dinner.'

'We also called by Mrs Keates' house to remind her about tomorrow night and Stephen's arranged to collect her.'

'Splendid. Now, while we're talking about tomorrow, do we have everything in place?'

'Well, the children have the bonfire all set up. Just need someone to put the guy at the top and it'll be ready to go. Bert has hijacked a stack of fireworks. I've no idea where they've come from, but it'll be a spectacular display, I'm sure of it.'

James cleared his throat. 'Yes, well, we won't ask any questions about those.'

'Elsie has lent us a huge cast iron pot to heat up

the cream of tomato soup,' continued Beth, 'and Graham is cooking the sausages in advance, so we just need to heat them up for the rolls. We have brown sauce and tomato ketchup, plus salt and pepper.'

'Wonderful. At the last count, we have about a hundred villagers coming. Will we have enough for everyone?'

'More than enough. A bowl of soup and a sausage roll for each, plus Mrs Keates' cakes. From what you've said and what I've seen today, she's likely to bring more than we need.'

James topped up their glasses. 'Are you making yourself scarce tonight?'

Beth's eyes took on a mischievous look. 'Absolutely not. I may not be keen on the old Professor, but I am interested in what he's got to say. And, I want to question him.'

James frowned.

'Well, honestly James, the man has lived here on and off for twenty-five years and we know nothing about him. Anyway, you never know, I may actually find I enjoy his company.'

Professor Wilkins arrived promptly at eight o'clock. A bulky well-built man of around forty-five, he'd studied at Oxford and taught at a number of universities including, for one year, a leading institution in the United States. His obsession with history, architecture, studying and teaching had shaped him into a serious and somewhat abrupt individual who had, in some regards, become old before his time.

His looks beguiled most women until they met

him properly. He was a handsome chap with matinée idol looks, soft greying hair and deep-set brown eyes. When he actually put his mind to smiling, he could melt the hardest heart. But, he did not suffer fools or small talk gladly, so most villagers rarely witnessed the lighter side of Professor Wilkins, if at all.

James cringed as Beth appeared to go overboard in getting the Professor to open up. Her welcome, he commented to her later, had been edging toward embarrassment and he'd been close to banishing her to the study.

'Professor Wilkins,' she said with over-zealous enthusiasm. 'I think this must be a first for you – you know, visiting like this. Let me take your coat and hat and, oh, your gloves too. Can we get you a drink? Tea, coffee? Or would you rather have something stronger?'

Wilkins thrust his coat at her and forced an abrupt smile. 'Thank you. I'll have a whisky and soda.'

Before Beth completely overdid things, James steered the Professor through to the lounge and prepared whiskies and soda on the rocks for all of them. He handed Wilkins his drink and placed the other two on the table.

'Take a seat, old man. I hope it's not been too inconvenient, coming here at short notice.'

'Not inconvenient, no,' replied the Professor. 'Although I'm not here for social chit-chat, I hope.'

'That's a shame,' Beth said. 'I mean, you have led such an interesting and varied life. And the knowledge you have, well, I'd have thought you'd

178

jump at the chance of sharing it with people.'

Wilkins frowned. 'Not really. I'm not a people person. Discovered that when I taught. Students were more interested in going down the pub than studying.'

'Well, I guess we're all young once,' replied Beth. 'Were you born in Cavendish?'

Wilkins cleared his throat and shifted uneasily. 'No. I'm a Kent man. Moved to Oxford when I was eighteen.'

'Oh, did you know the new vicar and his wife are from Kidlington? That's nearby, isn't it? And then you went on to teach there, too? How wonderful.'

'I wouldn't call it wonderful,' replied Wilkins gruffly. 'It was encouraging to have access to the reference books there, though. Shame our library doesn't come up to the same standard.'

James rolled his eyes as Beth continued with her gentle probing. 'And I guess you gleaned lots of information from other universities, too?' she said. 'I see, in your teaching, you were at an Ivy League university. Which one did you go to?'

'Dartford.'

'I'm sorry, where?'

'Dart... Look, I haven't got all evening, I'm afraid,' he said with exasperation. 'I have lectures to prepare for the historical society in Lewes.'

James held a hand up in apology. 'Absolutely, old man, don't want to keep you.'

Aware that Beth would probably launch into another batch of questions, he decided to distract her. 'Darling, any chance of some cheese and crackers to go with this whisky?'

179

Beth narrowed her gaze. She stood behind Wilkins smiling sweetly with a sarcastic glint in her eye. 'Of course. I'll be right back.'

James took his turn at engaging Wilkins. 'Professor, I have some questions about certain aspects of history that I thought you could help me with. In particular, witchcraft, pentagrams – that sort of thing. I'd like to know a little, also, about Hallowe'en, Roman artefacts, especially pottery. Can you assist?'

For the first time since arriving, Professor Wilkins appeared delighted to be there. He took a sip of whisky and confirmed that he did know a little about all of those things. What he didn't know could certainly be researched easily.

'Probably not necessary,' said James. 'I just want a sort of overview of things, really.'

'Well, as we're at that time of year, I'll start with Hallowe'en.'

Beth returned with a wooden board stacked with cream crackers, cheddar and a jar of Mrs Jepson's pickles. She handed plates out and invited everyone to help themselves. A rare smile crossed Wilkins' face, transforming it.

'Thank you, Lady Harrington.'

'Oh, call me Beth, please,' she said dreamily.

Professor Wilkins, oblivious to her swooning, sliced through the cheddar, helped himself to some pickle and crackers.

'Right, Hallowe'en. Believe it or not, it was the Celtic people who introduced this to us. The traditional name for it is Samhain. It basically marked the end of the summer and the beginning of the winter. The Celtic new year, you see, started on the first day of November.'

'So why do we view this as a supernatural festival?' James asked.

'Because, in a way, it always has been. The Celts believed that, when the evenings drew in, evil spirits came along with them. So, to frighten off that evil, they built bonfires. The actual ritual of building a bonfire for Hallowe'en died out in England, but was introduced again after the Gunpowder Plot in 1605.'

Beth swallowed her mouthful of cheese. 'So, if the bonfires faded, why did Hallowe'en continue?'

'That's a very good question,' replied Wilkins. 'Ironically, given their take on it now, it was down to the Christian church. They brought along Halows' Eve and All Saints Day to remember those who had died for what they believed in. Over the years Hallows' Eve became Hallowe'en and now it's evolved and perceived as something that is mainly evil. It's gradually grown into something more commercial but the tradition behind it continues.' His expression changed to one of superiority. 'If you can call it tradition.' He prepared a cracker. 'There used to be the ancient custom of distributing soul cakes, too. Do you know about that?'

'Ah yes,' James said, 'we know all about soul cakes. In fact, Beth made some to give out during our little shindig here the other night.'

Wilkins looked at her with a mixture of surprise and new-found admiration. 'Really? I'd no idea anyone carried that on anymore.'

'Well, we sure did,' said Beth, 'and so did Mrs Keates at Charnley. It's a shame you didn't come

181

and join us.'

Wilkins emphasised that it wasn't his sort of thing but he expressed his pleasure at the tradition continuing.

'What else did you want to discuss?' he asked. 'Pentagrams, did you say?'

James nodded.

'Can I ask why you're interested in all of this?'

'Wilkins, I don't know if you're aware of this but we found a number of pentagrams on the floor of Grimes' farmhouse. I'm just interested, really, especially as the Cavendish Players' production this year is all to do with golems and suchlike.'

'Hardly a Christmas theme, is it? You should be doing a Mummers' Play or something. Who on earth knows about golems around here?'

'Our cleaner's husband, would you believe. Mr Jepson. He wrote the play.'

Wilkins blew his cheeks out in surprise then leant over and picked up one of the library books James had brought back from the farm. He flicked through it slowly.

'There's all sorts of pentagrams and this business with the golem is a separate thing altogether. But again, we're harking back to ancient beliefs and traditions.'

James' ears pricked up. 'Really?'

'The pentagram is to witchcraft what the cross is to the church, or the six-pointed star to Judaism.'

James looked at Beth and stopped Wilkins. 'Are you saying that these are not used for devil worship?'

Wilkins frowned. 'Absolutely not. That's more of

a myth. Unfortunately, this type of symbol is associated more with Satanic ritual than its true meaning. Like the swastika. That has the most awful image now, but not originally in the eastern religions. No, see here.' Wilkins pointed at a picture of a pentagram in the book. 'Those you've seen at the Grimes place, are they like this – with the circle around it?'

'Yes, more or less.'

'Well, these are inverted pentagrams – they're more to do with warding off evil. They generally represent the spirits or gods that control the elements. And this circle that goes around the pentagram, well, that's a sign of protection. It shows the cycles of life and nature.'

'So, if Grimes was a religious man, although he never went to church–'

'He was probably a *very* religious man,' said Wilkins. 'Doesn't matter if he didn't go to church. He probably worshipped at home and drew pentagrams to prevent evil coming in.'

'Good Lord,' James said.

Beth topped up the Professor's glass. 'This is interesting. Have you taught this?'

Wilkins' face softened. 'No, I don't teach it,' he replied. 'But Sussex has such a wealth of this sort of history, especially around these small villages. It's interesting to see what's on the doorstep. One of the places that's renowned for Satanic activity is Clapham, near Littlehampton. I believe some people were arrested a few years ago for some sort of evil cult practice.'

James broke eye contact. He'd got Grimes all wrong. He was no devil-worshipper. If anything,

183

he was the other way; a religious fanatic who frowned on all things evil, even drink. He drained his glass, suddenly recalling the fact that he'd seen no alcohol at the house and the man had admonished Donovan about serving it in the pub.

'Well, Professor Wilkins, you're certainly shedding plenty of light on things. My last little quandary is this.' He felt in his pocket and brought out four shards of glazed pottery. 'Are these from a broken jug from Woolworths, or would you say they're something else?'

Wilkins swallowed hard as he took the pieces from him. He rolled them in the palm of his hand, got a small magnifying glass from his own pocket and began studying the fragments. From the expression on his face, James could see that this was not something from the local ironmongery store.

'What are your thoughts, Professor?' he said at last.

Wilkins placed the pieces on the table. 'Roman, no doubt about it. Where did you get them?'

James opted to ignore the question. 'Did the Romans come this far?'

Wilkins' expression was one of contempt. James held his hand up.

'I'm sorry Professor, but Roman history isn't my thing. I know, of course, that they've found things further south and west of here but I don't recall anything in this area.'

'Sussex is awash with relics from the Roman period. All across the county, we have Roman roads, towns, villas, farms, burial sites. The two nearest roads to us would be at Burgess Hill and

Slinfold – good examples, too.'

'Anything closer to home?'

'Yes, Bignor down on the south coast and a few items found near Lewes.'

Beth's face lit up. 'Of course, I'd forgotten about that. I remember wanting to see the site at Bignor some years ago. Would I be able to view it?'

'It's open to the public – you can view it any time,' replied Wilkins. 'It's worth seeing as they've been excavating for several decades now.'

'So,' said James, anxious to stay on the subject, 'these pieces of pottery. How do you know they're Roman?'

Professor Wilkins baulked. 'It's my job to know. It's what I studied for. It's everything, Lord Harrington – the glaze, the form, the clay that it's made from. It all contributes to knowing that it's Roman.'

'And looking at these shards, Wilkins, what is it that convinces you?'

Wilkins picked up the pieces and turned them over in his hands. He then went on to explain that the Romans were living in Sussex between the first and fifth centuries and that most of the pieces found to date were used for serving food and drink, which were stored in flagons or jugs which had narrow mouths.

'This,' he continued, 'I would say is Samian Ware. It's a term used to describe red-slip bowls and dishes imported from Gaul. This looks like part of a cup, used for drinking.'

James lit a cigarette. 'If I told you that this was found here in Cavendish, would that surprise you?'

Wilkins stared at James. 'Well, that's rubbish. Nothing has ever been found here.'

James shrugged his shoulders. The professor scrutinised him. 'Are you serious?'

'Found them myself.'

James wondered if he was imagining things, but Wilkins appeared a little put out by the statement. Even annoyed.

'Wilkins, what is this likely to be a part of?'

'A community – a villa, a farm, certainly living quarters of some sort. Can I ask where you found it?'

'I'd rather not say at the moment, old man, but rest assured, you'll be the first to know once I have the details. Could I ask you to do something for me?'

'What's that?'

'Can you trawl through your books, maps and whatever else you have? Just see if there's any record of a Roman settlement here, even if it's a rumour. I'd like to know about it.'

'I can tell you now, there isn't,' Wilkins snapped. 'I'd know if there was something on my own doorstep.'

'Well, give it a try will you?'

Wilkins seemed flustered, but assured him he would certainly check if it meant being part of a new find. However, he reiterated its improbability with some force.

With nothing more to discuss, he gathered his belongings and, in the hall, Beth helped him on with his overcoat and kissed him on the cheek. He flushed.

'Thank you for your hospitality,' he said, com-

186

posing himself.

'Professor, I know it's not your thing,' said Beth, 'but you are welcome to come to the bonfire celebrations tomorrow. After all, it is a part of our history, isn't it?'

'Yes, yes, I suppose,' he replied. 'I'm not keen on big functions. Can't stand chit-chat.'

'We'll make you welcome if you do decide to come,' continued Beth. 'Mr Hawkins the librarian will be coming.'

James bit back a grin as Wilkins reverted to type. 'The man's an idiot.'

'On the contrary,' James said, determined to stick up for Charlie. 'He may come across like that but he likes to read the books he stacks – you'd be surprised at the knowledge he has.'

Wilkins said he would see about coming, but they were not to hold their breath. They closed the front door and, when sure he was out of earshot, Beth burst out laughing.

'He certainly blows hot and cold. He's lovely, arrogant, wilful, childish, prudish, angry, lovable and rude all in one go. It's no wonder he's a bachelor! I wouldn't know any sane woman who would take him on.'

They returned to the lounge where Beth tidied up the plates and glasses.

'Did you get the information you wanted?'

'Mmm. Interesting, wasn't it?' said James. 'Grimes was clearly not into any satanic activities. He sounded more like a religious zealot. But, more fascinating for me was the Roman pottery. Do you think he found it on the farm?'

'But what has that got to do with anything?

Grimes died of a heart attack, James. There is no foul play and that's what you were looking for.'

James wanted to stamp in frustration. 'Yes, that's the trouble. For all my suspicions, I don't have an ounce of evidence about anything.'

'You have creditable suspicions,' replied Beth, 'and that counts for something. Shall I throw another ball into your juggling act?'

James looked at her with interest.

'What did you make of the Professor?' she asked. 'He seemed reluctant to admit that there could be a Roman settlement here.'

'Yes, he was quick to dismiss it, but he seemed sure. But perhaps he knows more than he's letting on.'

'I'll tell you something else, too,' added Beth. 'That man never taught at an Ivy League university.'

'How on earth do you fathom that?'

'He said he taught at Dartford. There's no such place – it's Dartmouth. When I asked him again, he changed the subject. Could be a slip of the tongue, but...'

'Can't imagine a Professor getting something like that wrong. He was pretty keen to move on, I grant you.'

Beth went to the kitchen and James raked the embers of the fire. Professor Wilkins had certainly been edgy and he'd been quick to move on from Beth's question about America. He'd also been quick to dismiss the idea of Roman remains in Cavendish.

Why would it be improbable if there were remains all over the county? Perhaps Wilkins wasn't what he claimed to be. Perhaps he already knew about a Roman settlement and was annoyed to find it had been discovered. But did this have anything to do with Grimes' death?

James' self-imposed deadline of Bonfire Night was looming. He hoped something would come up that proved, once and for all, his suspicions were worth pursuing.

CHAPTER SIXTEEN

'Couldn't be a more perfect evening for a bon-fire,' James said as Beth opened the door to the lounge and ushered in four excitable youngsters.

'James, the children want to know all about Guy Fawkes. Someone let slip that he was going to blow a building up and they want to know more.' She gave him a hopeful look. 'Do you have time?'

James couldn't resist the expectant gaze of the children and said he'd be delighted to tell them the story.

Luke and Mark Merryweather, together with Tommy and Susan Hawkins, ran to sit on the sumptuous sofa. They behaved impeccably as Beth handed them their glasses of lemonade, with strict instructions not to spill them.

Anne and Charlie had arrived early with their children to help with the preparations. Bert had also pitched up and had headed straight down to the bonfire to co-ordinate the firework display. Stephen had gone to collect Mr and Mrs Keates

189

from Charnley.

Beth planted a kiss on his cheek and wished him luck. He pulled his armchair closer to the children.

'Well now, I'm sure Mr Chrichton must have told you about Guy Fawkes.'

Tommy's arm shot up. 'He did but it got a bit boring because we had to learn dates.'

'I know he was going to blow up a King,' added Susan. 'I'm not very good at history things, I prefer needlework.'

'Well,' said James, 'did you know that Bonfire Night exists because of a potential murderer?'

They sat up wide-eyed. Now he had their attention.

'It all began hundreds of years ago when Elizabeth the First was the Queen of England and she was being quite horrid to those people who worshipped in the Catholic church. In those days, I'm afraid they weren't as understanding of religion as we are now. She was quite beastly to them and, when she died, a chap by the name of James the First became King. Unfortunately, he turned out to be just as horrible as the Queen and it all got a little unpleasant.'

Luke's arm shot up. 'How old was James the First?'

'Oh, not that old – in his forties, I think.'

'That's old,' Susan said.

James realised she must think he was ancient. He cleared his throat. 'Anyway, there was a group of thirteen men who decided they weren't going to put up with all this persecution. One of them was Guy Fawkes.'

Tommy put his hand up. 'What's persecution?'

'That's a very good question. I suppose it's a bit like being bullied. Lots of people having a go at someone because they don't fit in.'

'That's not very nice,' Susan announced.

'Were they part of a gang?' Tommy asked.

'Well, yes, in a way, they were,' replied James. 'The gang leader was called Robert, and do you know what they decided to do?'

Luke nodded eagerly. 'They decided to blow up the Houses of Parliament.'

'That's right.'

The children gasped as Mark asked why.

'That's another very good question. The answer is that they wanted to kill King James along with a lot of his friends who would have been with him at Parliament. You see, his friends had also been bullies, and awful bullies too.'

Seeing that the children were well and truly hooked, he leant in and whispered. 'This gang stored lots of barrels of gunpowder in the cellars under the Houses of Parliament but then something happened that changed everything. Some of the gang felt a bit rotten because a number of innocent people would die – people that weren't mixed up with the bullying. So, one of the men sent an anonymous letter to the King, who put plans in place to stop the attack.'

'Then what happened?' Mark asked.

'Well, on the Fifth of November, Guy Fawkes was in the cellar underneath Parliament getting ready to set the gunpowder off, when soldiers burst in and nabbed him. They rounded up the whole gang. To celebrate his safety, King James decided to make the Fifth of November a day for rejoicing. People across the land lit bonfires to commemorate that day and, as you can see, we've been commemorating it ever since.'

James settled back in his chair and rubbed his hands. 'So, my young scholars, while you're all toddling about singing 'Remember, remember, the Fifth of November', who is it you're singing about? Who's the chap sitting on the top of the bonfire?'

'Guy Fawkes!' the children shouted.

James decided it was time for him to lend a hand and chivvied the children out to the kitchen where Beth and Anne told them to put their boots and coats on and play on the patio.

Knowing how chilly the evening would get, James had opted to wear thick corduroy trousers and a brown cable-knit sweater. In the hall, he shrugged on his wax jacket, picked up his gloves and hat and popped back to the kitchen.

A constant chatter greeted him. Beth and Anne had been joined by Helen and her little daughter, Natasha. The doctor's wife came out of the larder, balancing bridge rolls on a serving dish. Natasha clung tightly to her apron.

'Ah Helen! Is Philip here?'

'He's helping Bert sort the fireworks out.'

'Splendid. Right, I'll leave you ladies to it.'

He slipped his gloves on and, armed with a large torch, strolled into the night. The outline of the bonfire became clearer as he sauntered toward it. The children had certainly made a splendid job of it. Over the last week, the small bundle of fire-wood had grown to an impressive height. Earlier, he and Beth had discovered that the children's 'guy' had been placed at the top.

He studied the effigy perched some height above him. The children always did a remarkable job of dressing him. This one looked particularly smart. Guy Fawkes' head wore a lime green cardboard mask topped by a beaten-up bowler hat.

About twenty yards away from the bonfire, Bert and Philip had sorted out the various fireworks and prepared launch sites for each. Old milk bottles stood to attention in rows of twenty, each one with a rocket sticking out of it. A number of wooden posts had been erected with numerous Catherine wheels hammered into them.

The Chinese lanterns from the Hallowe'en party, together with a string of Christmas fairy lights, added plenty of colour to the stark, bare fields around them. In the night sky, the constellations glittered and the more he gazed, the more stars seemed to flicker into vision.

Bert shouted across to him. 'Mind where you're standing.'

James shone his torch along the ground and saw three shallow trenches. At intervals, Bert had dug in a selection of fireworks and James aimed his beam to see what was in store for them: Roman Candles, Snow Storm Fountains, Star Bombs, Rainbow Pathfinders, helicopters and bangers were just a few of the exotic names.

'Bert, where on earth did you get all of this? I'm sure our funds won't have covered this many fireworks.'

Bert tapped the side of his nose. 'Ask no questions, tell no lies.'

Philip wandered across to join them. 'This is going to be a fantastic display. Bert, you've really done Cavendish proud. Natasha won't sleep tonight after seeing all of this.'

'Yeah, well, don't like to let the kids down,' replied Bert. 'Deserve it, too, with the bonfire they've built – blimey, it gets taller every year. And that guy's been well stuffed, too. Should take a while to burn.'

He bent down and, with a small crowbar, levered the lid off another box of Standard Fireworks. James gawped as he looked on layer upon layer of assorted rockets and bangers.

His friend stood up, took off his cap and wiped his brow with his sleeve. 'We've 'ad about forty boxes in total. Once it's up and running, we should 'ave around ten to fifteen minutes of display time. I'll need some 'elp with getting everything lit.'

Philip confirmed there would be plenty of helpers. 'I'm sure we can rope in as many as we need.'

'I say,' James said, 'do you have something there to add some sense of climax to the whole thing?'

Bert kicked the box by his feet. 'All I could lay my 'ands on were these things in the box called Astrals. They're bigger than the rest of the stuff, so we'll set 'em off together. Should 'ave about ten of each so, although they're not massive, it'll look good if they all go off at once.'

James announced that it all sounded perfect and returned to the kitchen where Stephen had arrived with Mr and Mrs Keates.

Anne and Helen helped them off with their

194

coats as Beth slid the lid off one of the round cake tins. Inside were iced fairy cakes.

'Oh, Mrs Keates,' she said. 'These look divine.'

Each cake was individually wrapped, coated in shades of pink, blue or yellow icing and topped with multi-coloured hundreds and thousands. Mrs Keates flushed at the praise.

'Oh, it's nothing, your Ladyship,' she replied. 'I'm pleased to be able to do something. And thank you for inviting us. I must say, I've always wanted to come and see your house.'

'And here you are, very much a part of the gang,' James said, taking off his gloves.

Mrs Keates nudged her husband and gestured for him to take his cap off. 'This is my husband, Stan.'

'Hello Stan,' James said, with an outstretched hand.

Stan grabbed his cap in one hand and mumbled a quick hello, clearly unsure about whether to bow or not.

James took his hand. 'Listen, please don't stand on ceremony. I'm James and this is Beth. We're more than happy with that, if you feel the same way.'

Mrs Keates baulked. 'Oh, I'm not sure that I'd be comfortable with that. Not at the moment. Do you mind?'

'Not in the least, but I'd rather like to be on first name terms with you if that's all right. Do you have a first name, Mrs Keates?'

'Yes, it's Primrose.'

'How charming. Well, Primrose, should you suddenly be overcome with the need to be less formal, don't ask permission, just get stuck in.'

She assured him that she would try. Stan glared at her and James saw the discomfort in his face. Obviously old school, thinking he mustn't mix with the upper classes.

Luckily, another fugitive from the alleged lower classes, Donovan Delaney, found his way into the large kitchen, his arms wrapped around a barrel of King and Barnes ale. 'Ah, yer man, James – I've got another one in the van,' he said heaving the wooden cask onto the pine table and disappearing back outside.

Anne gave James a helpless look. 'That really needs to be outside. We haven't room for barrels of beer *and* food.'

'I'll get him to sort that out.' He opened a cupboard, brought out two pewter mugs and turned to Stan. Determined to make the man feel more at ease, he offered him a beer.

Stan's face relaxed a little as he accepted the invitation. Mrs Keates, a natural domestic, began helping Anne by transferring cakes, pies and rolls onto plates and cake stands. Bert and Philip joined them in the kitchen and gratefully wrapped their chilled hands around steaming mugs of hot chocolate.

'Where d'you want these?' Graham boomed, standing in the doorway with a deep baking tray filled to the brim with browned home-made sausages.

'Oh, Graham,' Beth said, 'they look fantastic.'

'Those pigs were running around the farm a couple of days ago, so these are the freshest sausages you'll get. They're still warm, but you'll

196

need to heat them up again.' He handed her a flat parcel wrapped in paper. 'There's a couple of pork chops here for you and James. A little thank you from me for tonight.'

'You're a sweetheart!' Beth put the chops in the fridge. 'I've got the oven on, so let's put those sausages in now.'

She turned to Graham's wife, Sarah, who had appeared from behind her husband with their two children, Thomas and Georgina.

'Sarah, would you mind helping Mrs Keates with the trestle table – I need to get the food out there before the whole village descends on us. The rest of the children are playing on the patio, I think. Could you make sure the side gate is still unlocked?'

As Thomas and Georgina raced to join their friends on the patio, the women busied themselves scurrying back and forth with food, plates and cutlery, while the men sorted out where to serve the drinks and positioned the barrels of ale accordingly.

'Good to have a local brew,' Stan said, sipping his beer and looking a little more comfortable with his peers. The men agreed and Donovan told him that the ale they were drinking was conditioned in old wooden casks.

The children ran down from the patio and helped themselves to glasses of lemonade and squash. Pretty soon, families and individual villagers arrived in dribs and drabs. An orderly queue formed for drinks and nibbles. At seven o'clock, Beth, Stephen and Anne wheeled out the huge cast iron pot of cream of tomato soup, kept warm by a camping stove carefully positioned under-neath.

Before long, a crowd of villagers had congregated in the grounds. Excited youngsters raced up and down, yelling to their parents and whoever else cared to listen.

'Look at the bonfire!'

'Look at the guy!'

'Look at the food!'

'Cor, Mum, look! Sausage rolls and soup.'

Many wore grotesque Guy Fawkes masks and had smuggled in Jumping Jacks in their coat pockets. When they lit them, they threw them to the ground and squealed with delight as the Jacks darted and jerked noisily across the grass and in between people's ankles.

The villagers chatted and laughed while others stood and allowed the hot, creamy soup to warm them through. Beth distributed sparklers to everyone who had a free hand and Anne followed behind lighting them. The villagers waved them furiously, sending out twinkling shards of glitter as they drew shapes in the night.

Pete Mitchell turned up and, to James' relief, made no reports of mysterious goings-on at the Grimes farm. He also appeared a lot more relaxed than he had done during their previous meeting.

Stephen, minus his dog collar, ran and leapt like a free spirit among the crowd of children who giggled at his eccentric behaviour. James chuckled and found himself warming to the vicar even more.

Rose and Lilac Crumb arrived with their normal

dogged determination. James watched them in disbelief. Helping themselves to sherry and cake, they blatantly eavesdropped on every conversation and criticised the arrangements in their own inimitable way. One of those sentenced to an early ticking-off was Bert who had, unfortunately, cursed his burnt sausage for being too hot.

'Disgusting! Swearing is so disgusting! There's children about,' they said, more or less simultaneously as they moved on to their next target.

James joined his friend. 'That's you told.'

Bert clicked his tongue. 'I tell yer, if they were blokes, they'd 'ave had a bunch of fives by now. Ought to stick *them* on top of that bloody bonfire.'

Mr Chrichton waved a quick 'Hello' to James and offered Beth a box of toffee apples which, he hoped, would be a welcome addition to the refreshments. Following close behind, to James' surprise, was Professor Wilkins.

'Strewth!' said Bert. 'How'd you get him 'ere?'

'It won't astound you to learn that I really have no idea,' replied James. 'I think perhaps Beth must have dripped some charm over him yesterday.'

'Blimey. I'll lay you odds-on, he won't stop long. I've never seen 'im turn up for anything.'

James excused himself and went over to Charlie Hawkins to let him know that he'd retrieved his library books.

'Oh, that's great, thanks very much. I'll pick them up in the next couple of days, if that's okay. Just out of interest, how many did he have?'

'I think there were ten in total.'

'Honestly, I know he's dead and everything, but

199

that's theft, isn't it?'

'Yes, I s'pose it is,' James replied, wondering, as he walked away, just how 'Christian' Alec Grimes had been if he went about stealing things.

George arrived in a light grey trench coat and immediately ordered a pint of King and Barnes. Dorothy Forbes and her husband gratefully accepted a small sherry each and snuggled up to each other.

'We'll soon get you warmed up,' James assured them. 'The soup is being served and the sausage rolls are just there. I'd best get off and light this bonfire otherwise we'll never get started.'

He sought Bert out and spotted him talking to Graham. Catching his attention, he tilted his head toward the bonfire. 'Can you give me a hand?'

Bert waved an acknowledgement and put his beer down. A voice stopped him.

'Hello, Lord Harrington.'

James recognised Diana's Scottish tones. He swung round. She was wrapped in a white fur coat and holding hands with Ian Connell. They certainly made a striking couple.

'Ah, how lovely to see you,' he said. 'Listen, take yourselves over there and Beth will show you where everything is. It's very much help yourself, I'm afraid. I'm just off to light the bonfire.'

'D'you need any help?' Ian asked.

'Thanks, but I've got it covered. Go and make yourselves known. And Ian, do introduce Diana to Beth.'

Five minutes later, armed with torches, newspaper, petrol and matches, Bert and James strode into the darkness. James commented that the wood was dry and that the fire wouldn't take long to get going. Ducking under the roped barrier, they stuffed pieces of rolled-up newspaper around the base and splashed petrol up and down the slats of wood and bric-a-brac.

Satisfied with their efforts, James stood back and shone his torch around the bottom, looking for the best places to strike his match. Bert suggested they light it every few feet to get it going quickly. He took a box of matches from James.

'I'll start round the back there, you start here and we'll go clockwise.'

'Right-ho,' James replied as Tommy Hawkins ran up and tugged his sleeve.

'Ah Tommy, we're just about to light her up. D'you want to go and get everyone over?'

'What 'appened to our guy?'

James looked up. 'Nothing. It's up there.'

'That's not our guy,' said Tommy indignantly. 'Ours had my dad's tweed jacket on. Dad was really angry about it, that's how I remember. And anyway, our guy's been thrown over there, by the edge of the wood.'

James heard a match strike. 'Bert, stop!'

'Why, what's up?'

'For heaven's sake don't light it.'

James studied the guy lolling on top of the bonfire. Sometimes the kids messed about in the village and stole one another's effigies, but he had a bad feeling about this. He turned to Tommy.

'Tommy, I want you to do something very important for me. Go and make sure the children have plenty of sparklers before we start? Tell my wife not to let anyone come down until we say.

I'll get your guy on top before we start, all right?'

Armed with these instructions, Tommy raced off. Bert trudged over to him.

'What's the matter?'

'Bert, can you spot George in that crowd?'

'Yeah, 'e's over there, talking to Donovan and 'is missus.'

'Go and get him, will you, and keep everyone occupied up there. Get George down here and Philip Jackson. We need to get that guy down.'

'What for?'

James studied the form on top of the bonfire. 'Just do as I say, Bert, please.'

Bert gazed at the effigy and swallowed hard. 'That's not a guy, is it?'

James rubbed the back of his neck and felt Bert squeeze his arm. 'I'll keep everyone away,' he said.

A minute later he saw George walking briskly toward him. Beth, thank heavens, had picked up on the oddity of the diversion and Tommy's instructions. She announced that the bonfire would start in a few minutes and encouraged people to tuck into the refreshments in the meantime.

'Good girl, Beth,' he muttered.

He retrieved the wooden ladder that lay a few yards away and leant it against the back of the bonfire, out of sight of the villagers.

George and Philip, holding lanterns, stomped toward him. Bert brought up the rear.

'What's going on?' George said.

'I may be over-dramatic, but that is not the guy the children made. Our guy is lying over there.' James indicated to where the children's guy had been discarded by the trees. 'And that chap up there is awfully big and his hands look incredibly lifelike.'

His friend stared up to the figure, then at James. 'Is it safe to go up?'

'I'll go,' said Bert. 'He looks pretty stocky and I'm used to carting stuff about.'

He steadied the ladder and made his way up.

Stephen Merryweather joined James. 'W-what's happening?'

'I'm not entirely sure. May be a practical joke. I say, could you go and retrieve the guy that's over by the edge of the trees there?'

Stephen jumped to it and made his way across to the woods. Meanwhile, Bert had reached the top of the ladder. He leant over and pulled the mask from the guy's face.

'Bloody hell!'

George grabbed the ladder. 'What is it?'

'A body, a man ... a bloke,' cried Bert. 'I don't know who it is, never seen 'im before. He's got a great lump on his head, though.'

'Bring him down quickly,' George ordered.

Philip and James held the base of the ladder as Bert clumsily hoisted the body over his shoulder and steadily made his way back down the ladder. At the bottom, he laid the man out on his back. George looked at James.

'Seen him before?'

James shook his head. The unshaven, scruffy young man in front of him was a complete stranger. George squatted down and searched the man's pockets, finally bringing out a wallet. He flicked through some money and scraps of paper and found a driving licence.

'It's Keith Grimes.'

'Good Lord,' James said leaning in. 'Are you sure?'

'That's what it says here.'

Philip Jackson knelt down and felt for a pulse. 'He's still alive!'

CHAPTER SEVENTEEN

Philip announced that he needed to phone for an ambulance and tried to go but George pulled him back.

'Hold on, I need to think this through.'

'With all due respect, George, this man needs to get to a hospital and fast,' said Philip. 'His pulse is weak. The quicker we get an ambulance, the better.'

James took his Barbour coat off and laid it across Keith. 'He's right, George. We can't–'

'Listen,' George ordered. 'I want you to do exactly as I tell you. Stephen – hurry up with that guy.'

Stephen trotted back with the guy and stared at the man on the ground. 'Oh! Who–'

George grabbed the guy and pushed it at Bert. 'Take off Keith's jacket and put that, and this mask, on the guy and stick it at the top of the bonfire.'

'K-Keith!'

James rested his hand on Stephen's arm. 'We'll update you in a moment. George seems to have a plan.'

Bert quickly removed Keith's jacket and dressed the guy as George had instructed. George grabbed hold of Philip.

'Right, you ring for an ambulance and, using my name, instruct them not to sound the bell. Just draw up quietly. I don't want any attention from James' guests. No one knows about this except us. And don't go through the kitchen. If anyone does ask, just tell 'em the vicar's not well.'

'Use the study entrance,' James said. 'The door's open and you can keep to the shadows.'

Philip checked the main crowd, then scurried across the darkened field toward the house. Bert, meanwhile, had shimmied up the ladder and deposited the children's guy back on the bonfire.

'Right,' George said, prodding Stephen, 'you are the person who's been taken ill. You're gonna miss the party, I'm afraid. But it may help to catch whoever did this.'

'R-right you are,' Stephen said apprehensively as George ordered him to go in the ambulance when it arrived and stay with Keith Grimes.

'Bert,' George instructed, 'you got 'im down pretty easily. Can you carry Grimes to the house without being seen?'

Bert pulled a face. 'Blimey, he's a big bloke but, yeah, I'll have a go.'

James stopped him. 'The man's not well. Do you think we should be manhandling him across a frozen field?'

'Well, he was manhandled to the top of the bonfire and survived that,' replied George, 'It's a risk I'm prepared to take.'

Bert began his journey into the shadows. James groaned as the unmistakable voices of Rose and Lilac Crumb came closer. How did they always know when something was going on? George's brusque and ill-mannered request that they remove themselves back to the party went down badly.

'Who does he think he is?' Lilac remarked.

'How rude,' said Rose, as they retreated.

James shrugged his jacket back on and brought out his cigarettes.

'George, what the hell's going? Why is Stephen lying low? What's your plan exactly?'

George took a cigarette from him. 'A murder was going take place here tonight and I want the killer to think it's still happening. Stephen is the person who's been taken ill and that's our story for tonight. As far as the killer is concerned, Keith Grimes is still at the top of your bonfire.'

George pulled James toward him. 'Get this bonfire started and stick with me. Keep your eyes peeled and let me know if anyone takes too much pleasure from the sight of a burning guy. Come on.'

James baulked at the suggestion but, on their way back, he was conscious that just about everyone connected with Alec Grimes, the play, Hallowe'en and the assault on Stephen, had descended upon them that evening. Even Professor Wilkins, who never attended any social functions, had graced them with his presence.

To the delight of the villagers, the bonfire was lit and the dry kindling quickly sprang to life. The splashes of petrol encouraged the flames to creep up through the timbers. In no time at all the heat became more intense and the guests took that as their cue to get nearer.

George rubbed his chin. 'I'm going to commandeer your phone for a few minutes – get a constable to sit with Keith, just in case he wakes up.'

They surveyed the scene. The villagers had gathered close; each child waved a sparkler in one hand and gripped a sausage roll overflowing with ketchup in the other. The unmistakable smell of a smoky bonfire drifted across the field. Bert joined them.

'Keep an eye out,' George added. 'The suspect is likely to be standing here as we speak. Good job someone spotted it.'

James didn't even want to think about that. 'Are you going to be taking this Grimes business more seriously now?'

George winced and reluctantly confirmed that he was. 'Keith Grimes was obviously a target. Although I hate to admit it, it stands to reason his dad was, too. I'll go and make these calls. I'll be back shortly.' He strode toward the house.

James made his way across to Beth. Her expression was a mixture of worry and curiosity.

'James, what's happening? George looks so serious and Stephen's disappeared. Anne's been looking for him everywhere. Bert said something about an ambulance and then told me to speak with you – is someone ill?'

'Something pretty awful has happened,' replied James keeping his eye on the crowds.

He went through the events as they'd unfolded;

how the guys had been switched and how George took command of the situation. Beth remained speechless as James summed up. He waited for her response, having emphasised the need to get their story right.

'So Stephen's the fake patient and we're not to say a word about Keith Grimes,' she paraphrased.

'That's right. Keep an eye on everyone, there could be a potential murderer here. Can we rely on Anne to keep a secret?'

'Are you kidding! She'll want to play detective with you and try to uncover the murderer. But I shan't let her. I'll take her inside and let her know what's happening.' Beth held his hand. 'James, please be careful.'

He kissed her on the cheek. 'Don't worry, darling. Our killer isn't going to do anything drastic – not here.'

'He put Keith up there to burn alive in front of everyone! Whoever did this is evil. This isn't a game, James, this is real life. Promise me you won't do anything stupid.'

'Promise.'

Beth went to find Anne and James kept his eye on the bonfire and studied the reactions of their guests. Behind him stood four trestle tables laden with food and refreshments. In front of him, the bonfire. Away to the side, Bert, Ian and Graham discussed the plan of action in the firework area.

He checked his watch – 8.30 p.m. A little later than scheduled, but not excessively so. The flames had really taken hold and they lapped around the soles of the guy's shoes. In the flickering light, he spotted George threading his way through the crowd to join him.

'Ah, George, seen anything?'

'Not even sure what I'm looking for. You know these people better than I do.'

James observed the villagers as they tucked into their food and sipped their soup by the warmth of the fire. Most were families with small children, who stared in ghoulish glee at Guy Fawkes, almost willing the flames to envelop him.

Donovan Delaney appeared more intent on lighting sparklers for everyone than the main event, with Graham and Ian in the far field preparing the fireworks. Anne, Beth and Mrs Keates continued to dish out refreshments by the tables. Diana stood to one side, looking as if she was unsure whether to help or not. Mr Keates chatted with Charlie Hawkins, who kept a watchful eye on Tommy and Susan.

James swung round.

'What is it?' said George.

'Peter Mitchell. I don't see Peter Mitchell. He was here earlier.' James scanned the faces in the crowd. 'I don't see Professor Wilkins, either.'

He jumped as Bert sidled up to him. 'Fireworks are ready to go.'

'Splendid, you get on with that. George and I are undercover. I say, Bert, have you seen Peter Mitchell or Professor Wilkins?'

Bert said that he hadn't. 'Professor's prob'ly gone 'ome. I'm surprised he came in the first place.' He walked away.

George licked his lips. 'Perhaps he just came to see his handiwork.'

James nudged George and dipped his head

toward the woods where Pete Mitchell had just emerged.

'He looks a little furtive. What on earth's he doing in the woods?'

'And more specifically,' said George, 'isn't that where the children's guy was found?'

James felt a shudder go through him. 'Yes, yes it was. I have to say, George, he doesn't look terribly happy.'

At that moment, Bert, Graham and Ian began what was later considered to be the best display of fireworks Cavendish had ever seen.

Long, slender rockets projected skyward, leaving trails of streaming silver glittering into the night. Star bombs exploded violently as they reached the end of their journey; bright glowing stars silently rose from the ground and dissolved in the night air, while a crescendo of blue stars left wriggling tracks snaking hypnotically, before disappearing into the heavens.

The smell of gunpowder hovered above the frosted fields as Roman candles cascaded waterfalls of bubbling flares. Stars and comets scooted into the night, gently fading before limping to an end. Coiled Catherine wheels spun wildly, screaming and screeching as they chased their tails. Bangers exploded, Jumping Jacks leapt and whirling helicopters whizzed perilously with no sense of direction.

The villagers *oohed* and *aahed* and the children shouted excitedly with every bang, whistle, whoosh and crack. The clear night air turned hazy with smoke as Bert took them into the finale.

With a mighty explosion, twelve glowing balls

of fire sped into the sky and burst open, letting loose a canopy of stars that blinked silver, gold and blue across the sky before drifting slowly back to earth. Smoke hung in the air.

When the last speck of light disappeared, the villagers broke into spontaneous applause and cheered the display loudly. Bert, Graham and Ian bowed and patted one another on the back for a job well done.

'Oh, how fantastic!' Beth cried, linking arms with James.

'Wasn't it just. I think I'd better treat Bert to a bottle of something. I don't know where he got those fireworks from but I'm sure I didn't pay for so many.'

George, who had gone to collect a sausage roll, wandered across to them. 'I'll say this for you, you know how to put on a display. That really was something. I 'ope Bert didn't get any of this stuff from the warehouse job last week. There were some fireworks went missing there. I'm going to have to have a chat with him about that.'

James glanced at Beth with a grimace.

A huge cheer distracted them and they turned to see the guy erupt into flames, but James gritted his teeth in frustration. It was difficult to witness individual reactions. The villagers had spread themselves about and interpreting emotions and body language was impossible in the flickering light of the fire.

With the bonfire burning and the fireworks discharged, many of the villagers returned to the trestle tables, where Mrs Keates and Anne had continued serving food and drink.

'See anything unusual?' asked George.

'Not a dickybird, I'm afraid,' James said as he acknowledged the doctor's presence. Philip's daughter, Natasha, had wrapped her arms around his neck, her eyes closed.

'Did she sleep through all that noise?'

He laughed. 'Yes. James, I hope you don't mind, but I used your telephone to ring the hospital, just to see what was happening.'

'Not at all, old chap.'

George swigged the last of his beer. 'I'd better get down there and take a statement.'

'That's going to be difficult,' replied Philip.

George, James and Beth stared at him, fearing the worst.

'He's in a coma.'

'Oh Lord,' James said, sliding his hat back. 'That doesn't sound too good, does it?'

'Oi,' Bert shouted as he trudged toward them. 'Professor Wilkins, he went. Waited for the bonfire to go up and then scarpered.'

James turned to George. 'No. Not him. Why on earth would he want to kill Keith Grimes?'

George pulled his collar tight. 'Well, there's only one way to find out. I'll catch up with you tomorrow.'

Beth stopped him. 'George, please be careful.'

He smiled and patted her hand. 'I'm not as stupid as your husband, Beth. I'll have two burly constables with me.' He patted his stomach. 'I'm not fit enough to tackle a blade of grass, let alone a killer.'

They watched George go.

'Penny for them,' she said quietly.

212

'I don't know, darling. Wilkins just doesn't fit the bill for me.' He put his arm around her and they strolled toward the crowd. 'I think our killer is still here.'

CHAPTER EIGHTEEN

James stood in the small churchyard, beside the grave of Alec Grimes. Alongside him were Beth, George, Bert and Anne. A robin, perched in a holly bush, lifted the gloom with its chirpy song. Colin, the gravedigger, stood a respectful distance away, leaning on his shovel, his cap in his hand and his head bowed. Flurries of sleet tussled in the breeze, unsure whether to transform themselves into snow or misty rain.

He shivered. His toes were freezing and the winter chill had seeped into his bones. He adjusted his tie and smoothed his hair back as Stephen came to the end of a brief but poignant service. He'd clearly tried his best to be as personal as possible; James was impressed with the way the Merryweathers had already integrated. It was as if they'd been in Cavendish for years.

He dug his hands into the pockets of his overcoat and looked down at the coffin with a hint of sorrow and regret. Not one person from the village attended, or believed they had a need to attend. No other relatives had come forward to make themselves known. George had only appeared because of the circumstances surrounding Alec's death and, as with the Sunday service, his presence did not trigger any clues.

Lilac and Rose Crumb, to James' amazement, delivered a delicate hand-made wreath at the beginning of the service, but quickly disappeared before the only hymn. Clearly, they'd thought there'd be some gossip and, on seeing rows of empty pews, decided their efforts would be fruitless, so they left.

Stephen cleared his throat. 'Well, th-that's it, then. Shall we adjourn and have some tea?'

George excused himself due to work commitments, but the others made their way through the wooden gate to the vicarage, a small cottage next door to the church.

Anne's assumption that villagers would not turn out in force proved correct and her catering reflected that. She distributed pale blue plates, each with a paper napkin. Two small three-tier china cake-stands stood on the polished sideboard with a selection of fondant iced cakes, jam tarts and biscuits on them. Stephen poured the tea and told everyone to make themselves comfortable. Beth sat next to James on the sofa.

'I know that funerals are sad affairs,' she said, 'but did anyone else feel this was ... well, depressing?'

Anne smoothed strands of hair behind her ears. 'I thought so, too. I mean, I thought some of the farmers might have come to pay their respects.'

Bert prepared a cigarette. 'People aren't gonna mourn who they don't like, and 'e didn't go out of his way to be friendly, that's for sure.' He frowned. 'It's strange, though. He 'ad no friends, but he got involved in that play. Why would 'e do that? Has 'e been involved in other productions?'

'Not that I can remember,' Beth said. 'I guess that is strange. I wonder who asked him to take part?'

James crossed his legs and sipped his tea. 'I don't know. Dorothy Forbes usually does all the casting, but I can't see that she'd even know Grimes, let alone befriend him for a part.'

'P-perhaps it was this Mr Jepson?' said Stephen. 'I mean, th-they were both into this devil worship business.'

James almost choked on his tea. 'Oh Lord Stephen, that went completely out of my head. Grimes wasn't involved in devil worship. Not the way we were thinking. He was totally opposed to it.'

With the help of Beth, he went through the information that Professor Wilkins had given them on Monday night.

'That's a turn up,' Bert said, shaking his head. 'So, deep down, he was a zealous Bible-basher and believed he'd be sucked down to hell.'

James cleared his throat. 'Steady on, I'm not sure it was quite like that...'

'Oh d-dear, I wish you'd said before the service,' said Stephen. 'I could have made it a little more in keeping with the strength of his b-beliefs. I'll send up a separate prayer for him.'

'Sorry, Stephen, went completely out of my head. But you gave a wonderful service. I expect if Alec was listening he would have enjoyed your little rant about leading a good Christian life.'

'Mmm, I-I should be preaching to myself after

215

deceiving my parishioners last night. And I missed a rather g-good firework display, I understand.'

'Yes, I'm afraid you did, but all in the name of the law and all that. Has anyone dropped by to ask what was wrong with you?'

Stephen explained that he'd received a number of calls from the locals asking after his welfare. He admitted he felt embarrassed at having to lie. 'I told them I'd fainted and it was a precautionary examination, especially after my bash on the head last week.'

Anne asked if George was any nearer to knowing what happened.

James sighed and licked the crumbs from his lips. 'I don't think so, although he hasn't contacted me since last evening. We're catching up with him tonight at Harrington's.'

A glint appeared in Beth's eyes. 'Yes, that'll be interesting. George doesn't divulge a lot of information, but serve him a scrummy dinner and his tongue loosens up a little.'

Anne, totally intrigued and wrapped up in the whole mystery, insisted that Beth pop by the next day and let her know what happened.

'I know this is a dreadful business,' said Anne, 'but I can't help but be a little excited by it all. It's like an Agatha Christie novel, isn't it?'

'H-hardly,' replied Stephen, a little taken aback by his wife's relish. 'When it's on your doorstep, it's not quite so exciting. And, as the vicar's wife, you do need to t-temper your excitement.'

Bert's disgusting laugh broke the silence. He put his arm around Anne's shoulders. 'You're a breath of fresh air, Mrs Merryweather,' he said.

'Better than that crusty old bat that was in 'ere before. What with 'er and that bah-humbug of a vicar, you'd think hell had frozen over every Sunday at 'is service.'

'Bert,' James frowned, 'remember where you are, old chap.'

Stephen was happy to join in with the banter. 'Y-you needn't worry about me, Bert. God has a sense of humour. Probably felt the same way about our predecessors, you never know.'

Anne put her tea down. 'Have you heard from your Mrs Jepson yet?'

James sank back in his chair with a puzzled and concerned expression. 'No.' He looked at Beth. 'That's very odd, isn't it?'

'I can't think where they've gone,' replied Beth. 'But if Mr Jepson is responsible for what happened with Keith Grimes, he must still be here.'

'Nah, nah.' Bert picked up a cupcake and pondered which side it was best to eat it from. 'Mr Jepson's a small bloke and in his sixties. There's no way he could have dragged Keith to the top of that bonfire.'

Anne gave him a helpless look. 'Then who could?'

'P-plenty, my dear,' replied Stephen. 'If you're looking for men with enough muscle to carry K-Keith, there are plenty of villagers who fit that d-description.'

James sipped his tea and agreed that Stephen was right. A lot of the men in Cavendish were fit, sturdy chaps who wouldn't buckle at lifting such a weight. Perhaps George would have some ideas to share with them during dinner that evening.

Paul, the mâitre'd at Harrington's, bade James and Beth a warm welcome and escorted them to their usual table. The elegant restaurant area boasted twenty tables covered with pristine, snow-white Irish linen tablecloths. Each bore pale blue napkins shaped as swans and a petite fresh flower posy to add a splash of colour. Round each table stood four maple carver chairs with cushions. A luxurious deep blue Axminster carpet and Italian wall sconces in cobalt blue gave the room a homely yet modern feel.

When renovating the house, James had insisted that the stuffy oil paintings that once graced the walls be replaced by something a little more modern. The vibrant angles of Kandinsky proved a good choice. The dusty old glass chandelier had been an eyesore and the builders had removed this and fitted a number of wall lights. Near the entrance was a large, round table displaying a cascade of seasonal flowers and ferns.

In the corner, dressed in smart dinner jackets, the Eddie Harper Trio eased into a set of Dean Martin classics. The numerous guests chatted and laughed amongst themselves while others danced on the rectangular wooden floor in the middle of the room.

Their regular table, by a wide Georgian window, normally provided a grand view of the old estate and, in the summer, one could witness spectacular sunsets across the sprawling South Downs. Tonight, though, the view was only of dark shadows as heavy clouds moved across the sky. Then the moon peeked through and bathed the lawn with a soft blue light.

A young waiter, dressed in a crisp white cotton shirt, navy blue tie and an ankle-length black wraparound apron over his trousers pulled Beth's seat back for her.

'Thank you, Adam. How are you this evening?'

Adam handed them their menus. 'Very well, thanks, your Ladyship. You're looking very glamorous, if you don't mind me saying.'

Beth looked down at her cocktail dress – a black, velvet cocktail dress, its simplicity highlighted by her diamante bracelet. She thanked him for noticing. James repressed his amusement. He'd always thought young Adam had a soft spot for Beth. Adam blushed but remained composed.

'I hope you're both well,' he added.

James accepted a menu from him. 'We're splendid, thanks, Adam. Quite a few diners in tonight?'

'Yes, sir. We've been pretty fully booked up over Hallowe'en and Bonfire Night.'

'Excellent. Any recommendations, food-wise?'

'No, your Lordship. But you know our chef doesn't do drab dishes.'

James laughed. 'We could have that as a slogan. Didier doesn't do drab dishes. Has a ring to it, don't you think? Listen, Adam, we have a guest joining us, Detective Chief Inspector George Lane. Should be here any minute. He'll have a pint of Sussex bitter, I'll have a cream sherry – what about you, darling?'

'Sherry will suit me fine,' said Beth.

Adam bowed graciously and left them to peruse the menu. Five minutes later, George strode in and handed his trench coat and trilby to a waitress. Adam delivered the drinks just as he arrived at the table.

George took a couple of large swigs from the beer and closed his eyes in delight. 'That hits the spot.'

'I thought it would do,' said James. 'Hope you've an appetite, as our chef has a rather good menu this week.'

The decision over food always took a little longer as every dish sounded so mouthwateringly wonderful. But, after several minutes and much deliberation, they finally called Adam over.

'Beth and I are having the trout with the lobster and crab mashed potato,' said James, 'and our guest here is going all in with the home-cured pork and all the trimmings.'

Adam jotted the order down. 'Do you want soup or pâté to start with? I can recommend both.'

'No, no we're diving straight in with the main course.'

James returned the menus to him, pushed his chair back and sipped his sherry.

'So, George, what news?'

George heaved a sigh. 'Well, last night I went off to see Professor Wilkins, but he'd either stayed out or he'd gone to bed and was ignoring me. So, after the funeral this morning, I went round again. Still no answer. I want to know why he disappeared so quickly last night.'

'And,' Beth added, 'without the good manners to thank us or say goodbye. The man has no sense of etiquette.'

George gave her a quick smile. 'Mmm, quite.

Well, anyway, there's no answer and, as he doesn't exactly ingratiate himself with the neighbours, I've no idea when he'll be back. Same goes for Peter Mitchell. His lorry isn't about and, again, no idea when he'll be back. I've left a message with both of 'em.'

'Pete's been pretty busy with his orchard,' James said, 'and I know he's been helping to deliver sprouts too. You probably need to get to him early or late in the day. As for Professor Wilkins, Bert wasn't surprised that he'd decided to up sticks and leave early last night. First time he'd pitched up for anything, to be honest.'

'Which makes it even more suspicious, don't you think? Coming out to something like that when you never do normally? And on an evening when someone was about to be burned alive?' He rubbed his chin. 'And Keith Grimes is showing no signs of recovery. Whoever hit him, hit him hard.'

Beth grimaced. 'Do you know what with?'

'Not at the moment, but there looked to be a few splinters in his hair. Probably a plank of wood or something similar.'

'Who's top of your list?' asked James. 'You seemed to be homing in on the old Prof last night. Does he cut the mustard?'

George shrugged. 'To be brutally honest, I don't know. Last night was a knee-jerk reaction. I've got no reason to suspect him, or anyone else. On the other hand, there's lots of reasons I can suspect 'em all, but all circumstantial. I believe I'm looking for a man. There's no way a woman could have heaved Keith's body to the top of that bonfire.

'One thing I did find out, though,' continued George. 'And this was a turn up for the books.' He leant in. 'Kate Delaney, the landlord's wife. Did you know she's got a record?'

James and Beth stared at each other and then at George.

Beth ran her fingers around the rim of her glass. 'It's nothing serious though, is it?' she asked.

George lowered his voice. 'Shoplifting with violence.'

James gawped, hardly knowing what to say. 'Kate? I don't believe it.' He sought Beth's opinion.

'I'm with James,' she said. 'George, are you sure you've checked the right person?'

'Of course. It was a few years ago, mind, just before she married Donovan. I don't even know if Donovan knew her then. I shouldn't be telling you really but I know you'll keep it to yourself.'

James puffed out his cheeks. 'Gosh, this is all getting a little serious.'

'Getting?' George whispered, conscious of the proximity of his fellow diners. 'It got serious last night. Now, I need you to spill the beans tonight. I want to know who's done what, where and to whom, and don't hold back. I take it this meal is on you, by the way, 'cos I can't afford these prices.'

James grinned and waved an acknowledgement that it was. Their meals arrived on white bone china plates edged with gold leaf. The smell of pork and of Didier's special gravy prompted George's stomach to growl in appreciation. And the more subtle aroma of fresh, delicate trout reminded James that he must get out and do some fishing.

The band launched into Frank Sinatra's 'Witch-craft' and they gave one another wry looks. James put his sherry down and sprinkled his fish with salt and pepper.

'Right, George. I shall tell you everything I know; no holding back, no secrets. But let's eat dinner first. I cannot, under any circumstances, allow this trout to go cold and we shouldn't discuss murder during dinner; it's uncommonly distasteful.'

CHAPTER NINETEEN

Over dinner, they spoke of Christmas preparations and potential holidays and days out. James and Beth updated George on Harry and Oliver and their Oxford exploits; how the Merryweathers were settling in and Bert's dubious activities – although James quickly moved away from this subject to something a little less compromising, namely the delicious food on the table.

'You know,' he said to George, 'I interviewed Didier personally after my sister, Fiona, recommended him to me.'

He went on to describe how he'd come across Didier's talents in a small restaurant close to where Fiona was living at the time. 'I poached him, excuse the pun, by giving him a free rein in the kitchen and paying a little over the odds.' He paused as he let the delicate flakes of trout dissolve in his mouth. 'All I have to do in return,' he continued, 'is allow Fiona free food here when she visits – which, I hasten to add, she would have received anyway.'

Didier Le Noir, a rather aloof Frenchman, had trained alongside the best in the top restaurants in France and blazed an unbroken culinary trail at Harrington's. Since their re-opening after the war, he had produced and delivered high-quality meals that guests praised long after their dining experience.

Le Noir personally inspected every dish before it was served. Every day he trawled the markets, farms and fisheries for the freshest ingredients, from succulent south coast cockles to juicy, tender beef from the farm down the road.

'He runs a tight ship, mind you,' James continued. 'Even I've been on the end of a tongue-lashing from Didier should I get in his way. Worth it, though. Look at these people in here. They will all leave with absolute contentment and there won't be a morsel left on their plates.'

George observed the diners. Amidst the laughter and conviviality, all of the guests were enjoying their meals with great enthusiasm.

After dinner, they ordered port, coffee and a plate of cheese and crackers. James felt in his pocket for a slim tin of cigarillos and offered one to George.

'Right, down to business. Do you have a notepad or can you file everything in your memory?'

George lit his cigarillo and pulled out a small notebook and pencil. 'Now listen, don't keep

224

anything back. Tell me all the details you have, no matter how trivial you think they are.'

James did as he was told, taking George back to the day he'd discovered Alec Grimes and why, in particular, he'd harboured suspicions. He reminded George of the condition of the painting, the lack of red paint, the canvas being signed, the unfinished breakfast and the door being left open on such a cold morning.

Beth stirred her coffee. 'And don't forget that Grimes is a farmer. I'm not saying farmers don't have hobbies, but I have to agree with James – it seemed an odd time to be painting.'

'And don't forget his shoes,' added James. 'That's something that did slip my mind the last time we discussed this. They had mud built up around the heels and the buttons on his jacket weren't fastened properly. That suggests to me that someone had bundled him into that jacket and dragged him across to the chair. Now do you think he was murdered?'

'That's a difficult one because both Jackson and our doctor confirm a heart attack. There was no evidence of foul play but with everything that's happened, I believe someone's covering their tracks.' He helped himself to a slice of cheese. 'Going back to the shoes, did you notice drag marks in the ground?'

James admitted that he didn't. 'To be honest, George, I had Mrs J with me. She was in a bit of a state, so I thought I ought to get her away. She was distraught, poor woman.'

'Ye-es,' replied George thoughtfully, drumming the table with his fingers. 'I've put out a search for the Jepsons. You haven't heard from them, have you?'

Beth clasped her hands together. 'I can't believe they'd have anything to do with this. I mean, she's been our cleaner for fifteen years—'

George stopped her. 'How did she react when you found Grimes?'

'She was shocked,' said James. 'I mean, genuinely shocked.'

Beth continued. 'And she was all of a dither when she arrived at our place that morning, wringing her hands with worry.'

George pondered. 'Could that be because of her husband? She knew he was with Grimes that morning. She as much as admitted to people that they'd had an argument. That could be why she was in a state.'

James started to protest but he knew George had a point. He reluctantly agreed that it did appear suspicious. 'Anyway, going back to your question,' he replied, 'no, we haven't heard a word from Mrs J – not a phone call or letter. That's strange in itself.'

'But sweetie, what motive could they have?' said Beth.

He met the question with bewilderment. 'I've no idea. And what did Mr J and Grimes argue about? I assumed it was to do with the play. What else could it be?'

George drew a line in his notebook. 'Well, until we get hold of 'em, we're not going to know. Who else is on your list?'

'Donovan Delaney. Now, he's had a couple of run-ins with Grimes about one thing or another.

No love lost there. Put him in hospital at one stage because he insulted Kate.'

'Who,' George reminded them, 'has a criminal record, which includes violence. The pair of 'em seem to have hidden tempers.'

James agreed and commented that Donovan was built like a heavyweight boxer. 'One punch would knock you out, I'm sure. Did Kate go to prison for this robbery with violence business?'

George explained that it was her first, and only, offence and it wasn't taken any further. 'I had a chat with her about it today,' he continued, 'just discreetly, while Donovan was in the cellar. She said she'd got in with the wrong crowd and helped to rob some bloke's house. Apparently, he kept all his cash there – didn't believe in banks. Anyway, they thought he'd gone out but he was still at home. Got disturbed and Kate knocked him over the head with a frying pan.'

James was too astonished to speak.

Beth expressed her surprise too, but commented that Grimes appeared to have had nothing of any value in his house. James confirmed that when he poked about, the house and its contents were in a sorry state.

George shrugged, suggesting that money was always a strong motive for murder. 'You can be sure that it's money, love or power that lands someone in the dock.'

Beth gave a start of surprise. 'Graham Porter lent Grimes a lot of money.'

'And,' added James, 'he'd threatened to kill him a couple of weeks ago because he never got a payment. And the morning Grimes died, he was on his own.'

'Yes, I know all about that,' replied George. 'Graham admitted to threatening Grimes, but swears blind he didn't go to the farm that morning. No witnesses, though, and he's got more motive than anyone.'

George made a few more notes.

Beth nudged James. 'What about Ian Connell? You said he acted strange when you went to see him.'

George held a finger up. 'That's the architect bloke, isn't it?'

'Yes,' James said, 'although I'm not sure that he knew Grimes terribly well. But he was owed money for some plans he drew up. I saw them – very detailed they were. He was asked to do quite a lot of work around the place.'

James went on to explain where Ian worked and the relationship between him and his secretary. 'One thing that may be important,' he added, 'although I'm not sure why at the moment. He said that Sutherland's was going to leap in and put the farm up for auction. They were getting all the paperwork ready to submit. He was surprised when I mentioned that Keith Grimes existed and that the farm would surely go to him.'

George raised his eyebrows. 'May be worth pursuing. What sort of motive would Connell have?'

'I have absolutely no idea. He's not been in the area long.' James topped their glasses up with port. 'Darling, who else is there?'

Beth looked up, inspired. 'Well, Professor Wilkins! He lied to us.'

George flipped over to a new page of his notebook. 'What d'you mean, lied?'

'Well,' said Beth, leaning in like a village gossip, 'he told us he'd been a lecturer at one of the Ivy League universities in America. When I asked him which one, well, he gave me the name of one that didn't exist. And, I know I've said this already and I'm being terribly biased, but the man has no manners. I know you think he's an unlikely suspect, but someone so rude and dismissive could also be very ruthless. He's a man who, I believe, would stop at nothing to get what he wants.'

'Mmm,' George mumbled, 'he left just after the bonfire was lit, too.' He turned to James. 'Tell me more about what you discussed with Wilkins.'

James said he was impressed with the Professor's knowledge and expertise. He described the finer details of inverted pentagrams, the fragments of pottery and the various locations of Roman settlements around the south of England. He fished the pieces of pottery out of his pocket and placed them on the table. George picked up a fragment.

'So, you think that these pieces of pottery have something to do with it?'

'Well, it was Charlie Hawkins who sparked my interest,' replied James. 'He told me to speak with Wilkins. Well, the old Prof went banging on about Roman villas and farms left, right and centre. It makes you wonder, doesn't it?'

Beth cut herself a sliver of French Brie and placed it on a cracker. 'Do you think Grimes' house is sitting on a Roman villa?'

George looked at James, hoping for an enlightened answer, but James simply shrugged.

'According to Wilkins, there are no settlements here. The nearest one is at Lewes. He seemed disproportionately cross when I suggested there could be something local – but I've asked him to look at some of his reference books.' He caught his breath. 'That's another thing. Grimes had a stack of reference books from the library. Most of them were to do with all this pentagram business, but there was one that related to all things Roman. I think that's our link! It has to be.'

George frowned. 'That could be a motive. I suppose this stuff is worth something if it's found?'

'Search me. I can't see what a lot of broken pottery can be valued at. According to Wilkins, there are a few settlements in Sussex so there might be an abundance of the stuff. That, in itself, dilutes the value.'

'Charlie Hawkins – any thoughts?' asked George.

Beth leapt to librarian's defence, describing him as a wonderful character and devoted father, who had no other ambition than to ensure the welfare of his children. 'He's been a widower for some years now and he's done a wonderful job of bringing up Tommy and Susan.'

James agreed. 'It must be hard for him.'

George apologised and insisted on taking the opposite view. 'He recognised the value of the pottery in your hand. He's read up on Roman history. He's finding life tough as a widower – and miffed with Grimes for nicking his reference books.'

'That doesn't make him a killer. And anyway, he didn't know Grimes had the books. No, no, you're clutching at straws there.'

George put his pen down and described a young, good-looking man, suave and debonair; whose family belonged to the Plymouth Brethren; who'd won a scholarship to the Queen Elizabeth Grammar School; who'd won a further scholarship to Wakefield Cathedral, where he was a choirboy. He'd become a motor mechanic and then an insurance salesman.

'Does this man sound like a solid individual to you?'

James exchanged a quick glance with Beth and they both agreed that he sounded like a gentleman.

George went on to explain that the man was fired for allegedly stealing from the cash box at the insurance company. That he later moved to London and became a bogus solicitor, where he was arrested and sent to prison.

'During his prison sentence,' continued George, 'he thought up what he believed to be the perfect murder.'

James stopped him. 'You're talking about the acid bath murderer, John Haigh.'

George nodded. 'What does that tell you?'

Beth sighed. 'I guess that tells us that anyone from this list is capable of committing murder.'

'I'm afraid so, yes.'

Beth shivered. 'I don't want to think about that. All of the people we've spoken about are wonderful human beings in their own way. We have no reason to suspect them of any wrongdoing.'

They paused for a while to enjoy their coffee and finish the cheese and crackers.

George flicked through his notes. 'What about Chrichton, the teacher? Did you know he studied archaeology? That was one of his subjects at university.'

James told him about Chrichton's run-in with Alec Grimes over the treatment of his son and his genuine concern over Keith's safety. George nodded.

'From what I found out yesterday, Keith Grimes was no angel and Chrichton did give him a good whacking the day he left school.'

James and Beth gave him a questioning look.

'Apparently young Keith damaged the classroom. One of life's angry young men. Chrichton lashed out at him with his cane.'

James shifted uneasily in his seat. 'But surely Chrichton had good reason for that: that's what teachers do. Getting the cane is part of school life.'

'I said lashed out. Keith broke some of Chrichton's personal stuff in some sort of rage. Chrichton had the cane in his hand and simply struck out without thinking. Keith ended up having stitches across his cheek.'

'Well, that doesn't sound like the Chrichton I know. He's such a mild-mannered man.'

Beth reminded him of the question they must all ask themselves. 'How well do we really know these people? Mind you, that was years ago, so perhaps he's changed.'

Adam arrived with a silver tray and cleared the table. The restaurant had slowly emptied and, checking his watch, James realised they'd been sitting there for three hours.

'Adam, if you want to start tidying up around

here, don't mind us. When you've two seconds, bring our coats over, will you?'

The young man gave him an appreciative smile and returned to the kitchen.

George took a deep breath. 'Is that everyone?'

'I believe so,' replied James. 'But about Peter Mitchell – I think you need to dig further with him. He was acting strangely on Bonfire night, looked very furtive when he came out of those woods. He also collared me on Sunday, more than a little concerned that you were going to question him some more.'

George acknowledged all of this and put his notebook away. 'Has Bert found anything? He's normally one for sniffing people out.'

'Not that I know of.'

'George,' Beth said, 'what about the assault on Stephen? That is connected, right?'

'Mmm, I think so.' He gave them a grim look. 'I agree with you. I don't think there's a supernatural element to this, but someone wants us to think there is by building a golem and sticking Keith Grimes on top of a bonfire to burn like a witch. We're dealing with an evil mind, make no mistake about it. I'm with you, I think those pieces of pottery have some sort of bearing on this.'

'I say, what's happening about Keith?' asked James. 'Are we keeping his situation quiet?'

'Yes we are,' said George. 'Everyone who knows about what happened is sworn to secrecy. I want the villagers to know that we've found a body, but that's it. I've issued a press release to say that the body of a man was found in the village of Cavendish. I didn't say where – I didn't think

233

you'd want the publicity. I've not said whether he's alive or dead; left it completely ambiguous. But the report will suggest that he's dead. I'm hoping that our killer will think it's Grimes and assume the same.'

James leant forward. 'Wouldn't it be a good idea to say who it is and that he's survived? You know, draw the killer out. He may come back and try to finish the job.'

'I don't like putting lives at risk, James. We don't have the manpower. A lot of my constables are helping the Met out at the moment. I'll think about it, though.'

'What's your schedule tomorrow?'

George rose from his chair and accepted Adam's help with his trench coat.

'Well, my first stop is to question all of these people we've talked about and try to get hold of those who are proving elusive. There's motive and opportunity here for most of them. If Grimes was sitting on something of historical importance, that means there's money involved. These social events happening on dark winter nights makes it difficult to place individuals. People come and go without being noticed. Villains always slip up, though, and I intend to be there when they do.' He motioned with his hat at James. 'And you are not to play amateur detective. Don't offer yourself up as the next victim.'

James held his hands up in surrender. 'Say no more,' he chirped and bade his friend goodbye.

George kissed Beth on the cheek and ordered her to keep her husband under control. He strode out of the restaurant, grumbling about all the work he had to do. Beth picked up her clutch bag.

'Are you going to take George's advice and leave it to the professionals?'

James gave her a sheepish grin. 'No.'

He quickly shushed her protest. 'It's all to do with that farm. There's something there, Beth, and I want to find out what it is.'

'Well, if you're going, I'm coming too. And Anne,' she added excitedly. 'She wouldn't want to miss this. Safety in numbers.'

'Darling, after what happened to Stephen, the last thing I want is Anne waking up in a hospital bed. No, I was intending to take someone with a bit of muscle.'

Beth's shoulders slumped. 'Bert.'

'Don't look so disappointed. I promise I'll let you and Anne know if something crops up.'

He pushed himself up from his chair and, as he helped Beth slip into her coat, a tingle of excitement ran down his spine.

CHAPTER TWENTY

Late the following morning, James battled with the steering as his car slid onto the muddy grass verge at Grimes' farm. An overnight downpour had saturated the ground and the hard frosts of the last few days had now moved on. Although it was currently dry, ominous grey storm clouds gathered to threaten more showers. Bert rubbed his hands.

'All right, Jimmy boy?'

James' eyes flickered with hesitation. 'At the moment, yes. Did you bring that cosh with you?'

'You expecting trouble?'

James knew he looked sheepish and he was relieved to see Bert expose the implement inside his jacket as he opened the passenger door. A gust of wind almost snatched it from his hand.

'Cor blimey, you've picked a fine day to trudge around 'ere. Couldn't you have organised some sun with 'im upstairs?'

James climbed out of the car. 'I have no divine influence, Bert. Come on, the sooner we do this, the sooner we can toddle off to the pub for a pint.'

The promise of a beer spurred Bert into action. They leant into the wind and marched toward the farmhouse. James opened the front door, pulled his gloves off and slipped them in his pockets.

Bert pulled him back. ''ere, put your gloves back on.'

'Why?'

'This is a crime scene, Jimmy boy. I'm sure George would 'ave something to say about you trampling all over the place. Keep your gloves on and take your shoes off.'

James followed Bert's advice.

'Now, what're we looking for?'

'Right, Bert, we're looking for anything that could possibly be of value. Roman bits and pieces. You know, pottery, mosaic, that sort of thing.'

'Shall I take downstairs and you take up?'

'Splendid – shout if you find anything.'

James unbuttoned his jacket and trotted up the stairs. The threadbare carpet provided no cushion-

236

ing and each step on the creaking floorboards echoed through the house. He peered into the main bedroom. It smelt musty and damp; a thin layer of dust coated the surfaces. Beside a solitary single bed, there was a slim bookshelf, a wardrobe and a chest of three drawers. On the wall hung a crude sculpture of Jesus on the cross; opposite this, an oil painting that prompted him to look again.

'Well, well,' he murmured, recognising a similar painting to the one in front of Grimes on the morning he'd died. This one depicted the copse in all its glory with the rays of the sun catching glossy green leaves on the treetops. He knelt down and peered under the bed. An enamel chamber pot and a tatty pair of tartan slippers greeted him. He snaked his arm under the mattress and beneath the pillows; no hidden treasure there.

The contents of the wardrobe only served to confirm that Alec Grimes hadn't two farthings to rub together. He examined the bad tailoring of Grimes' only suit and felt in the pockets to find some faded receipts and a cigarette butt. Aside from the suit, he counted three collarless shirts and two pairs of work trousers. The shelves to the side, normally reserved for hats and shoes, stood empty.

He clicked the doors shut and shifted his attention to the chest of drawers. Sliding the top drawer out, he leafed through everyday garments – underpants, vests and socks, all in need of repair. James cleared them to one side in the hope that something might be underneath but, again, no joy. Jumpers, cardigans and long johns filled the next drawer, along with a 1953 first day cover stamp-set of Queen Elizabeth's coronation.

He pulled at the third drawer. His eyes lit up – a solitary cardboard box. He squatted down and pushed the lid off. Photographs. Not valuable, but at least something that might give some insight into Grimes' life.

The aged bedsprings groaned as James sat down to flick through the handful of grainy black and white photographs, clearly taken years ago. James uncovered Alec Grimes in happier, more carefree days; a young man with jet-black hair, in an ill-fitting suit, grinning broadly, his arm around a pretty young blonde in a cardigan.

'Mrs Grimes, I presume,' James mumbled and the next photo proved him right: their wedding day. Joy radiated from their faces. What hopes and dreams did they have back then? Very much in love and from the expression on their faces full of life. He cast an eye around the shabby bedroom. How on earth did Grimes end up like this?

The next image he found most poignant. His finger traced the outline of a young boy, standing proudly in his school uniform and cap. He turned the photograph over: in pencil, someone had written 'Keith, aged 5, first day at school'.

James recalled his own emotions on seeing Harry and Oliver leaving home for their first day at school. A mixture of pride, joy and poignancy had washed through him. Pride at seeing his two sons looking so smart and grown-up; joy at their own excitement; and a poignant sense that this stage heralded the start of a new period in all their lives. He wondered if Alec had felt the same way.

He pushed the drawer shut with his foot, replaced the lid and secured the box under his arm.

The second bedroom appeared to act as storage space for Alec's hobby. Several canvases rested against the wall and various oil paints and frayed brushes lay on wooden trays on the floor. James slowly browsed through the paintings, ten in all, each one providing an exquisite image of the copse from a different angle. He frowned. Why did he keep painting the same place?

On the table under the window, a smaller canvas caught his eye. He picked it up and, without knowing why, decided to take this with him.

Stepping over the paints, he pulled open the door of a small wardrobe that stood in the corner. His fingers gently parted hangers of clothes that must have belonged to the late Mrs Grimes. How touching that Alec had kept them; he wondered how long he'd been a widower. He then wondered if Alec had been too affected by her death. The loss of a loved one, he knew, was traumatic but time eased the hurt and clothing was normally given away or discarded. In this case, Alec had clung to the clothes. Bert rapped on the door.

'Any luck?'

James picked up the box. 'Photos of happier times. D'you think Keith will want them?'

Bert scratched his ear. 'Maybe, maybe not. What's all that?'

'Mrs Grimes' clothes. I'm guessing she died a few years ago. These appear to be all pre-war items.'

'No Roman togas anywhere?'

James chuckled and closed the wardrobe.

'There's another picture of the copse in his room. Same view as the one I found him with – just a different season. And look at these – different aspects of the same copse. Do you think that's relevant?'

Bert pulled a face. 'Might be. He might be like that bloke Magritte. He went through a phase of painting people with sheets on their 'eads. Don't mean anything, just meant he liked painting the same thing. P'haps that's all Grimes could do.'

'Like you on that damned ukulele.'

Bert laughed. He had managed to master one song on the ukulele so well that those who heard him thought him a master musician until they asked for an encore, whereupon the listener discovered it was the only song he'd ever learnt. James secured the box of photographs and the small painting.

'Come on, we'll have a quick scout outside.' On the landing, he pulled his friend back.

'What?' Bert asked.

James looked directly above him. 'We forgot the loft.'

'Blimey, how'd we forget that?'

Excited at the possibility of finding something, James bundled the photos and canvas into Bert's hands, dashed into the bedroom for a chair and placed it under the hatch. Slipping out of his coat, he stepped up and manoeuvred the badly-fitting trapdoor to one side.

'Give me a hoist up.'

Bert deposited the photographs and canvas on the landing, linked his fingers together to provide James with a stirrup to heave himself into the darkness.

'Oh Lord, I can't see a blasted thing.'

Bert ordered him to stay put. 'There's a torch in the kitchen.' A minute later he threw the silver tube up.

James shone the torchlight through the beams of what was a tiny loft with very little headroom. He stooped, treading carefully over the rafters, shining the light into every recess. From what he could tell, Grimes didn't hoard anything, not even the obligatory Christmas tree. He pursed his lips together, annoyed at the fact that virtually no clues were emerging about this man.

'Any luck?' Bert shouted.

'Not a dickybird. I'm beginning to get very frustrated with our man Grimes.'

As he made his way back to the hatch, he stepped awkwardly and felt his ankle twist. He reached up to a supporting beam to keep him from tumbling. 'Damn.'

'You all right?'

James leaned against the beam and rubbed his foot. 'Yes thanks, just twisted my ankle. Blast.'

He pushed himself off the wooden frame, wiggled his foot around and gingerly placed it down. The light of the torch caught a glint in the shadows beyond the trapdoor opening and he moved across to see better. It was a silver box, oval in shape, about nine inches wide and seven inches deep. He picked it up.

Bert hollered. 'What's going on? You found something?'

'Yes, I'll bring it down.'

His hands ran over what appeared to be an antique biscuit box. He didn't know much about silver, but he remembered his grandfather owned something similar.

'What an exquisite thing you are,' James murmured as he marvelled at the beaded borders, drop-ring lion-mask handles and tortoiseshell finial. He gently opened the lid and stared in stunned silence.

After a few seconds, Bert shouted again. 'Whatcha doing up there?'

James closed the lid and, ignoring the pain in his foot, clambered back to the hatch and passed the biscuit box down to Bert, with strict instructions to be careful with it. Bert placed it on the floor and helped him locate the chair with his feet as he clambered down from the loft.

James replaced the hatch, jumped onto the landing and brushed himself down. His friend studied the box.

'So, he's not as 'ard up as we thought. Got a stash of money in there 'as he?' Bert's face took on a look of suspicion. 'What is it then?'

'A motive, Bert. A motive for wanting someone dead.'

He opened the lid and ignored Bert's colourful language as they gazed incredulously at its contents. James knew little of antiquities, whether Roman or Celt, Victorian or Georgian. He was more of a modernist in art and fashion, so he only remembered snippets of information during school lessons and the few photos he'd seen in the books that Charlie had shown him.

He did know, however, that the gold rings, sapphire necklaces and brooches of rubies and emeralds that glittered enticingly inside the silver box did not come from the local market. If his memory served him correctly, they bore similar shapes to those images in the library books.

'Well, my friend,' he said. 'Professor Wilkins was wrong about there not being a Roman interest here.'

Bert studied a large bracelet he'd pulled out and gave him a knowing look. 'Either that, or he doesn't want you to know it's 'ere.'

'Ssshh!'

Footsteps had sounded in the hall.

James gently closed the lid of the box and passed it to Bert. He leaned over the wooden banister and let out a sigh of relief. 'Philip, what're you doing here?'

Philip Jackson peered up from the hall. 'Could ask you the same,' he replied. 'Saw your car outside, wondered what you were up to.'

James felt Bert prod him in the back. He turned to see him covering the box with his coat while mouthing a silent 'Ssh'.

James frowned but played along. He picked up the canvas and box of photographs, waving them nonchalantly as he wandered down the stairs.

'Just found these odds and ends of Alec's that Keith may want. Has he come out of his coma yet?'

'No, he hasn't. Must have taken one hell of a bash. Anything I can do?'

James, feeling a little embarrassed at being so secretive, told Philip that they'd finished there and were heading off to the pub for a lunchtime snifter.

'Why don't you join us?'

Philip groaned a reluctant refusal. 'Got to dash, I'm afraid, I'm off to see a patient just along the road here.'

They made their way back through the hall and out of the front door.

James locked up as Philip returned to his car. 'Probably see you tomorrow.'

'Tomorrow?'

'The rehearsal – tomorrow night.'

'Oh yes, I'd forgotten about that. I'll be there. I suppose I'd better learn the script.'

He saluted Philip as he drove off then turned to Bert.

'What was all that about, playing innocent with Jackson? You don't suspect him, surely?'

'Jimmy boy, the less people that know about this, the better. If this gets out, something pretty nasty could 'appen. People turn ugly if there's money to be 'ad. You said yourself, there's a motive 'ere and, judging by your chat with George last night, no one knows anyone deep down. You need to speak with George. This is serious.'

James tossed his car keys high and caught them as they fell. 'You're right of course. Listen, I'd best give the pub a miss. I don't like the idea of leaving this box in the car. Come on, those clouds are almost upon us.'

James placed the box on the back seat and covered it with a tartan blanket. He started the car, checked the road, then jumped when Bert grabbed his arm.

'Oi, look over there.'

He followed Bert's gaze. Emerging from a dirt track that led to the copse, a green Land Rover turned away from them towards Cavendish. Bert stared at him.

'You know who that was, don't you?'

James released the brake and crept forward. 'Yes,' he answered, not quite believing what he'd seen. 'That's Professor Wilkins.'

CHAPTER TWENTY-ONE

Stephen and Anne perched on the sofa, sipping cream sherry and nibbling toast and pâté. Anne, her eyes sparkling mischievously, couldn't contain her excitement.

'Oh come on, James. Let's have a peek before you hand it over.'

James held up a finger as if to admonish her. 'All good things come to those who wait, my child.' He checked his watch. 'Anyway, he'll be here any minute, so this agonising lull in proceedings will soon be over.'

'B-by the way,' said Stephen, 'I popped by to visit Keith Grimes today.'

'And how's he doing? Still in the land of nod?'

Stephen put his drink down. 'N-no change, according to the nurse. Th-they've been chatting to him as if he's with us. Th-that's supposed to help, I'm told. Anne's been reading to him – an Agatha Christie, of all things.'

The door swung open and Beth shepherded George into the lounge. He was looking more gruff than normal but with good reason. His face was flushed and he had dark circles under his eyes.

'Ah, George.' James headed for the cocktail cabinet. 'Look like you could do with a whisky, old chap.'

'No thanks,' replied George. He looked at Beth. 'You haven't got any flu remedies, have you? I think I'm going down with something. I've been in and out of this weather all day and every person I want to talk to is out. Does everyone in this village disappear into a secret cave or something?'

Beth assured him they didn't and promised him a hot aspirin drink with honey and lemon, insisting that a dash of whisky would also help. From the kitchen, she called out, 'You shouldn't have come all this way, George. This could have waited until the morning.'

'I'm glad you did come,' Anne gushed. 'I'm dying to see this.'

George commented that her choice of words was a little inappropriate bearing in mind the attacks that had taken place, but Anne wouldn't let that diminish her excitement. George flopped back in an armchair and rested his gaze on James.

'Right. Let me clear one thing up. I tell you not to go playing amateur detective and what's the first thing you do? Break into a victim's house and search it – without, I might add, any authority. You know that this is a potential crime scene.'

'Steady on, old chap. Anyway, I didn't break in, I still had the key. And I kept my gloves on and pottered about in my socks.'

George held his hand out. James sighed. He retrieved the keys and tossed them over.

'Thank you. Now, you left a message with my sergeant about finding some jewellery. What–'

'Oh, do come on, James,' said Anne. 'Let's have a look.'

'Mrs Merryweather!' said George sternly. 'This is a police investigation, not a fashion show.' He sneezed and quickly rummaged in his pocket for a handkerchief.

Beth returned with George's drink while James retrieved the silver biscuit box from the sideboard. A murmur of anticipation spread around the room.

'I found it in the loft, George. There was nothing else up there. In fact, I was on my way down when I stumbled upon this – almost literally.'

He placed it on the coffee table in front of them and opened the lid.

Anne brought her hands to her mouth and gasped.

'H-heavens,' said Stephen.

'Bloody hell,' George said, pulling the box toward him. 'Has anyone else seen this? Apart from you lot?'

James confirmed that Bert had been with him at the time and that it was thanks to his advice that the information had gone no further.

'Someone with a bit of sense,' George remarked. 'Now, before we go off into the realms of fantasy, this wouldn't be family jewellery, heirlooms and all that?'

'Not unless Grimes can trace his family back to Caesar. These, my friend, are Roman.'

The gems glittered and, one by one, they reached out and picked up individual pieces to study, turning them over in their hands and commenting on their intricate artwork and craftsmanship. James, meanwhile, went to his bookshelf and returned with a large, hardback book and an eyepiece.

'Charlie Hawkins left a couple of books with me,' he explained. 'This one here is his most detailed reference book about Roman artefacts. Luckily, it has a mass of photographs and I had a good look through this before you all came. I can identify a lot of these items from the pictures. Not because they're replicas but they're the closest I can get to explaining what they are.'

He peered inside the box and poked around at the objects and realised that Anne had what he wanted.

'Ah, Anne, let me have that for a second.'

Anne handed him a long, dangly earring. James had marked several pages of the library book with scraps of paper. He opened the book and swung it round so that everyone could see.

'This, ladies and gentleman, is an earring dating back, quite possibly, to the third century.' He held it gently between his thumb and forefinger and rotated the S-shaped hoop.

'Isn't it lovely?' Beth purred.

Dangling from this were flattened rosette shields with perforated ends. A piece of wire held a blue glass bead at the base. He returned the piece to Anne, picked up a gold band and leafed through the book to another marked page.

'This book suggests that this also dates back to the same period,' he said. 'You see that it's not a solid band of gold, but there are five wires here, all woven together.'

'Do you know what the blue glass is?' asked Anne. 'It's beautiful.'

'I'm afraid I don't but...' he flicked through some more pages. 'Ah, here it is. If you look closely at that piece, there's some rather wonderful engraving. Not sure what it is, maybe a horse.' James handed the ring to Stephen who, in turn, passed it around the group. 'There are quite a few in here with garnets fixed in. Quite extraordinary.'

One by one, rings, earrings and bangles were exchanged and, where possible, James tried to find a corresponding image in the book – or, at least, one close to it. The eyepiece went back and forth from person to person, followed by mumbles of appreciation and wonder. Anne pinned an oval pendant to her deep yellow cardigan. Beth leant in to take a closer look.

'This is staggeringly beautiful,' she said. 'The yellow sets it off, but look here. There are two figures there. One has a spear and shield, the other one looks like it's holding something – not sure what.'

Beth took the eyepiece and studied the brooch carefully as James checked the book. 'That may be Minerva and Fortuna,' he said. 'She should be holding a cornucopia.'

'Yes!' said Beth. 'That's exactly right. Oh my goodness, it's stunning.'

James closed the book and leapt up. 'And now, ladies, I've saved the best until last. There's one more little treasure in here, but it really is too lovely to throw in with the rest.'

He dashed across to the sideboard and took out a bundle of tissue paper. Eager eyes followed his every move as he returned to his seat. Slowly, with the utmost delicacy, he unfolded the tissue and let the contents slip onto his palm. There was a collective intake of breath. Beth reached out and carefully laid the most beautiful, intricate necklace across the palm of her hand.

'This,' James said, 'would date back to around the first century. It's pure gold, and I'm sure you ladies don't need to be told that those precious stones are pearls and diamonds.'

George puffed out his cheeks; Stephen shook his head disbelievingly as they discussed the style, age and artwork of the jewels and compared them with those in the book. While Beth, Anne and Stephen were engrossed, James positioned himself by George who was sipping his flu remedy.

'I say, George,' he said quietly. 'Couple of odd things to tell you – apart from the jewellery, that is.'

His friend cradled his mug in his hands.

'Bert seemed to think it was nothing, but all of Grimes' paintings – well, there must have been a dozen in all – showed the same view of the copse. Different aspects, seasons and all that, but … well, anyway, it may be nothing.'

'And the other thing?'

'We were just pulling out from the farm and we saw Wilkins' Land Rover driving out. Nothing much to that, but he came out from the road leading to that same copse.'

'Professor Wilkins?'

'Yes.'

Anne had overheard the conversation and gave them a wary look. 'Do you think he's the killer?'

Beth opened her mouth and announced that the man was rude and contemptible. She caught James' reproachful eye. 'Well, you have to admit,' she said, 'he's a bad-tempered specimen of a man.'

'No, he isn't, darling,' replied James. 'He's simply a man who hates social niceties. There are plenty of them around.'

Stephen agreed. 'A-Alec Grimes sounded like that.'

'And it doesn't make Wilkins a killer,' James added, although he didn't know why he was sticking up for him.

'But,' Anne said, replacing bangles in the box, 'it's interesting that both are victims.' All eyes were on her. 'Well, Alec Grimes wasn't the most social man in the world, and he's been murdered. His son, from what we know, was a loner, and he was nearly murdered. And this man, Wilkins, well ... he's ill-tempered enough to kill someone.'

George held his hands up despairingly. 'Mrs Merryweather, that's the most illogical argument I've ever heard. Everyone is capable of killing, not just loners who don't socialise. It's not your personality that makes you a murderer, it's motive. If someone was to attack your children and threaten to kill them, what would you do?'

Anne winced.

'Exactly. You'd do what any mother would do if their child was threatened. It doesn't mean you're a natural killer. Circumstances make a killer. It could be love, jealousy, hate...'

'Greed,' James added.

'That's right,' he said, 'and that's what we have here. A form of greed. Money equals power to people who kill for it. Who do you know would want this sort of money? This sort of power?'

'M-most people, unfortunately, are sw-swayed by money,' said Stephen.

James stood up and put his hands in his pockets. 'For the love of money is the root of all evil, eh, vicar?'

'W-which, while some coveted after, they have erred from the faith, and pierced themselves through with many sorrows. First T-Timothy, verse six. People always forget that bit.'

George rubbed his chin. 'Well, someone has well and truly built up a pile of sorrows if they think they're getting away with this.'

After checking the time, he heaved himself up from the chair and swayed on his feet.

Beth squeezed his arm. 'Are you all right, George?'

'Head's swimming a bit. I'll be all right.' He massaged his neck. 'James, you have a safe, don't you?'

'Yes, it's in the study.'

George's eyes grew heavy. 'It's just that I'm feeling pretty rough. I can't face a drive back to Lewes and that jewellery needs to be somewhere safe. Lock it up overnight and I'll pick it up tomorrow. Is that all right?'

'Absolutely, old man.'

Beth felt George's forehead. 'We have spare rooms, good food and I have an excellent bedside manner. Stay here with us for the night. I'd be much happier if you did.'

He held his hands up. 'I'll be fine, Beth. If I feel worse tomorrow I may take you up on that. But my notes and files are at home. I need to do some thinking.'

Beth instructed him not to think *too* much. He waved a cursory goodbye to everyone. Beth retrieved several more sachets of Beecham's Powders and handed them to George in the hall. James followed him out.

'Anything you want me to do?'

George rolled his eyes. 'Nothing. I'm grateful for what you've done, but please, leave it to the professionals now. One thing I will do is get that Professor in for questioning – if I can find him, that is.'

After a bout of five sneezes, George excused himself and left.

'I'll get that jewellery back in the box,' James said to Beth. 'Then we'd best lock it securely in the safe.'

She turned to go into the lounge and then paused. 'Oh, by the way, Ian's popping in to chat about the work you want completed on the patio. He's coming tomorrow evening, before the rehearsal. Is that okay?'

'Oh, jolly good. It'll be nice to get that up and running before the summer. Listen, I'm just going to make a quick call. Be through in a moment.'

Beth returned to the lounge as James picked up the receiver and dialled. There were several rings before a young boy answered.

'Ah, hello Tommy, is your father there? Run along and get him, will you, it's Lord Harrington.' James leant on the banister and waited. 'Charlie?'

'James, this is unexpected.'

'Yes, sorry about that. I just wanted to pick your brains, if I may. You're a bookworm, you know, read a lot and all that. Regarding this Roman business – do you know how much something like a Roman pendant would be worth?'

'Yes, I do, as it happens,' replied Charlie. 'There was something in the paper the other day about stuff like this being sold at auction. It wasn't a pendant, I'm afraid – more of a brooch of some sort, sold at Sotheby's. Good condition, you know, fetched around a hundred pounds.'

'Good Lord, for an old brooch?'

He heard Charlie laugh down the phone. 'Nice work if you can get it. Why d'you ask?'

'What? Oh, nothing, just been flicking through your book and the question cropped up.'

'Oh, right. You're not the first person to ask me that.'

James straightened. 'Really? Anyone I know?'

'Can't remember, to be honest. I know it was in the library, but I get asked loads in there. It was quite a while ago, so ... no, I'm afraid not. Is it important then?'

'Not really. Well, actually, it could be. If you can remember, give me a call, will you?'

Charlie assured him he would, quickly explaining that he had to go as the children should be in bed. James replaced the receiver and joined the others in the lounge where they were studying the two paintings of the copse.

Beth picked up on his concern. 'What's wrong?'

James went through his chat with Charlie. The price of the brooch caught everyone by surprise, but the fact that someone else had made the same enquiry prompted an urgent look from Stephen.

'Y-you know, you ought to be careful, James. Th-the walls have ears and all that.'

Anne caught her breath. 'The killer may hear.'

James slipped his hand into Beth's. 'I've promised George that I'll leave it to the professionals and that's what I intend to do. There really is nothing to worry about.'

Stephen picked up the small eyepiece and leant in to study the paintings more closely.

James eventually asked what he was doing. His friend appeared enlightened. He picked up the two canvases and laid them side by side, inviting James to take a look. He held up the eyepiece.

'L-look at the signatures.'

James leant forward to study the first canvas and then the second. At first, he couldn't make out what he was supposed to be looking at. His brain told him that he should be reading the signature of Alec Grimes. His study took him from one canvas to the other before he stood up, surprised.

'Well, well.'

Stephen grinned at him as Beth and Anne insisted on being let in on their discovery.

'Our victim has spoken from the grave.'

'What on earth do you mean?' asked Beth.

'Grimes has signed his name at the bottom, that's clear. But he's added some very finely written Latin underneath. You can hardly see it.'

'What?' Anne asked. 'What has he written?'

'Aurum. And circled around the word is a delicate gold band.'

Beth looked on blankly. 'Latin is not my strongest subject.'

'Aurum, correct me if I'm wrong,' replied James, 'is the Latin word for gold.'

James allowed the news to take its effect on the women, who insisted on seeing this for themselves. He took a sip of whisky and felt it glide into his stomach. What an exciting mystery this was turning out to be.

CHAPTER TWENTY-TWO

On Friday evening, the church clock struck six as James entered the chaos of the village hall. The cast members and backstage crew for *The Devil Incarnate* busied themselves and the scenery on stage was taking shape.

Villagers huddled in groups, rehearsing their lines, their faces creased with concentration; to his amusement, some were exhibiting some rather overzealous acting skills. Others shouted directions, while a handful took the easier and more relaxing option of drinking tea by the WI table.

Graham fixed spotlights into place and his wife studied a table of props and ticked them off the list on her clipboard. Their two children, Thomas and Georgina, sat cross-legged in the corner playing Snap with Luke and Mark.

Rose and Lilac Crumb, for once, appeared to be focussed solely on providing tea and biscuits. But, he reminded himself, they had perfected the art of eavesdropping so probably were, at that very minute, digesting items of conversation before turning them into rumours.

Amateur builders and carpenters drilled and hammered large sections of scenery into place. Women in oversized overalls transformed those blank pieces of wood into trees, houses and fields, using paints left over from their last production.

Kate Delaney proved to be quite an artist with the paintbrush as well as shifting bulky wooden frames across the boards. Although slight and bonny, she certainly had brawn and, now James knew about her background, he could imagine her holding her own if she had to.

An unwelcome thought crossed his mind. Could she kill someone? He quickly dismissed the notion as too horrific to contemplate. No, a woman couldn't do this – that was a ridiculous notion. Wilkins was the man, had to be. He'd lied, he'd dodged the police, he'd acted suspiciously, and his knowledge of the Roman period was not in doubt. He clearly knew something about the copse and had discovered that Grimes owned the land. He'd got greedy and wanted the kudos of being known as the man who discovered a new Roman archaeological site.

Philip's voice brought him out of his thoughts. 'Are you word perfect?'

James closed his eyes and groaned. 'Hardly. To be honest, Philip, I've not looked at this script since last week. What with Hallowe'en and Bonfire Night, not to mention this business with Keith Grimes, it's all been rather a nightmare.'

'Yes, Graham's the same. He's having problems with his bank manager and hasn't been sleeping well. I think he and Sarah had a bit of a bust-up earlier about it. She's furious about him giving Grimes that loan.'

'Mmm, I must admit, I'd be loath to do such a favour for someone I didn't know well.'

'Perhaps he knew him better than we thought?'

Dorothy's no-nonsense request for the Players in the 'Golem' scene to gather spurred Philip into action. 'Come on, James, that's us.'

James stroked his chin as he followed Philip. Could Graham have killed Grimes? He didn't think so, unless it was in a fit of temper, or an accident. But if he had murdered him, how would he get his money back – unless he knew about the jewellery? But if he did kill Grimes, why not take what was owed to him? Perhaps he'd searched the house and couldn't find the jewels.

Dorothy thrust a script into his hand.

'You don't appear to have your script with you, Lord Harrington.' Her face lit up as she retrieved it from him. 'Oh, but of course, you've learnt your lines.'

James snatched it back with an embarrassed smile. 'Sorry, old thing, haven't had a chance. I promise I'll knuckle down this week.'

Dorothy pursed her lips as she pulled Bert toward them and counted the members of the group. 'Oh, for heaven's sake,' she said. 'Where on earth are George Lane and Ian Connell?'

'Ah, Ian's up at my place,' James said and checked his watch. 'He and Beth will be along at around seven.'

Dorothy maintained a polite demeanour but James detected a flash of irritation.

Bert leant close and whispered. 'Oi, don't annoy our eminent director. She's already spitting daggers that we 'aven't learnt our lines, and now she's short of two actors and a wardrobe mistress.'

Before James could answer, Dorothy's frustration erupted.

'Really, is it too much to ask for people to give up an evening a week and be here on time?' She waved her hands dismissively. 'You'll have to rehearse, two short. And, if George isn't here tonight, then his part will go to someone else.' She stormed off, leaving James, Donovan, Graham, Philip and Bert gawping after her.

'Blimey,' Bert said, 'if I'd 'ave known I'd get out of this just by not pitching up for a couple of rehearsals, I wouldn't 'ave bothered.'

They chuckled at one another, each knowing they had all thought the same. Their chuckles dissolved into general chit-chat.

Graham turned to James. 'Is Ian doing some work for you?'

'Yes, I've asked him about getting a nice patio done at Harrington's. I picked up the idea from an Italian hotel brochure. When the evenings are balmy, the guests can dine outside – use it as an extra room, so to speak.'

Graham pulled a face to indicate he was impressed by the venture. 'Nice. Is Beth doing all the arranging, then?'

'No – well, yes and no. It's just that Beth is the more artistic one, so she's thinking about the brickwork, patterns, that sort of thing. I think there's some intricate sort of paving style she'd like. I'm the one dictating the size of the thing and the cost implications.' Graham's reaction to his last statement was not lost on James. 'I heard you went to the bank manager?' he said.

'Tch, more like the bank manager came to me.'

'Listen, if you're short of the readies, I can–'

Graham's enormous hands stopped him mid-sentence. 'No. Thanks all the same, but I should've stuck to my old mum's mantra. Never a borrower or a lender be.'

'There's a lot to be said for it, old man. Where's Stephen and Anne?'

'I think they're backstage. I saw them earlier. Ah, there's the vicar, just come through from the green room.'

Philip cleared his throat and got their attention. He straightened his script out.

'Gentlemen, I think perhaps we'd better make a start, show willing. Otherwise, I'll be treating Mrs Forbes for a heart attack–'

The main door crashed open and two constables barged in, followed by a flu-ridden DCI Lane. The room hushed except for Dorothy Forbes who, despairing of this latest frustration, marched toward George.

'Well, really! Inspector Lane – what do you think you're doing?'

George brushed past her and approached James' group with his warrant card displayed.

'It's Detective Chief Inspector Lane,' he said to Dorothy as he passed her, 'and I'm here on official business.'

He sneezed violently and a few of the older villagers murmured 'Bless you.' James grabbed his arm.

'I say, George, what's going on?'

George ignored him and faced Donovan. The landlord shifted on his feet and found it difficult to look at George.

'Donovan Delaney, I'm arresting you on suspicion of the murder of Alec Grimes and attempted murder of Keith Grimes.'

The villagers reeled with astonishment; a few mumbled their surprise at the mention of Keith Grimes.

'No!' Kate Delaney bellowed ferociously as she jumped down from the stage and lunged toward George. 'Leave him be! He's done nothing.' She pulled her arm back and formed a fist.

A constable grabbed her before she had the chance to land a punch on George. James looked on in astonishment as the burly PC struggled to maintain his grip.

George gave Kate a look of disdain before returning to the matter in hand.

'You are not obliged to say anything unless you wish to do so, but what you say may be put in writing and given in evidence.'

Donovan's jaw dropped as the second constable placed handcuffs on him. 'No – this isn't right,' he began. 'I didn't kill him.' His eyes urgently sought James'. 'James, I didn't kill him. Honest to God, I didn't.'

'Take him away,' George ordered, then jutted his chin at Kate. 'Bring her, too.'

Kate spat her opinion of George and attempted to kick him.

James caught her arm and swung her round. 'Kate! Stop it. You're not helping Donovan with this behaviour. You go along with him and I'll get in touch with our solicitor.'

He put his hand under her chin and forced her to look at him. Her fierce eyes turned fearful and tears welled up.

'The children...' she cried.

Stephen took control. 'W-we'll take them, Mrs Delaney. We've got a spare room. D-don't worry.'

Donovan twisted and wrestled with the constable. He shouted back to James as they marched him out. 'Your man Grimes, he was already dead!'

The door slammed shut and a numbed silence took hold. Men, women and children looked at one another and slowly, the murmur of gossip and opinions spread around the hall.

Bert pulled James toward him. 'Did you know this was gonna 'appen?'

James mumbled that he hadn't known and his glazed eyes stared ahead. What was George thinking? What did Donovan mean *'He was already dead'?* His head swam with the complexity of it all.

Villagers began asking random questions, trying to make sense of it, while others commented on the mention of Keith Grimes, the arrest, the attack on Stephen and whatever else they could think of. Bert snapped James out of his thoughts.

'Jimmy, d'you think we should go down to Lewes – moral support or something?'

'Oh Lord, I don't know.'

Stephen put a hand on his shoulder. 'M-might be best to, for Kate's sake.'

James checked his watch – just gone six-thirty.

'Well, the first thing I'd better do is get our solicitor down there. I'll call Beth, tell her and

262

Ian not to bother coming down.'

He felt his pockets for change, before making his way out to the cloakroom, still in a daze. He dialled home and waited for Beth to pick up. The pips went and he pushed a few coppers in the slot.

'Hello, darling?'

'Oh, am I glad to hear from you!' she gushed. 'Good news, we–'

'Darling, George has arrested Donovan Delaney.'

'What!'

James waited to let her take the news in.

'But, what evidence does he have?'

'I've absolutely no idea. Donovan said something very interesting, though. Something about Grimes already being dead. So he must have been there, mustn't he? But listen, darling, I need you to call our solicitor, Mr Bateson. Ask him to get down to Lewes a.s.a.p. Can you do that?'

'Of course.'

'Oh, and tell Ian not to bother coming down. I don't think anyone's up for any more drama tonight. If you're all right with this, Bert and I are following George down to Lewes.'

'That's fine, I'll let Ian know,' Beth said, hesitantly, clearly distracted by the news.

'Darling, are you all right? Do want me to come home?'

'No, no, you carry on there. Donovan will need support, I'm sure.' Beth said that Ian had proved to be good company and she'd pass the news on and get hold of their solicitor straightaway. James started to say goodbye, but stopped himself.

'I say, what was that about good news?'

Beth forced an upbeat chuckle. 'Oh, it's not going to seem important now, but Mrs Jepson called. She's been calling when she can, but either we've never been in or she couldn't get through. She did leave a message with the local police, but wanted to speak personally.'

'What did she have to say for herself?'

'John Jepson's mother died suddenly. Of a heart attack. She lives in the Forest of Dean, in a cottage in the middle of nowhere, with no telephone. That's why they disappeared so quickly. John told her they didn't have time to call in and that they'd ring but, of course, they couldn't reach us and she forgot all about sending a telegram.'

'Oh Lord, and here's us trying to put them in the frame. Well, that's one mystery sorted.'

The pips beeped.

'Blast,' James felt his pockets. 'I've no more change, darling. I'll catch up when I see you.'

The line went dead and James returned to the subdued villagers in the hall. The news had hit home and it was clearly difficult for them to take it in.

Philip, who was with Dorothy, waved him over.

'James, we were just saying, should we carry on? What d'you think?'

Anne rushed across to join them. 'I've just heard. Is it true?'

Dorothy sighed. 'Yes, it's all very distressing. I'm not sure we should continue. I mean, people's minds aren't on the play tonight, are they?'

Stephen insisted that they weren't, so all eyes settled on James for the decision.

He picked up his jacket. 'Well, I don't know

264

about you, but it wouldn't seem right to continue. And I want to get down to Lewes, see if I can help in any way. How about knocking it on the head tonight? We'll rearrange for Monday, yes?'

'I think that's wise,' said Dorothy. She clapped her hands and announced that the rehearsals would be postponed. 'We will all meet back here on Monday evening at seven o'clock. I know we're all in shock, but the show must go on and hopefully we'll have good news about Mr Delaney by then.'

Stephen rallied the villagers and delegated jobs to help tidy up. Bert encouraged the children to fold up chairs and stack them in the corner. James gritted his teeth. Rose and Lilac Crumb were feeding off the arrest of Delaney like vultures on a carcass. Rose sidled up to James with a cup and saucer.

'Not what we thought he was, is he, that landlord?'

'Yes,' added Lilac, 'always thought he was a bad one.'

James felt his blood pressure rise. 'Ladies, this is not appropriate and I'd appreciate it if you would be courteous enough to keep your opinions to yourself.' Ignoring their indignation, he shouted over their heads to Bert. 'Come on, Bert, let's get down to Lewes.' He couldn't help but give the sisters a piercing glare. 'I need to get out of here.'

Although he had a cup of tea, George slid open his desk drawer and brought out a half-bottle of whisky and two glasses. 'I thought you said Bert was here.'

James explained that Bert wasn't comfortable in the confines of any police station, let alone the Sussex headquarters, so he'd decided to have a pint in the pub on the corner. George smirked and hinted that he wanted to speak to him about the warehouse robbery.

'What, the one with all the fireworks?' asked James.

'That's the one.'

'No, George. Bert wouldn't use stolen items on my property. I know he's a scoundrel but he wouldn't jeopardise our friendship like that.' He brushed some dust from his trousers and silently prayed his friend hadn't been involved. 'Besides, the evidence has gone up in smoke.'

George poured a double in each glass and pushed one toward James. 'Beth called. Your solicitor's in London, not back until tomorrow.' He met James' gaze. 'So, you want to see Delaney?'

'If poss, yes.'

His friend stared at the bottle. After a moment of thought, he swigged his drink down, picked up his tea and invited James to follow him.

They wandered along a narrow corridor with offices on either side. There was a constant hum of subdued chat, the clatter of typewriters and the odd shrilling of a telephone.

At the end of the corridor, George opened the door to a small, windowless room with one solitary light, a desk and four wooden chairs. Behind the desk was Donovan Delaney, who leapt to his feet.

'James! For pity's sake, tell me you're taking me home.'

'Sorry, old chap. Just come to lend a sympathetic ear and all that.'

'Where's Kate?'

George put the tea down in front of him. 'There's a constable looking after her. She's down in the canteen.'

Donovan slumped back on the chair as James and George took their seats opposite him. His red-rimmed eyes had lost their sparkle. He fiddled with the cup, rotating it this way and that, swirling the tea almost in a dream. He looked like a man lost in the wilderness. James leant forward and put his elbows on the table.

'Bateson's in London, won't be here until to-morrow. Why don't you tell us what happened – the day you went to Grimes' farm?'

'I tell you the man was already dead,' replied Donovan.

George invited James to continue. 'Well, what did you see? I mean, why did you go over there? And, more to the point, why not report it?'

Donovan took a slurp of tea. 'You know he had awful opinions about my Kate. He was dead against her. And the kids. I mean, they were nothing to him. He knew nothing about them, but he took to hating Kate the minute we took over at the pub.'

George flipped his notebook open. 'In what way?'

'Well, Kate's a no-nonsense sort of a woman, gives as good as she gets, you know. They had a couple of run-ins about things.'

'What things?' George asked.

Donovan closed his eyes in exasperation. 'I

don't know.'

James couldn't help but think that Donovan was being deliberately awkward. The man knew very well. He leant back, crossed his legs and cradled his glass. 'Well, you need to *think*. It could be important.'

Donovan stared at the ceiling. Then, with a resigned sigh, he looked at James and then at George. 'Religion. Kate and me, we're not that religious. I think religion's a personal thing. You shouldn't talk about it publicly – it's between yourself and your God. That's what I think, anyway. Kate said something, I don't know what, but it riled Grimes no end.' Donovan slammed the table with his fist. 'I don't like airing dirty linen. D'you know what I mean?'

James assured him that he knew exactly what he meant, but surely it was better to tell the truth than refuse information and be charged with murder.

Donovan wrestled with his conscience. 'Kate said, in the pub, we weren't gonna get the kids baptised until they were old enough to make their own minds up about their faith.'

James puffed his cheeks out. 'I can't imagine Grimes being terribly impressed.'

Donovan let out a shaky laugh. 'You're not wrong there. But, you know, that's what started it. Ever since then, he just kept dishing out the sarcasm. Preaching his Christian ways to us. I don't mind that, James, I really don't. The people that come in the pub, they're friends and good Christian people but they're good Christian people *inside*. D'you know what I mean?'

James understood. 'You mean Grimes should have kept his opinions to himself and certainly to have practised what he preached?'

'That's exactly what I mean.'

George's eyes narrowed. 'So what's this got to do with the morning Grimes died?'

Donovan took another deep breath and described how, after closing time the evening prior to his death, Grimes had hammered on their door.

'By the time I'd got dressed and gone downstairs, he'd gone. But—'

'How did you know it was Grimes?' asked George.

'Because he'd slipped a note through the letter-box.'

James frowned. 'A note? What sort of note?'

Donovan looked close to tears and James could see that George was as worried about the landlord as he was.

'It accused Kate of bringing her children up outside the true Christian faith, not worshipping God.' His eyes pleaded with them. 'I mean, what sort of sick person was he? I could see it upset Kate – well, I was going to have it out with him there and then, but I didn't. Kate said to leave it.'

'So you decided to venture out in the clear light of day,' James stated and Donovan confirmed that that was what he'd planned. James' index finger ran around the rim of his glass. 'And what did you do?'

Donovan's shoulders relaxed. 'I didn't do anything. I got out there and there he was, dead as a dodo. He was in the chair at the back of the house.'

There was a lull.

'What I don't get,' George finally said, 'is why you didn't report it?'

Donovan leant on the table. 'Because someone else was there and I was scared. Something didn't seem natural to me.'

'Who?'

Donovan shrugged. 'I don't know. I heard something, someone in the house, I don't know who. I went in the kitchen and shouted out, you know, hello and everything, but it went really quiet. I didn't like it, to tell the truth. There was definitely someone there. It gave me the creeps so I didn't say anything. And when yer man Jackson said it was a heart attack, well, I thought I'd stay quiet.'

'I say,' said James, 'I know you didn't see this chap or anything, but did you hear him say anything?'

'A couple of swear words and drawers opening and closing.'

'Mmm,' George mumbled. 'Like he was searching for something?'

'Yeah, exactly like that.'

James folded his arms. 'That all sounds pretty straightforward, George. What on earth are you doing arresting him?'

George flicked back through the pages of his notebook.

'We received the report of some blood samples taken at Grimes' farm a couple of days ago.' He looked at James. 'That knock on the head that Alec had. He was hit by that hideous figurine of a robin – the one that was on the kitchen worktop.

There are small traces of Grimes' hair and some blood on it. That blood is of the same group as yours, Donovan.'

The statement confused James and, from Donovan's expression, he clearly felt the same. 'I'm sorry, I don't understand.'

'Donovan's fingerprints are also on the robin,' George added.

Donovan wagged a finger. 'No, no, that would be the cut I got when I changed the barrels.' He spread his hands, where a recent gash was beginning to heal. 'It was still bleeding. I do the barrels in the morning. And your robin, it was on the edge of the work surface, so I just pushed it back.' He swallowed hard. 'You've got to believe me, George.' His eyes pleaded with James. 'For God's sake, this is nothing to do with me.'

James pressed his lips together. This was the sort of evidence that could convict a man. He clasped his hands together.

'Listen Donovan, you must tell all of this to Bateson when he gets here. And try to think, *really* think, about what you heard when you got to the farm. Everyone has a tone, an inflection in their voice which could trigger recognition. Do you understand?'

Donovan indicated he did. The circles under his eyes appeared darker, as he became resigned to the fact that he would be spending the night in the cells.

James pushed his chair back. 'Stephen and Anne are looking after the children and we'll rally round Kate. Try not to worry.'

'D'you want another cuppa?' asked George.

Donovan's answer was barely audible as he stared at the table.

'I'll get one down to you. We'll do the statement tomorrow, when your solicitor gets here.'

They took a slow walk back to the front desk where James slipped his coat on. He felt the stirrings of a headache form at the back of his neck. At the desk, George asked the sergeant to bring Kate out.

He took out a handkerchief and sneezed. 'Thoughts?'

James met his gaze. 'I believe him. He was clearly at the farm, George, the evidence shows it. He admits it. But that's not our man. I can't prove it, I can't explain it, it's just instinct.'

George remained stone-faced. 'I know what you mean.'

'Have you found the Professor yet?'

George pursed his lips. 'No, he's proving bloody elusive. But Grimes' late night visit to Donovan has given me an idea.'

James tilted his head.

'I think I'll pay Wilkins a visit late at night and drag him out of bed,' continued George.

Kate, looking drawn, tired and with no fight left in her, joined James, who put an arm around her. She leant into him.

'Let's get you home,' he said. He nodded a farewell to George. Outside, he found Bert waiting for them by the car.

They arrived at the vicarage twenty minutes later, to find that Charlie had stayed with the Merry-weathers to help look after the children. Kate

272

gratefully accepted a strong sedative left by Philip and went straight to sleep in the spare room.

James telephoned Beth to say he'd be home shortly and updated her on what had happened. She told him not to worry as she still had Ian for company and he was proving to be a funny and knowledgeable guest.

Over a welcome cup of tea and toasted tea-cakes, he took everyone through what had hap-pened at the station.

'I can't believe it,' said Charlie. 'I had Jepson down for it. I mean, he's argued with him and done a runner. It's obvious.'

'Oh,' said James, 'you haven't heard, have you? Mrs Jepson rang earlier. John Jepson's mother died suddenly – that's why they left without any notice.'

Surprise and relief swept round the room.

Bert helped himself to a teacake. 'I'm with George. I think Wilkins 'as a case to answer.'

'H-his behaviour does seem a little erratic,' added Stephen.

Charlie said he simply couldn't believe any of it. 'And Donovan Delaney ... it doesn't seem possible. Do you believe him?'

James didn't know what to think and he shifted on his chair as all eyes bored into him for an an-swer. Donovan had a temper. But did that temper manifest itself as murderousness? He didn't think so. But if Grimes had threatened his wife and children, perhaps it would. They'd already had that conversation with George. Everyone, James reminded himself, is capable of murder given the right circumstances.

273

He rested his cup and saucer on his lap. 'I want to believe him, of course, but the evidence with blood and fingerprints, doesn't look good for him. But I'm no expert: it may turn out to be insufficient.'

Charlie pushed himself up from his chair, saying he ought to be getting the kids to bed. He called up to Tommy and Susan who raced downstairs and were quickly told to stop the noise. 'Mrs Delaney's sleeping and we're not to disturb her.'

James nudged Bert. 'Come on. I think we all need a little peace and quiet after such an eventful evening.'

Bert snatched another teacake and smiled cheekily at Anne. She picked up another and thrust it into his hand. 'You obviously missed dinner,' she whispered with a grin.

They congregated in the hallway and Stephen leaned against the wall. 'This is certainly a r-rum do.'

Anne agreed. 'I don't believe it's him, James. Donovan seems such a lovely man. He doesn't have an ounce of hatred in him. He's a gentle giant.'

'Don't worry, old thing,' said James, 'I'm sure there's a logical explanation. He'll be back with us in no time.'

He caught Bert's expression. Clearly, he was less optimistic. Stephen opened the front door and pulled a face at the rain lashing down.

'Right, I'm off,' Charlie said. 'I'll see you in church on Sunday.' He pulled his collar up and steered his children out.

James and Bert dashed out after him and side-stepped puddles, while Stephen and Anne watched from the shelter of the porch. James saw Charlie's children climb onto their bicycles, while Charlie squatted down to check something.

'Everything all right?'

Charlie gave the thumbs up and got on his bike. James closed his eyes in frustration and returned to the vicarage where Stephen was waving a set of keys.

'F-forget these?' he asked.

James let out a *tut* as he collected them.

Charlie called back to him. 'By the way, I remembered who it was that asked me about the jewellery. You know, valuations, auctions an' all that.'

'And?'

'It was Ian Connell.'

The news stopped James dead. *'What?'*

Charlie sauntered up the path, already drenched from the downpour. 'Yeah, while ago now. He had some woman with him, good-looking woman: she was at your Bonfire Night. Didn't recognise her at first, cos she'd dyed her hair. Anyway, I looked up the books he'd had out. Apart from building stuff, architecture and the like, he borrowed a lot of books about archaeology, Roman sites. Wanted some information on land registry.'

The rain drizzled down James' face. 'When was this? Recently?'

'Nah, about three months ago. See you Sunday.' Charlie trotted back to his bike.

James swallowed his rising panic and felt Bert's presence beside him.

'You all right, Jimmy boy?'

A sickening realisation hit him. He grabbed Bert's arm. 'It's Ian. Ian Connell. He's at home with Beth!'

Anne let out a stifled cry as Stephen pushed them toward James' car. 'Anne, s-stay with the children.'

Bert stopped him. 'We'll take two cars. We may need 'em.' He grabbed James' keys. 'Give me those, you're in no state to drive.'

James snatched them back. 'I know these roads better than you. Stephen, don't try to keep up, just arrive safely.'

CHAPTER TWENTY-THREE

James sped onto the drive so fast he nearly skidded out of control. A feeling of elation washed over him when he saw the lights shining from the hall and the kitchen. He'd overreacted. Everything was fine.

But then his stomach lurched.

The front door was open.

The tyres locked as the car slid to a halt. With Bert close on his heels, he bounded up the steps and into the hall.

'Beth?'

He flung open the lounge doors and caught his breath. His armchair was on its side with a smashed glass beside it and the large canvas of the copse was ripped, the frame snapped. He dashed

276

through to the kitchen and dining room then took the stairs three at a time, all the while calling for Beth and praying that she was safe, that Connell had left her unharmed. But he knew. He knew deep down, that Connell had taken her.

Bert shouted for him to come to the study. He sprinted down to find him at the far wall. 'Check your safe. I'm calling George.'

James stared. The painting that usually covered the safe had been thrown across the room. He edged toward the strongbox where the door hung open. The jewels were gone. He flicked through the remaining papers with a snarl. 'Damn it, Connell! If you've so much as touched her...'

In the hall he collided with Stephen.

'W-where is she?'

James blinked back the tears, feeling wretchedly helpless. 'I don't know.'

The vicar put a reassuring arm round his shoulder. He heard Bert on the telephone.

'We're 'ere now. He must've taken 'er somewhere. Yeah, all right.' He hung up and turned. 'George says to sit tight, they're on their way.'

James could have hit him. 'Sit tight! My wife is out there with a killer and he wants me to sit tight?' He grabbed his keys and made to leave.

Stephen blocked him. 'J-James, the police know w-what they're doing.'

'Do they? They've already arrested the wrong man. I have to find Beth, I can't just sit here.'

He fought to leave but Bert wrestled the keys away, grabbed his lapels and slammed him hard against the wall, winding him. 'Jimmy boy, you think 'ard. Where're you gonna go? Where's 'e

277

likely to be? You're not driving away from 'ere without thinking.'

James rested his head back. His heart crashed in his chest. Think. For God's sake, *think*. His gaze darted around the hall, unable to focus on anything. This can't be happening. *Think,* damn it. Where would he go?

He butted the wall with the back of his head and eventually stared long and hard at a discarded painting on the floor.

He picked it up. 'That was in the lounge.' He gripped Bert's arm. 'On the piano. There's no reason for it to be here.'

Bert picked up Grimes' small canvas. They looked at each and came to the same conclusion.

'The copse!'

Bert flung open the door, pushed James through it and stabbed a finger at Stephen.

'You wait 'ere for George. Tell 'im we're at the copse.'

James shouted after him. 'Tell him that Diana, at Sutherland's, is in on this too.'

A hundred yards before they reached Charn Wood, Bert switched off the Jaguar's headlights and slowed the car to a snail's pace. The windscreen wipers worked hard to clear the screen, but their view became a permanent blur as the rain fell. Connell's abandoned car came into view. They stopped and turned off the engine. James studied the field to the side then grabbed Bert's arm.

'There!' he whispered. 'I saw a light, I'm sure of it.'

Bert wound the window down. 'Rain's easing off.'

'There! There it is again,' said James, groping to open the door.

Bert yanked him back. 'Look at me. Look at me.' James did so. 'Right. Now you listen up. This is my area of expertise. You get out of this car quietly. You close the door quietly. We do everything by hand signals and no die-hard acts of bravery. Got it? You listen to me and me only, you don't go off doing your own thing.'

James felt himself trembling. His friend handed him a torch, then they slipped out of the car and nudged the doors closed.

Bert opened the boot; his torch beam settled on a large spanner. He thrust it into James' hand. 'Put that inside your jacket.'

For himself, Bert chose a long, iron wheel wrench. Clicking the boot shut, he told James to keep his torch off and to follow him. 'If we need to switch these on, shine 'em straight down and shield the beam with your 'and.'

They scurried along the road then onto the saturated muddy lane that led to the wood. James looked up to the night sky. Thankfully, the moon remained hidden by the clouds. He stayed close to Bert who, every few seconds, squatted down before planning his next move.

Approaching the copse, they switched their torches on. The shadows of the trees provided camouflage as they trod a slow and careful path, occasionally crouching in dense ferns and peering into the woods. The heavy rain had stopped but water continued to drip down from the branches.

279

James took a step forward; a twig snapped and a bird took flight. Bert glared and pulled him back. 'What did I tell you,' he whispered.

James mouthed 'Sorry' as they sat on their heels, watching and listening.

At first, he heard nothing, just the patter of rain-drops. His feet were soaked and water trickled down the back of his neck.

Bert squeezed his arm.

Yes, he'd heard it too. Voices.

Torches off.

Bert beckoned for him to follow.

The further they went, the more the feeling of dread penetrated James. What was he going to find? He stopped and reached for a tree to keep his balance. Nausea swept through him. Bert sensed his mood and pulled him close. 'I know what you're doing. You musn't think it. Not now. She needs you to be strong.' He pointed to his head. 'You get it? Take a deep breath.'

James took in some air then motioned for Bert to continue. A minute later, the voices were louder and they could see torches being waved. Bert found a natural dip and pulled James into it. His friend nudged him.

James caught his breath. Beth! He fought hard to contain himself. The elation was so strong he wanted to shout to the heavens. Strength surged through him, so strong he felt gung-ho with bravado. Again, Bert grabbed him with a fierce glare. He prodded his head.

'Focus,' he mouthed.

James realised that Bert must have kept his eye on him since they'd arrived. Any change of emotion, any unnecessary move and his friend had roughly manhandled him and brought him to his senses.

Bert edged forward another few yards. James followed.

At last, a clear view.

Beth looked dishevelled, sitting on a dead tree-trunk. Her ankles and wrists were tied and a gag covered her mouth. Her eyes were wide with fright as Ian and Diana began shouting at each other. James and Bert stayed low and listened in.

'You stupid, stupid man!' Diana screamed. 'We wouldn't be in this mess if you'd thought this through. Why bring her here? Now we've no choice.'

'She told me they'd found the jewels,' Ian replied. 'Grimes had had them all the time. I thought we wanted them.'

Diana rolled her eyes. 'For God's sake, Ian, if you thought *that*, all you needed to do was hang on! We could have gone back for the jewels when the Harringtons were out. You just didn't think, did you? You never do!'

'I'm sorry! I panicked, that's all.'

'Yes, panic is about the only thing you're good at,' she spat. 'Grimes keeled over and everything was going our way, but you had to get in a blind panic. You couldn't even do your homework right at the start.' She began rummaging in her bag.

'What do you mean?' Ian asked.

'Keith! Keith, you damn fool.'

'How was I supposed to know he'd have a son... Diana ... no!'

Diana had pulled a large knife out of her bag.

281

She turned towards Beth, whose eyes widened in horror above the gag that prevented her from screaming.

Ian stepped forward, hands out. 'You can't...'

She shrugged him off. 'You're the coward in this sorry partnership, so I'll have to do it.'

'I'd rather be a coward than a killer.'

James, as he listened, every muscle trembling, realised they thought Keith was dead, that Diana had killed him. He tensed, gripping the root of a nearby tree. Bert grabbed his collar to restrain him and held up three fingers, then closed his hand again, before inching forward. James retrieved the spanner from inside his jacket. Bert held up a finger.

One.

Diana, still moving towards Beth, had paused to pick up and throw a spade to Ian. 'Get digging. This is a Roman burial site already – suitable last resting place, don't you think?'

'Diana, you can't do this...'

Bert's second finger went up: *two.*

'Watch me,' Diana replied, the knife rising in her grip.

James didn't wait for Bert's count of three. He charged out of the undergrowth straight at Diana, ignoring Bert's curse as he passed. He saw the whites of her eyes as he wrestled her to the ground in a rugby tackle. Ian leapt on his back and dragged him off as she kicked him in the side of his knee. The excruciating pain sent his leg into spasm, forcing him to the ground, where an extra kick to the stomach winded him. The spanner fell from his grip. He heard Beth's muffled screams and struggled to his feet.

Diana stood beside him. 'Well, this is nice. Come to play the hero?' She picked up the spanner. 'You don't play very nicely, do you, Lord Harrington?'

James limped to Beth and put his arm around her shoulders. 'You don't exactly play nicely yourself. You're a ruthless woman. I suspect if Grimes hadn't had a heart attack you would have killed him anyway.'

Diana shrugged. 'He got greedy. We found out about this site months ago, but he'd already applied for the land. He'd found a few bits of pottery and saw us poking around. We found something more than old pottery – coins and a couple of bangles – we knew we'd hit the jackpot.'

'But he researched what he'd found and discovered something more.'

'We told him we'd split the haul fifty-fifty to get him off our backs. But it was us who'd put all the work in. We deserved it. We researched the site, we dug it. He did nothing except plough a few pieces up by chance. I told Ian to make friends with him.'

'Let me guess. You offered to do up the farmhouse, keep him on your side, befriend him. Get his trust.'

Ian's head dropped. 'It almost worked. But he started pushing me for a bigger percentage because it was on his land. He thought me and him were bosom buddies, told me to cut Diana out of it altogether so we both got a bigger payout. He said he wanted to use the money to do the place up and sell it. He didn't wanna be a farmer. I let Diana know and she said to go along with it. If we had the farm and the copse, we might find loads more. We told him we'd agree to it if he allowed Sutherland's to auction the farm off. That way, we'd be able to buy it. Put it through the books somehow. We wrote up the paperwork for him to sign so it'd be legal.'

James saw the box of jewellery by Beth's feet. 'I assume he found those gems before you.'

Diana sniggered. 'That's why he bought the copse. That's why he borrowed money so anything he found was on his land. Then he wanted a bigger percentage.' She closed her eyes in frustration. 'Ian went round to have it out with him.'

'I didn't kill him,' Ian emphasised as Diana let out a sarcastic laugh. 'I went round there and we argued. He said he didn't trust us, said he wasn't gonna sign any paperwork or let us auction the farm. I got angry and I picked up the nearest thing...'

'That robin?' James said.

Ian nodded. 'I hit him over the head. Not hard – I didn't want to hurt him, just frighten him. But he started weaving about, clutching his chest, fighting for breath. Then he just collapsed right in front of me.'

Diana threw her hands up in the air. 'And if you'd left him there, no one would have asked questions. It was a heart attack.'

James scanned the clearing. He knew he was buying time. Bert was still hidden and George would surely be on his way. His confidence began to build. 'You're not cut out for this, are you, Ian? You panicked, you dragged Alec out and tried to make it look as if he'd died painting. I think you

284

were going to make a very believable scene but you wanted to search for the jewels first and then tidy up; but Donovan pitched up before you had a chance to finish setting the stage.'

Ian closed his eyes, his face wretched with anguish as James continued.

'You knew Grimes had a considerable haul of jewels and you went inside to find them. Then Donovan arrived and discovered Grimes dead. It was you he heard in the house, but it spooked him and he left. Once he'd gone, you decided not to hang about and scampered off. That's why you came back later, when I was there. You wanted to search the place again.'

Ian perched on a log and put his head in his hands while Diana sneered at James. 'Aye, you came along and stuck your nose in. You had to keep asking questions and poking about. If you'd left well alone, we'd have had that farm up for auction and everything would be ours. Well, you'll not be probing any further. You two will be buried deep in the copse and no one will be any the wiser.'

James stood up. 'But you're forgetting about Keith Grimes.'

She narrowed her eyes. 'He's dead. That was one good turn you did for us. We didn't realise there was a son until you mentioned him.'

'I presume that Alec had let Keith know what was happening,' added James. 'Keith returned and came to see you.'

Ian looked resigned. 'He came in a couple of hours after your visit. Alec had told him about the jewellery and the deal we were trying to strike.

Alec wasn't an idiot – he knew we were trying to con him.'

Diana glared at Ian, who chose to ignore her.

'I contacted Diana while he was still with me and when he left, she followed him and bashed him over the head.'

James felt his shoulders sink. He couldn't believe the depths people would go to. 'And asked you to put him on the bonfire.'

Ian swallowed hard and appeared relieved to get the whole thing into the open. James glimpsed past Ian and Diana. Bert was on the edge of the clearing and, in the distance beyond the trees, he could see the blue lights of the police cars. Trembling with relief, he felt confident enough to play his trump card.

'But didn't you know? Keith is still alive.'

Diana rounded on him. 'That's impossible! I killed him. We watched him burn.'

'No, Diana. What you saw go up in flames was a pile of straw that the children had made. We retrieved Keith's body before we lit the bonfire. He was still alive.'

Her hard eyes glared. 'How? How did you know that was Keith?'

'The children said it wasn't their guy.' James massaged his knee. 'So you see, Diana – you're no further forward. Keith is the rightful owner of the farm now and you won't get away with attempted murder. The police will put two and two together and Keith will, I'm sure, provide a statement.'

Diana erupted. She let out a horrifying scream and lunged at James with the knife. He leapt to one side and watched as she stumbled into the leaves behind him.

Bert vaulted a tree trunk but was quickly slowed down when Ian punched him in the stomach. He groaned and tried to avoid Diana as she rushed toward him with the swiping blade. He let out a yelp when she caught his thigh, and collapsed. Ian threw himself on top of Bert and began punching him.

James caught Diana from behind and held her in a vice-like grip. She brought her foot up and kicked his damaged knee. He winced and tightened his grip to take away the pain. She kicked again and again; he caught his breath as his knee buckled. Ian groaned as Bert brought the iron wrench down on the back of his head.

He clambered to his feet and made a beeline for Diana. 'I don't normally hit ladies,' Bert said, 'but in this case, I'll make an exception.' His fist slammed into her cheek. Her angry eyes dulled; the knife fell from her hand and she dropped to the ground, unconscious.

Catching his breath, James grabbed the knife and limped over to Beth. He slipped the blade through her bindings and untied the gag. She burst into tears and flung herself at him.

'Oh James,' she sobbed.

He held her as close as he possibly could. 'It's all right, darling, it's all right.' He stroked her hair. 'Ssh, ssh, you're safe now.'

Over her shoulder, he glimpsed Bert pull Diana's scarf off and attempt to patch up his bloodied leg while, in the distance, he heard George's gruff voice ordering his team to keep up. Never had he been so pleased to see his friend.

CHAPTER TWENTY-FOUR

On George's instructions, Beth, James and Bert were driven straight to the local cottage hospital where Bert received seven stitches to a knife wound. James gratefully received a walking stick to aid his twisted knee ligament, while Beth was happy to accept a prescription of sleep aids to see her through the next few nights.

The following day, James insisted that Beth remain at home to rest while he caught up with various residents in the village – in particular, Donovan and Kate. There, he shared their joy over Donovan's release and confirmed that the case against Connell and Diana was watertight.

Dropping by Graham's butcher's shop, he discovered that Bert had already paid him a visit to deposit an antique gold bracelet with him.

'He told me it was worth a few hundred,' said Graham. 'I don't know where 'e got it from. It must be nicked, mustn't it?' He winced at the thought. 'I'm gonna have to return it, aren't I?'

James recognised part of the jewellery haul and wondered when Bert had swiped it.

'Look, Graham, I can tell you that it's not stolen. At the same time, you may have a little trouble selling it. Keep hold of it for now. Let me make a few enquiries and I'll let you know in a couple of days. You'll get your money, I'm sure of it.'

Graham's relieved face beamed as he thanked

James, reiterating his need to get his finances in order. James, too, wanted some justice for Graham. He wondered about buying the bracelet himself but hoped a solution would come about naturally.

Two days later, he closed the curtains and joined their guests at the dining table. With the events of their ordeal still fresh, James hadn't thought it wise to be entertaining so soon. However, Beth had insisted on hosting a small dinner party, dismissing James' concerns over the trauma of the night, preferring, instead, to get back to normal.

Joining them were George, Bert, Stephen, Anne and, although a little tired and washed out, Keith Grimes. He'd woken from his coma and had been released from hospital on the understanding that he would be placed in the care of Dr Jackson and that he wouldn't be on his own. James assured the doctor that Keith could remain with them until he was fit enough to return to Scotland.

In his late twenties, Keith had short, chestnut brown hair and hazel eyes. A manual worker, with calloused hands and a ruddy complexion, he wore blue jeans and a navy Guernsey sweater.

James had banished Beth from the kitchen that afternoon to prepare one of his favourite meals: roast beef, roast potatoes and parsnips, Yorkshire pudding, sliced carrots and a pan of red wine and shallot gravy.

With the conversation in full flow, he uncorked a couple of bottles of claret and placed them at either end of the table.

'Stephen, old chap, would you do the honours?

Say grace and all that?'

'Of course.' Stephen bowed his head. 'Father, we thank you for b-bringing us together this evening and delivering our friends to us, s-safe from their ordeal. We thank you, too, for this sumptuous meal and ask th-that you continue to pour your love and tenderness on us all. Amen.'

James removed the lids from the various dishes and invited everyone to help themselves. Stephen jumped up to pour everyone a drink.

The smell of roast beef drifted across the table and everyone murmured their appreciation as they tucked in.

Anne licked her lips. 'Oh James, this is lovely. Did you do all of this yourself?'

He said that he did as he helped himself to parsnips. 'I love to cook. Perhaps I should have been a chef.' He held his glass up. 'Cheers, everyone.'

'You'd 'ave been better as a detective,' said George.

Anne's mischievous eyes lit up. 'I thought you'd never get onto the subject. I have to say that I suspected Graham for a short while.'

'Well, you had every right to think so,' James replied. 'Graham had a just reason to wanting to harm Grimes.'

The previous day, he'd updated everyone on what had happened but he expected further questions, especially from Anne, who seemed enthralled by the whole thing.

He looked at George. 'I'm interested in knowing what put you on to Donovan.'

'Your cleaner, Mrs Jepson. She'd been so desperate to get in touch with you that she went to the local police in Gloucestershire. Anyway, I was there when they rang through. I asked if Mr Jepson was with 'er and 'e was so I got to speak to him. He admitted arguing with Alec Grimes that morning and, as we thought, it was about the play. Grimes wasn't happy about the topic and wanted him to change it. That was it, really. Nothing malicious. But when Jepson arrived back in the village, Delaney flagged him down. Asked if he'd been past Grimes' place and whether he was in. That's when we knew he'd been over there that morning.'

Anne frowned. 'But Mr Grimes was renowned for being solitary, so why agree to be in the play?'

'He wanted to change the story,' replied George. 'Convince Jepson that it wasn't right.' He glanced at Stephen and then at Keith. 'Didn't like anything evil or superstitious and said the players should stick to a more Christian theme, especially near Christmas. He felt that being on the inside, he'd disrupt things a bit.'

'W-well, I can't say I b-blame him,' said Stephen.

'That sounds like Dad,' said Keith. 'He went off the rails when Mum died. Felt it was his fault, that he was being punished and that Mum had been punished. He steadily got worse, paranoid even. He became more and more religious, more obsessed with banishing evil from his life and everyone else's. Unfortunately, he didn't go about it the right way.'

'But why?' asked Beth. 'Why would he feel that way if he hadn't before?'

Keith pushed the food around on his plate.

She placed her hand on his. 'I'm sorry, you don't have to say why. I'm sorry if we've stirred up memories.'

'No, it's all right.' He took a deep breath. 'They weren't married when Mum fell pregnant with me.'

Anne mouthed an 'Oh' at Beth as Keith continued.

'Dad, from what I know of his upbringing, was a churchgoer and his parents were pretty strict with their beliefs. But when Mum became pregnant, the reaction he got from his parents ... well, they cut my Dad off, wouldn't have anything to do with him or Mum, even when they got married. Then when Mum died – I was about ten – everything changed. He said God was punishing him.'

Stephen appeared shocked and expressed his sympathy.

'But they loved each other, right?' said Bert. 'Got married an' all?'

Keith assumed so and Bert announced that that was all that mattered. He told Keith he couldn't be blamed for his parent's actions. 'Or your grandparents' actions for that matter.' Bert turned to James. 'Why didn't Donovan tell you he'd been to the farm?'

'Scared. He'd had a few run-ins with Grimes over the way he treated his family. I didn't help matters by questioning how Grimes had died. Can't help the chap for being slow in coming forward. A man will want to protect his family.'

George grunted. 'I wish people would just tell the truth. Save a lot of trouble.'

James carved some more beef and topped up Beth's wineglass. 'You know, if Ian had called an ambulance when Grimes had his heart attack, no one would have been any the wiser.'

Beth agreed that Ian couldn't cope in a crisis. 'I mean, he had no reason to kidnap me. A cool head would have reacted differently.'

When they finished their meal, James insisted Beth remain seated as he and Anne served dessert. He'd spent the previous day making his grandmother's sherry trifle layered with jellied sponge, raspberries, blancmange, meringue and cream, topped with mandarin slices.

'K-Keith, when did you hear from your father?'

Keith sipped his wine and cleared his throat. 'Dad sent me a letter. He was worried about this deal he'd been offered and he told me what he'd found on his land. He suspected he was being dealt a dodgy hand and he told me he had a bad feeling about it. I'd left home after a few arguments, but we used to have a good relationship. He wrote me a long letter, explained what Ian and Diana were trying to do and that he felt pushed into a corner. He'd purchased the copse but Ian was trying to secure some sort of deal that would mean him giving up the farm. He didn't understand it so decided to contact me. He used to be a strong, assertive man but he'd got older. He was vulnerable and didn't know what to do and I think those two were taking advantage of it. I got the letter late because I'd been on holiday. By the time I got down here, Dad had already been buried. I didn't know what to do at first but I ended up going to Loxfield to have it out with Connell.'

James explained that Keith had visited the same day as him. 'It was Diana who battered Keith into a coma and brought him here.'

'How did they get him on top of that bonfire?' Anne asked.

James rubbed his chin. 'Easy. The villagers were in and out of these fields during the days leading up to Bonfire Night. The side gate wasn't locked so everyone had access. That's what made this whole thing so bally difficult. People buzzing in and out like honey bees. But you don't expect a real body to be hauled to the top of your bonfire, do you?'

A contented lull was finally interrupted by Anne. 'How are you feeling now, Beth, after that awful night. I was worried sick waiting for news.'

Beth raised her palm to her forehead. 'What an evening that turned out to be! I feel a fool for being so open with Ian. Once James had rung to tell me about Donovan, well, I let Ian know. He started asking questions, you know, wanting to know the details, and I told him. Told him about James' suspicions, the jewellery he'd found at the farm. At first, he seemed to take an innocent interest and said he was fascinated by history.

'He seemed such a nice man, but he suddenly got really angry. I honestly thought he was going to kill me right here in my own home.'

James nudged his chair closer and held her hand. 'Unfortunately, Ian doesn't think in a crisis. He'd shown his cards to Beth and then went into a blind panic. Forced Beth to open the safe. He rang Diana and she told him to meet him at the copse and to bring poor Beth with him.'

The doorbell rang and James asked Bert if he'd mind showing their visitor in. A few seconds later Professor Wilkins entered.

'Good evening,' he said.

James grabbed his walking stick and limped across to greet him.

Beth gave the Professor a warm smile. 'I'm so glad you came.'

'Pull up a chair, old man, let me get you a drink.'

Their guests shuffled their chairs to give him room to sit down. James poured a glass of claret for him and asked what he'd discovered since they'd last met.

Wilkins undid his jacket, and pulled his chair in between George and Anne.

'Quite a bit.' He grimaced at George. 'I'm so sorry that you had the run-around trying to find me. I understand I may have been your chief suspect for a while. The fact is James sparked my interest with his pottery find. I knew I hadn't seen any articles about Romans in Cavendish but then it occurred to me that I should check local documents rather than the national or county ones.'

He felt his pocket and brought out some loose sheets of paper.

'I managed to find copies of some parish pamphlets printed at the turn of the last century. It appears that back then, there was rumour of some sort of settlement here.'

'A settlement!' Beth said. 'How exciting.'

Wilkins told them about telephone calls and visits to the British Museum, Fishbourne Palace and Lewes, as well as visiting colleagues with private book collections where he came upon some very old booklets and newsletters.

'You see, these little essays and pamphlets get lost in the system,' he said. 'Because no one had any real proof, the fuss about any Roman settlement died along with the writers of these little essay things. Of course, then Grimes ploughed up some pottery pieces and discovered this jewellery. It's remarkable that evidence has finally surfaced.'

'Not as remarkable as the last piece of news,' James announced with a broad grin. 'I asked Mr Smithson, the builder in the village, to take his little digger over the field where the pottery was found. He went up there yesterday. Had to dig quite deep but it's there all right.'

The guests waited for more.

'He uncovered what appear to be remnants of a Roman community. Quite extraordinary.'

Wilkins confirmed that the whole thing was incredibly exciting. 'There is a small burial mound hidden in the copse. Whoever was there would have been someone held in high regard. Many of the coins date back to the fourth century, to the time of Emperor Constantine. It's not a nationally important site or anything but certainly something to add to the history of our village.'

'I can't believe it,' said Beth. 'But Professor, I have to ask something. Why did you leave so quickly the other evening? As soon as that bonfire was lit, you disappeared.'

Wilkins cradled his drink. 'I'd received quite a bit of information to research and I wanted to get back and continue with it.' He bowed his head. 'I'm sorry I didn't say goodbye. That was rude of me. I'm like that sometimes, I'm afraid.'

'And which university did you teach at in the States?'

'Dartmouth.'

Beth looked confused. 'Oh, only last week you said Dartford.'

'Ah, I'm always doing that. I'm from Dartford. A lot of my family still live there so it rolls off the tongue, even when I don't want it to.'

James couldn't help but grin at Beth's embarrassment.

'D-do you know who coshed m-me over the head?' asked Stephen.

'Ian,' George answered. 'He decided to play up to all this supernatural business what with the play and Hallowe'en. He obviously knew you were asking questions, James, and he popped over to the Grimes farm to mould that mud man as a joke and see if he could find that jewellery too. Parked up in the copse and wandered across to the farmhouse.'

'He must have slipped out of our Hallowe'en event for a while.'

Beth sat up with a start. 'He did! He had to drop his niece and nephew off.'

'And then gone straight to the farm after that. That's when Mitchell saw the lights.'

'Ian was still at the farmhouse when you lot pitched up,' George continued. 'He waited for you to go but you, Stephen, came too close for comfort so he clobbered you.'

Stephen let out a relieved sigh. 'So, a-all's well that ends well. And,' he said to Keith, 'you, thank the Lord, are alive and well.'

Keith thanked them all for rescuing him from a nasty death. Bert slapped him on the back.

'You've got Tommy Hawkins to thank for that.'

George took out his pipe. 'Are you moving back here, Keith? You've inherited the farm and have the added bonus of a huge Roman haul on the land.'

Keith shook his head. 'Just to oversee the excavation,' he replied. 'Professor Wilkins seems to think that we'll find quite a few artefacts, but not a lot else. But I'm going open up that whole area, see what we can find, and the Professor will be the lead where the museum and historical society are concerned. I'll sell the farmhouse and the original land eventually but I'm keeping ownership of the copse and that will hopefully become a Roman attraction. Be a great place for people to visit – bring some funds in for the village.'

James proffered his cigarettes. 'I say, Wilkins, what's the score with this little treasure find? Will Keith have to hand it in? I mean, finders keepers and all that and it is on his land.'

'You have to declare it,' replied Wilkins, 'but Keith here should get some sort of value from it. I understand it depends on whether it was intentionally buried or just left.'

Anne laughed. 'Well, how on earth will anyone know?'

Wilkins allowed his charming smile to surface. 'Exactly. Keith should get a tidy sum. Plus, of course, you'll get a percentage from takings once we get a visitor centre open.'

Keith explained that this would be great for him, as he was getting married the following year and the group congratulated him on his good fortune.

He leant in to James. 'I heard Dad owed Mr Porter some money. I'll make sure he gets that back.'

James clocked Bert's sheepish expression and decided he would sort that situation out the following day.

Beth held her hand up. 'I have one more question. What about Peter Mitchell?' she asked. 'He acted so strange on more than one occasion.'

'Ah yes,' said James, 'Peter Mitchell, I'm afraid, was up to no good with a certain young lady.'

Anne gasped.

'Thought so,' said Bert. 'When someone's that shifty and their wife's away, they're normally up to no good and normally involves a woman.'

'Mmm, he'd had a liaison with someone in the village, but won't say who. He assures me it's finished and that's why he looked so annoyed when I saw him coming out of the woods. He'd arranged to meet this lady in the little hollow there to call it off and it all got rather heated.'

He turned his attention to George.

'I've no doubt Diana will be tried for attempted murder but what about Connell? I detest the man for what he did to Beth and would like to see him pay for it. He was easily led by Diana, but even so.'

George gritted his teeth. 'The man kidnapped Beth, knocked Stephen unconscious, attacked you and Bert and he knowingly put Keith at the top of a bonfire. You can be sure we'll be throwing the book at both of them.'

James hobbled across the dining room and reached for a bottle of champagne. Anne helped Beth to distribute flutes as James unscrewed the wire seal.

'Well, I believe that a toast is in order,' he said as the cork popped. He filled the glasses with foaming champagne. Standing behind Beth, he rested a hand on her shoulder and raised his glass.

'To getting back to normal, to the new Roman display and to Keith, a man who will always be welcome should he wish to return with his new wife.'

'Cheers!' the guests chorused.

The publishers hope that this book has given you enjoyable reading. Large Print Books are especially designed to be as easy to see and hold as possible. If you wish a complete list of our books please ask at your local library or write directly to:

Magna Large Print Books
Magna House, Long Preston,
Skipton, North Yorkshire.
BD23 4ND

This Large Print Book for the partially sighted, who cannot read normal print, is published under the auspices of

THE ULVERSCROFT FOUNDATION